Welcome Home, Bailey

Hope A. Milam

Yellow Rose Books
by Regal Crest

Copyright © 2020 by Hope Milam

ISBN 978-1-61929-438-7

First Printing 2020

9 8 7 6 5 4 3 2 1

Original cover design by AcornGraphics

Published by:

Regal Crest Enterprises

Find us on the World Wide Web at
http://www.regalcrest.biz

Published in the United States of America

Dedication

This book is dedicated to two wonderfully amazing people: my wife, Delaina, and my daughter, Emerson.

I would also like to thank several others for their help, support, and guidance. So many thanks to Thom, Kyla, Christine, Darci, Brandy, Steph, Kaytee, Melanie, and Q. Thanks everyone and I love you all.

Chapter One

BAILEY RAY COOPER leaned back in the seat, pulled her sunglasses on, and adjusted the detested seatbelt. She hated wearing her seatbelt when in the back seat as it made getting comfortable difficult. She angled her hips, tossed one long leg on the seat, and crossed her arms over her chest. She closed her eyes and tried to concentrate on something other than LA traffic.

While Bailey loved driving, she hated traffic and made use of the label's limo service whenever she had to be in a car for more than a few minutes. This limo driver was not the chatty sort. That made it easy for Bailey to do a bit of daydreaming before she fell asleep.

She fell easily into one of her favorite memories. She was on a balcony in Vienna and it was lightly raining. She felt the soft lips on her own and the light shivers coursing through the woman in her arms. However, before memory could become fantasy, she dozed off and found herself in a much less pleasant memory that her brain always twisted into a nightmare.

"Ms. Cooper? We're here," the driver said.

"What?" She looked around. It took a moment for images of a near certain death to fade. "Oh. Thanks. Listen, do you mind hanging around for an hour or two to give me a ride home?"

"Not at all, Ms. Cooper." The older gentleman got out of the car and opened Bailey's door. "I am at your disposal for the day."

"Thank you." She had never gotten used to some things. "Would you like something to eat? This is a lunch thing."

"No thank you, ma'am." He smiled as he offered his hand to assist her. "Thank you for the offer."

"If you change your mind just go in and have them send me the tab," she said.

"Over here, superstar." The familiar voice came from behind her. Bailey turned and saw the drummer and co-founder of their band, Creature Feature, already seated outside the restaurant. As always, Kat had her mane of hair coiffed in a retro punk style. This time it was a lurid green mohawk that clashed spectacularly with her red leather jacket and pale complexion. Kat had chosen a patio table, complete with a boring green umbrella. Bailey had to laugh at that. The umbrellas at an establishment back home would have been garish in colors and advertisements.

"You didn't tell me this place had an outside area. I could have brought Elvis," she said as soon as she got within comfortable speaking distance. She walked past the hostess stand and joined her friend.

"You've never been here?" Kat asked as she stood and gave Bailey a quick hug. "Though I'm surprised you didn't bring him anyway. I can't think of a more well-traveled bulldog."

"No, I've never been here. And yes, I did think about bringing him anyway," Bailey admitted. She often took the bulldog with her when she went out. It made things a little less lonely.

"Of course, you did," Kat said as if she had known the answer. They'd known one another for years, after all. "So what's new with you?"

Bailey shrugged. "Nothing much. I just finished the final score for Laci's new movie. Some big space odyssey." Bailey had developed an interest in composition several years prior and sometimes took the occasional movie job between records and tours. It kept her from getting too bored, and it certainly padded her bank account.

"Oh yeah," Kat said. "Ross said it's going to be huge. It's pretty cool that she was able to change careers like that."

"It's even cooler that no one's broken that story," Bailey said. "Where is Ross anyway? You two are never together, even when you're around one another."

"Japan. They're filming some samurai love story epic thing." Kat flipped over the menu.

"When are you going over there?" Bailey asked. Kat always tried to maintain a cool detachment where her married life was concerned, but Bailey knew better. There was real love and passion there, at least on Kat's part. She was never sure about Ross's feelings."

"Never could hide anything from you, could I?" Kat grinned. "In a few days. What are you going to do?"

"I don't know," Bailey answered honestly. With the band on an extended break, she didn't have much to do. She had finished the score for her latest movie job and had no plans. The break pretty much caught her off guard. Usually she had trips and adventures planned for breaks.

"You gonna write some more?" Kat asked. The waitress appeared and took their order. Kat paid more attention to her lunch order than to her friend's answer for a moment.

"Maybe. My lyrics have been so bad lately they'd make

country seem happy, but the melodies have been pretty good." She waited until after the waitress left. She knew from long experience that Kat was reticent to speak in front of anyone they didn't know. They'd been burned in the press more than once because someone had turned an overheard remark into a big deal

"You need a distraction, my friend."

"I was toying with the idea of taking a few online classes, but I hadn't given much thought to what I want to study," Bailey said. She kept her eyes on the menu. It was a startling admission, but she wasn't ashamed. Like Kat, she hadn't finished college; instead she had gambled on her chances of fame and fortune.

"And I'm sure that would keep your days occupied. I was speaking of your nights." Kat idly picked at a callus on her thumb.

"You're going to regret doing that," Bailey cautioned.

"So you tell me every time." Kat sighed and stopped. "You can't avoid the topic forever, Bailey, my love."

"Don't start with the fake Irish thing." Bailey laughed in spite of herself. Kat's Irish accent was so bad it always brought groans.

"Anyway, you've been single for over two years now. What gives?" Kat asked. "Breaking up with what's her name couldn't have been that heart-wrenching." The waitress placed their lunch order on the table and departed.

It took a moment for Bailey to remember the name. "Jade." She had been so preoccupied with other thoughts that she'd almost forgotten her most recent ex-girlfriend. Of course, they'd only dated for six weeks or so.

"Whatever. She was a waste." Kat began rearranging her sandwich. "Hey, speaking of waste, what was up with Heather dumping champagne over you the other night? I swear I've had that clip sent to me ten times."

Bailey shrugged. "Heather's band needed some press. I didn't have anything else to do so I volunteered. I'm sure a lot of people would give a ton of money to be able to do the same to me. It worked though. Their new single has had a lot of recent downloads."

"A true friend in need," Kat said when she stopped laughing. "Seriously though, why haven't you been dating?"

"Ah, that's a tough one." Bailey sighed and leaned back in her chair. For a moment she really wanted a cigarette. Then she remembered she didn't smoke, and even if she did, she was pretty sure it wasn't allowed in LA anyway.

"It's not really tough. You've been different since your fortieth. You haven't even been picking up groupies. What happened?"

"Kat, that was almost two years ago."

"A lonely two years," Kat said. "What's that woman's name? The one you went to school with? The one you're still in love with? Bev?"

"Beth," Bailey answered without thinking. "Kat, really."

"Really. It's because of her, right?" Kat leaned forward. "What happened in Vienna? Because you've been different ever since you came back."

"Nothing." Bailey shrugged off the lie she hated to tell. "I can't cheat anyone anymore, Kat. I'm too old for that. I can't get involved with anyone until I figure out what's the deal. I'm not looking for flings anymore. There has to be more there. Maybe I'm just getting old."

"I hope it happens for ya, my friend. I really do. The long-term thing anyway; not the growing old part. That's going to happen anyway."

"Thanks," Bailey said dryly. "So enough about me, let's get on to business. Do you think Tiny's going to quit? He's been with us for quite a while." Their most recent bass player was rethinking his life's ambition.

"I don't know," Kat said. "I mean Creature Feature has always been mainly you and me. Would it matter too much? Any number of bass players would kill for the rhythms you write." She was correct.

"I like Tiny." Bailey shrugged again. "How long are we going to keep going?" She asked somewhat wistfully. They'd been Creature Feature for over twenty years. It was hard to maintain, what some would call, a normal life with everything they'd been required to do, to at first make, and then keep, their careers and reputations.

Kat looked surprised. "You don't want to stop, do you? We're barely in our forties. Look at the groups before us. A lot of those guys are still kicking ass." The waitress walked up and placed the check on the table without asking any questions. They ignored her.

"A lot of those guys are bigger than we'll ever be and still only produce albums every few years," Bailey said. "A lot more of them are dead."

"Well, we've stopped touring so much, but I don't want to just release rehashes of old stuff or fade into obscurity." It was

Kat's turn to shrug. "I'm just not ready yet. I always envisioned us as white-haired old ladies rocking hard and kicking ass."

"I can see that," Bailey admitted. She had no trouble at all picturing that. "I guess when you get back from Japan we'll talk some more. See what Tiny wants to do."

"That sounds like a plan. Stay in touch, superstar." Kat rose and added a few bills to the folder the waitress had placed on the table.

"You too. And don't go trying to mimic stunts again. Remember what happened last time." Bailey reached for her wallet, but Kat waved her off.

"Yes, mother." Kat rolled her eyes. "Wasn't as bad as when you wheeled off the steps and crashed. Thought you were going to have to play sitting down the whole tour."

Bailey groaned, "I couldn't sit down, it hurt too much. Damn, we are getting old."

"It's a state of mind, my friend. See you when I get back." Kat wrapped her in a big hug.

Bailey returned the hug. "Have a great time." She watched as Kat crossed the parking lot and climbed into a large SUV. Kat had no problem driving in LA, but then again, Kat didn't have Bailey's history either.

THE PHONE BEGAN chirping before the sun was up the next morning. Bailey pulled the covers over her head and ignored it. It didn't work. Whoever it was kept calling back.

"What?" She answered it without looking at the screen. She was intent on telling someone off for waking her but stopped the tirade when she recognized the voice.

A light, teasing voice came through loud and clear. "Wow. Good morning to you, too, Grump."

Bailey placed the phone on the nightstand and put it on speaker. Cindy's voice was just a bit too chipper sometimes first thing in the morning.

"Cindy, it's not morning here yet. The sky's still dark."

"Oh yeah. Sorry," Cindy said, but didn't sound it. She did love to wake her. "Anyway, Bailey, how are you?"

"What can I do for you, Cindy?" Bailey knew that tone well. She would not be getting off the call easily. With a sigh, she got up, grabbed the phone, and let the dog out.

"You can tell me congratulations to start." Cindy sounded smug and overwhelmingly happy. In short, she was more chipper than normal. It was almost irritating.

"Congratulations. What am I congratulating you for?" Bailey hadn't talked to anyone from home in the past week or so. She had emailed her cousin Liz a few times, but nothing earth shattering was even hinted at.

"Mike and I are getting married," Cindy's voice rang out in singsong. "In three months. I kinda need you home because you're going to be in my wedding, whether you like it or not."

"Man. Congrats. I never thought he'd propose. Why so quick? Don't these things take time to plan?" Bailey wasn't an expert on weddings or relationships, but she'd always been told quick weddings were weddings of convenience. She certainly knew that wasn't the case with Mike and Cindy. Then the rest of what her friend said struck her. "You want me in your wedding? You're nuts."

"Bailey, Mike is your cousin. You're one of my best friends. Of course you're going to be in my wedding," Cindy said patiently. She was a kindergarten teacher and frequently called on that skill to explain things to Bailey. "You're not doing anything, right? Liz said you were taking a break. Where's a better place to take a break than home? Come on, Bailey, we need you here, me and Mike. You've helped him so much, and you mean so much to both of us. Please? I hate to ask it of you, but you do help keep him under control when he stresses out. I'm worried about the stress and how he handles it. You and I both know how stressful weddings can be."

"Shit. You're right. How is he right now?"

"He's holding it together," Cindy said. "It's hard you know. My mom...I just. Bailey, please."

"If he's holding it together okay, then I can take a day or two to pack and get ready. I'm not sure how good I'll be at helping with a wedding, but if nothing else, I can keep my volatile cousin from freaking out about it."

"Excellent. Thank you, Bailey. Oh, have you spoken to Beth lately?" That question caused Bailey's interest to spike.

"Not in a month or so. I saw an email from her about a fundraiser for Rebecca's class. Why?"

"Um, no reason. Just let me know the details when you make them. Or Liz. She'll let us know like always."

"Okay. You're all getting just a little weird, you know that, right?" Bailey let it go. She had a trip home to plan. She couldn't get lost on what ifs regarding Beth at the moment.

"Maybe you're finally rubbing off on us. Gotta go. Oh, and

Scott has some new designs for you," she said as an aside.

"Great. I've been saving some space for him." Scott was Mike and Liz's little brother. He was a well-respected tattoo artist. "I'll let someone know my impending arrival."

She waited until the dog came back in before leaving the bedroom in search of food. The house was quiet. If Bailey were being honest with herself, and for the last several years she always tried to be, she knew it was too quiet. With just her and Elvis, it was a rather lonely existence when the band wasn't actively recording or touring. It would be good to go home for a little while.

Aside from Kat, she didn't have a lot of good friends in LA. She had developed a low tolerance for half the music scene in recent years and she was almost there with the other half. It was hard to stay sane and sober with constant parties, groupies, and every other temptation she could name, a second away.

After a meager breakfast she called the band's manager. She liked the idea that someone knew where they all were even though it wasn't required. They were all adults, but since they depended on one another for their jobs, more or less, it was the responsible thing to do.

That chore done, she went out on the small patio that halved the tiny yard. One thing she hated about LA was the lack of space. She paid a fortune for a house that was smaller than most apartments. At least it had some yard. That and the canyon overlook was what had drawn her to it. This was the longest amount of time she'd spent there. It was starting to bother her.

She pulled her phone back out of her pocket and quickly made airline reservations, pleased that she could do it all electronically. That left just one thing to do and it was the one she dreaded.

"Hello?" Fiona Cooper picked up just before it went to voicemail.

"Hey, Mama," Bailey said quietly. She made it a point to call her mother once a week. It wasn't time for their weekly call.

"Bailey? What's going on?"

"Nothing. I thought I'd fly in and spend some time at home. Is it okay if I stay with you?" She hated that she had to ask, but she couldn't just assume a warm welcome would be waiting for her. Her mother was nothing if not mercurial.

"Yeah, if you want to. You'll have to get your room ready when you get here. You bringing anyone?" Bailey didn't hear interest in her mother's voice. She could tell her mother's attention was elsewhere.

"No, just Elvis," she said. Not for the first time recently, she felt lonely.

"Guess they finally told you Beth's divorce is final."

"Um. What?" Bailey felt her heart drop. Her stomach dropped. Everything dropped at that moment. "No. No one said anything to me about that."

"They tell you about Dwight, then?" She heard her mother pour a drink in the background. Fiona never stopped tending bar.

She felt blindsided. "What's going on with Uncle Dwight?"

"He's in the hospital. Got a cold." Fiona didn't sound concerned.

"They don't put you in the hospital for just a cold, Mama."

"You think you know more?" Bailey heard the challenge in her mother's voice and backed down. She would find out later.

"No. I just thought maybe it was more than a cold." She wasn't even back there and already was regretting the trip. It would be different though. Her mother always came off cold over the telephone. At least she hoped it would be different.

"Nope. He's sick. So he's there. When you getting here?" Bailey heard the pressurized air leaving a bottle of beer as it was opened. She missed that sound.

"Day after tomorrow. I'll have Liz pick me up at the airport if she can. If not, I'll get a cab."

"Good. I'll have to have the bar open. Can't trust those idiots who work for me. See you in two days then."

"Bye, Mama. Love you."

"Love you too." Her mother disconnected the call first.

Now that her day was officially started and she'd handled the important duties, she just needed to pack for an extended stay. If she were honest with herself, she was glad for the opportunity. She missed her friends and family. She didn't really have much left in LA anymore. Her bandmates had families or hobbies that kept them busy when not on tour. When not traveling, her hobbies were gaming and writing songs. She could do that as easily from her mother's couch as she could from her own living room.

The real problem she had was baggage restrictions. So she called the shipping company she'd used last time and arranged a time to pick up a big box of her clothes, Elvis' toys, recording equipment, gaming systems, and books. By the time she was done packing it was lunchtime. She gazed around the small house and shook her head. The only things it seemed she hadn't packed were the awards and other band memorabilia, photos, and heavy winter clothes. Her house was surprisingly free of knick-knacks, souvenirs, and other things that made it more personal. All that was still in boxes. She had never taken the time to decorate.

LIZ COOPER PULLED the car into the parking lot of Fiona's bar. The old brick building looked as run-down as always. Bailey remembered asking her mother why she never updated the outside. Fiona had said that sprucing the place up would put off her clients. She ran a bar that catered to the working class. She didn't want any rich kids coming in and pushing out her regulars.

Liz followed a well-worn track around back to the house that stood behind and to the side of it. Bailey shook her head. There were seven cars at the bar and two at the house. She had to remember the time difference. It was later now with the time change. She was still on California time, but she knew that would change as soon as her body adjusted.

The car stopped behind her mother's beat up green Chevy parked beneath an overhang. She could see her old truck parked just in front of her mother's car. Bailey got out and opened the back door. Elvis was relieved. He'd had enough moving for one day. She agreed. Two flights and a long drive had worn them out. She hoisted her bags, Liz helped, and they entered the house. It was almost like walking back in time.

Bailey walked around the living room of her childhood home. It didn't seem that much had changed. Her mother had most of the same childhood pictures on the wall covering the faded wallpaper. The same shabby furniture still rested on that horrible green shag carpet Bailey had always hated. The house even smelled the same. She closed her eyes for a moment against the overwhelming thought that she was seventeen again and everything had been a dream.

Liz's voice brought her back from the half fantasy. "Same old place?"

"Of course. It's comforting," Bailey answered. "Thanks again for the ride."

"No problem. How long are you staying?" Liz brushed her long blonde hair behind her ears. Bailey smiled at that. Liz had always had that habit.

"I don't know. How's your dad? Are they letting him have visitors?" They hadn't talked much in the car. Liz worked constantly and spent most of the ride on the phone with a patient.

Even when they'd made the arrangements, Liz had been distracted and remarkably closed mouth about everything. Mike was Liz's twin brother, and between the stress of the wedding and Dwight's illness, Bailey didn't want to push Liz about anything.

"Yeah but only every two hours. It's too late to go this afternoon. They shut the whole floor down for a few hours for lunch, doctor visits and so forth. If you're wanting to go, they open it back up this evening." Liz sat down on the couch, took her glasses off and used her shirt to wipe off her lenses. Her green eyes stared in an unfocused way. It made Bailey a little uncomfortable because it was so different from the mental image she carried with her of Liz. They had often been told they looked so much alike, but age and motherhood seemed to have changed Liz more than life as a rock icon had changed Bailey. There was more weight in Liz's round face and a sight slump to her shoulders Bailey had never seen there before.

"I'll go tomorrow then. I should let Elvis get used to these surroundings and spend some time with Mama." Bailey ran her hand through her hair, causing it to spike more than normal. She sat down on the chair facing the couch and leaned forward. It still felt strange to be there.

"Cindy said you were meeting her for lunch tomorrow," Liz said. She was no longer distracted and looked at Bailey with some concern.

"Yeah, you're going to be there?" She had learned it was better to ask than assume. Cindy and Liz were not as close as they were to some of the others in the little group.

"Of course. Look, your mom didn't tell me what all she told you. You must have a ton of questions."

"A few, yeah." Bailey looked at Liz, wanting to see the truth in her answers. "How come you didn't tell me about your dad? You know he's the closest thing I have to a father." It was true. Uncle Dwight was her mother's brother. The family had been very close once.

Liz shrugged. "He asked me not to. He didn't want to worry you needlessly."

"Being in the hospital doesn't cause needless worrying."

"I know, but until he came down with pneumonia it looked as if he was going to easily beat the cancer."

"Cancer? That's why Cindy and Mike are getting married so quickly. Why didn't anyone tell me?" She felt as if the floor had given way and the whole building had sunk ten feet. She took a deep breath and steadied herself.

"Yep. You know Cindy. She's an alarmist and she didn't want to tell you over the phone," Liz said in a reassuring manner.

"So you think he'll be okay?" Liz was pretty grounded and didn't often overestimate things. She usually took her time to reach a conclusion and Bailey trusted her judgment.

"If he can beat the pneumonia. I think he can beat the cancer."

"Man, I hope so."

"He'll be okay. Anything else? I should really get back to the office and you need rest, I'm sure." Liz stood and brushed off her pants. As always it was a little disconcerting to see her look so professional and grown up.

"I think that's enough for now. I'm not sure I want to know what else you guys have been keeping from me." Bailey stood as well. "I'll walk next door and see if Mama needs any help. Elvis will love it. He loves people."

"Great. I'll see you tomorrow then." Liz paused at the door, suddenly looking every bit her age. "Bailey?"

"Yeah?" Bailey looked up from where she'd been attempting to put on Elvis's leash.

"I'm glad you're home. We've missed you." And with that, Liz closed the door behind her.

While Bailey hadn't used the leash to get Elvis out of the car, she opted to use it on the way across the yard to the bar. There were always stray cats living around there. She didn't want him to chase one and have either of them get hit.

The bar was a long brick building. It looked as old now as it had looked to Bailey when she was a child. Like a lot of other things, it hadn't changed. She smelled the cigarette smoke ten feet from the door. It made her nose itch. She could no longer stand the smell. Right below the smell of stale cigarettes was the stench of cheap aftershave and cologne. Above both, almost tart in its power was the smell of stale alcohol. It was, in a strange way, the smell Bailey associated most with home.

"Hey, Mama," she called from the door, waiting for her eyes to adjust to the dim light. Elvis stayed right by her side.

"Bailey. There's my girl." Fiona strode around the bar and flung her arms wide. She had clearly started drinking already but was fortunately in a good mood.

Bailey peered through the gloom and noticed only a few people sitting at the bar. "How's business?"

"Good. Good. Come on in. Want something?" She returned

behind the bar area.

"No thanks. You look good, Mama." Bailey was amazed. As hard as her mother lived, it never showed on her face.

"Listen at you flattering me. I'm on to you, girl. You'll have to get someone else to feed you. The grill's all greased over and the guys haven't been by to clean it." Her mother jerked her thumb over her shoulder at the ancient grill.

"It's okay. I'll pick something up. You want anything?"

"Nah. Got plenty to eat here." Fiona waved an expansive hand. "Go on. Go explore and go eat before you waste away. I don't know how you stay so thin."

Bailey chuckled. "It's easy when you're on tour. And I work out a bit. Helps the stamina."

"Uh huh. You can tell me about it later. I gotta keep an eye on these fellas." A few of the guys on the barstools made grunting noises. Bailey assumed that indicated their amusement.

"Okay. I'll see you later, Mama." Bailey shrugged and turned to leave. She hated feeling as if she'd walked back in time, but it was just how it affected her. She didn't know another way to be present in her mother's life without constantly feeling like an awkward teenager.

Bailey made sure Elvis was still beside her and left the building. She walked back toward the house, heading for the detached garage. Bailey only left one thing in her mother's care. It was a custom-made motorcycle they'd used in a video several years ago. Bailey had fallen in love with it and managed to talk the production team out of it. They even included the sidecar. Elvis loved it. She had installed a special harness for him not long after she'd gotten him.

Bailey opened the garage door and walked inside. Her motorcycle was waiting for her beneath the tarp. She removed it, sneezing a little at the dust and sighed. It still gleamed as if it were brand new. Mike checked on it once a week for her to make sure it was always ready to be ridden. She heard a clatter and turned around to find Elvis already sitting in the sidecar.

"You wanna go for a ride, boy?" She got the helmets from the shelf by the door. "Okay. Let's cruise."

She buckled him in and then put on his helmet and goggles. He waited patiently for her to open the mechanical door. She put on her own helmet, climbed on board and kicked it to life. It roared instantly. Bailey sighed in complete bliss, but then sighed again and adjusted the mirrors. It was odd. They were aimed for someone much taller. She knew it hadn't been Mike. He wasn't much taller than she was. She shrugged it off and put it in gear. It was possible she had accidentally moved them when she removed the tarp. She decided not to let it worry her. It was too good an evening to waste.

She steered the motorcycle toward the beach. It always surprised her how different the beaches of home were compared to the beaches of LA. It was clear and the visibility was high. It smelled like salt and water, sand and the indefinable air of home. The water wasn't blue and there were no waves to speak of, but it was beautiful all the same.

Bailey pulled over and parked. The walkway along the beach was deserted. She unbuckled Elvis from the sidecar and then buckled him into his harness. He was well trained, but the city did have leash laws. Together they walked along the path, taking in the sights and smells of home.

It was still hot. In this area, summer died a slow and painful death every year to be replaced by an abbreviated winter and then a short spring. Bailey was no longer used to the humidity. Neither was Elvis. They stayed for as long as she felt comfortable keeping him from drinking water. The sun was just touching the horizon when they started for her mom's house. They were both hungry, so she made a quick detour through a drive through.

Chapter Two

THE AUTO PARTS store wasn't terribly far from the bar. It was a small town, so truthfully nothing was very far from anything else. Bailey parked the truck and went inside. The bell tingled when the door opened, and she was hit with another wave of nostalgia. The store smelled like her grandfather and her great uncle. It smelled like parts, new oil and clean machinery.

Bailey saw her cousin Mike as she blinked tears from her eyes. He was behind the counter as always, helping a customer. "Hey, Mike."

"Bailey!" Mike's face split in a wide grin. "Dude, I've missed you."

"I've missed you, too, big guy." She stopped a moment to admire the neatly trimmed beard he sported. It was different than his usual clean-shaven look and it suited him. "I like the beard," she said as he came around to envelope her into a crushing hug. The dirty blond beard made him look a little older and a little less like a surfer.

"Thanks." He turned to someone else behind the counter. "Tim, can you help Ms. Lewis? Her car keeps making a funny, squeaky sound."

"Sure, boss," Tim said, and stepped up to the customer.

"Come back into my office," Mike said. He leaned over and held the divider between the counters open. "You know the way."

"That I do." This auto parts store was one of the last locally owned and operated ones on the Coast. Their grandfather had started it. The only reason Bailey hadn't worked there over the summer like the rest of the Cooper clan had was because she worked at the bar, much to her aunt's dismay.

"So have you seen everyone yet?" Mike asked as he opened his office door.

"Everyone keeps asking me who I've seen so far." Bailey shrugged. "But the answer is no. Liz picked me up at the airport. I'm supposed to go to lunch with your charming fiancée." She let her accent out a little more pronounced than normal. "In about an hour. I thought I'd swing by here and see how you were doing."

"I'm great. Aside from Dad's issues." Mike sat behind the

desk and sighed. "I hope he makes it. I'm not ready to lose him yet."

"Me either. Not sure we get to vote on that though. Remember what happened when Cindy's dad died?" She took a good look at him as well. It was the first time she'd seen him in almost a year. He had bulked up a little. The shoulders of his uniform shirt were tighter than they had been. He looked good. The part of her mind that always worried about Mike relaxed.

"You know, I still think that old woman killed him." Mike didn't get along with his future mother in-law. In fact, most people didn't get along with Cindy's mother. "She's mean. Hates me."

"Me too," Bailey said. "But she loves Liz."

"Everyone loves Liz. She's the perfect one." Mike made a face to show there was no bitterness in that statement. "Anyway, there's a serious question I need to ask you. So I'm glad you're here."

"Okay, shoot. I think by now you know there's not much I wouldn't do for you," she said. She hadn't meant to remind him of anything in particular, just that she was there for him.

"I know. And look, Bailey, I love you like a sister. I owe so much to you for everything. Really. I don't think I would have made it this far without you. So, Cindy and I were talking. Actually, it's my decision. Look, I'd like you to be my best man."

It took her a moment to understand what he was asking. "Seriously?" She had expected to fight off Cindy and a revolting bridesmaid dress. "Do I get to wear a tux?"

"Better. We might be going full morning suit." Mike grinned. "Top hat and all. I haven't decided yet."

Bailey smiled back. "Excellent. I'm honored. Really. And yes, I'll gladly stand beside you and help ensure you have an outstanding day."

"Bailey, you've made my dreams come true. I can't think of anyone else I'd want to stand up there with me except my dad. And well..." He shrugged and looked down at his desk.

"I know." She did. It was still a bit difficult for them at times. She glanced at the clock on the wall. "Shit. I need to head to the café, speaking of your wonderful future mother-in-law."

"I should make sure Tim's not trying to fix a squeaky belt with solvent. It's happened." He stood and ran his hand down his beard.

Bailey stood as well. "Oh man, yeah, save your customers. I'll go eat with your bride-to-be."

"Have fun. Thanks again, Bailey." He pulled her into a brief hug.

"My pleasure, my man. My pleasure."

Bailey climbed into the old truck and waited until it was time to crank it. It was an old diesel and needed to be treated very gently to keep it going. She loved it. It was another relic of her childhood. She had learned to drive in it and had her first kiss on the hood. There were more memories in that truck for her than there was rust on the bumper.

She cautiously made her way downtown, the streets narrowed due to curbside parking. It was an outdoor city and it seemed as if everyone was out and about. By the time she found a decent place to park, it was time to meet her friends for lunch.

Bailey sighed a little with nervous energy, crossed the street and entered the old building. The café had been in the same place for almost seventy-five years. The same family had owned it for that length of time. The Arnoux family was a proud one with deep roots in the community.

"Bailey." Ms. Arnoux smirked as Bailey walked past her. She was too startled to return it.

"Cindy, why does your mother look happy to see me?" Bailey asked as she joined Cindy and Liz. They were sitting at a table for four not too far inside the doors.

Cindy Arnoux stood to greet her old friend. "Why wouldn't she? My mom likes you."

"Your mother only looks happy when I'm leaving somewhere. She hates me. This isn't news," Bailey said when the hug ended.

"Maybe she thinks having a famous rock star eat at her café will be good for business," Liz teased.

"Please. I'm so not famous here." Bailey shrugged it off and sat down at the table. Not much seemed to have changed. Just to be sure, she grabbed a menu.

"No, you're notorious," Cindy said. She was toying with the end of a thick braid of black hair. "Did you really get champagne dumped on you at the awards show?"

"Yeah. Hollywood dykes have so much drama." Bailey tried to shrug that off as well. She thought about telling them the story behind it but decided against it. "Is the special still The Special? Your mom may hate my guts, but she makes one hell of a country fried steak."

"Yes," Cindy said. She took the menu and then made a sign to the waitress who had their table. "Does Beth know you're back yet?"

"Not as far as I know. We just flew in last night. I've only seen you two, Mama and Mike."

"Who is we? I don't see anyone with you. And your mom didn't say she was expecting anyone else." Cindy looked around as if expecting to see a surprise visitor.

"Duh. I brought my dog with me. Like I was going to leave Elvis with some Hollywood dog sitter. I'd come back home and he'd have issues and phobias that would probably turn him neurotic."

"I don't think that's how it works," Cindy said as the waitress placed a very hot plate in front of Bailey. "So where are you staying?"

"With my mother." Bailey rolled her eyes at the sour look on Cindy's face. Bailey assumed Cindy was still mad at Fiona for not sharing family information. "So, what's going on?"

"Damn, I've got to go." Liz stood as her phone began making alert sounds. "See you later, Cindy. Bailey, mom would love to see you. Stop by the hospital later, okay?"

"Absolutely." Bailey stood and gave her a hug. "Tell Aunt Ellen I'll be up there later."

Cindy waited until Bailey had resumed her seat before attempting to change the conversation. "So, how was the flight?"

"The usual. They kept staring at me like I was going to set the bathroom on fire." She sighed happily as she looked down at her plate. "So what gives?"

"Nothing more than I said the other day. We need you here, Bailey. It's a tough time for all of us with Liz's dad's health, my wedding and Beth's divorce. You complete our group. We've never been as strong without you as we are with you."

"I just don't get it. I mean in the last week you've called, my mom's called and even Beth emailed me." She shook her head and then asked the question she'd wanted to ask since she arrived back home. "How's she doing?"

"Beth? You can ask her yourself. There she is." Cindy smiled and waved.

Bailey glanced behind her and felt her stomach drop to her knees. Beth Forsyth was there as if she'd been conjured. She waved at Cindy. She looked as beautiful as always. She could have just stepped out on the balcony in Vienna. Bailey felt her heart constrict as she took in Beth's appearance for the first time in two years. The auburn hair gently curled against her shoulders and framed the heart-shaped face appealingly. The green eyes sparkled and, as always, there was a slight smile hovering around the full lips. Suddenly Bailey wished she had stayed in California.

"Bailey?" There was definite surprise in that voice. "Bailey? I almost didn't see you there."

"Hi, Beth." Bailey stood. It was an awkward hug. "Good to see you."

"You too. Am I interrupting?" She looked down at the table.

"Don't be silly," Cindy said. "Of course you're not. Sit down. Want something to eat?" Cindy had long since stopped working at her mother's café, but she still liked to direct the wait staff on occasion. She held up a hand and gestured for the waitress to bring another Special.

"Yeah. I'm just on lunch. I thought I'd get out of the office today."

"Good plan," Cindy said. "It is a beautiful day. I was so grateful for the student holiday. We only had to work half a day today."

"Yeah. It is a nice day." Bailey eyed Cindy suspiciously, but the other woman merely smirked. Something was at play here. She could tell.

"So, Bailey, did you see your uncle yet?" Beth asked.

"No. I got in late yesterday afternoon. I'm going up there after this though." She felt the sudden need to justify everything. Somehow Beth always made her feel vaguely guilty about something. "How have you been?"

"I'm good." Beth looked down at the plate that had suddenly appeared before her. "Better now. This has got to be my favorite meal here."

"Cindy told me you and Bastard split." It was hard to make small talk to someone to whom she was once able to bare her soul.

"Yeah. Bastard flew in long enough to sign the papers and then flew back out." She said cheerfully.

"Ah." There wasn't anything to say to that.

"I hear you wear champagne well. Funny. I always imagined a whipped cream pie myself." A dig. Beth was playing it cool. She was still mad about something.

"You know champagne does tend to go with everything." Bailey felt the ground rise back up beneath her feet. This she could handle. She was clueless as to where Beth's anger was coming from, but she could handle the cutting remarks.

"So I saw." Beth leaned over and placed a cool hand on hers. "I bet that was rough. She was an attractive young girl. How long did it take you to find someone to take her place? Minutes? Or did you hire it done?"

"Excuse me?" Bailey almost choked on her tea. She looked over at Cindy who also looked fairly shocked at Beth's comments. They were so out of character, she didn't know how to react. Her fight or flight instinct kicked in and told her to leave quickly. "Cindy, I'll catch up with you later. I'm gonna help Mama open the bar and then go see Uncle Dwight." She pulled a few bills from her pocket and tossed them on the table. "Later."

"Bailey, wait." Beth called.

"What?" Bailey half expected more derision.

"Truce?" Beth offered. Her green eyes were dulled. With shame or embarrassment, Bailey couldn't tell which. "At least stay long enough to eat your meal."

"Okay." Had it been anything other than Arnoux's famous chicken fried steak, she may have left. Instead she reclaimed her seat. There was also the feeling, however fleeting, that she deserved Beth's attitude.

Things were tense after that. Cindy did her best to keep the conversation flowing, but Bailey was a little too confused and hurt to pay much attention. When they got on the topic of the wedding, Bailey turned her attention fully to her meal. She only realized there was silence at the table when she reached her mashed potatoes and gravy.

"Huh?" She asked around a mouthful of potatoes and gravy.

"I asked if you've talked to Mike yet?" Cindy seemed more amused than angry at having to repeat herself.

"Yes. I went by there first to give my congrats to the big guy." She said after a long drink of tea.

"So what'd you say?" The bride-to-be's eyes sparkled.

"I said yes of course." Bailey was astounded she had to ask.

"Yes to what?" Beth asked.

"Mike wants Bailey to be his best man." Cindy looked ready to cry. "I'm so happy you said yes. Thank you."

"That's nice." Beth had gone a little pale. She pushed her chair back and stood. "I'm glad that you'll stand up with him. Excuse me, I need to get back to the bank. Cindy, I'll call you later. Bailey, it was good to see you in daylight and dry clothes."

"What?" Bailey stopped when Cindy put her hand up.

"She's still pissed at you, my friend." She said as soon as Beth was out of earshot. "I wonder if I should have them box up her lunch?"

"That much is obvious. What did I do this time?" This time. It seemed as if it was always something. She regretted the trip back.

"I'm the wrong person to ask. Talk to her." Cindy shrugged. "I'll have them box it up and drop it off at the bank. Hey, I've got another favor to ask of you, since you're here and all."

"What?" She asked suspiciously.

"Come play for my class? You brought a guitar, didn't you?" Cindy asked.

"Of course." Bailey scoffed. "As if I travel without one. Please."

"So?" Cindy pressed.

Bailey gave in easily. "Okay. When would be good for you?"

"I don't know for sure. Maybe you can do it sometime next week. You have any plans?"

"Nope. I'm supposed to be writing some stuff, but so far, zilch." She shrugged. "I don't know why. Seems like everything's already been written."

"You'll come up with something great. You always do." Cindy got up from the table. "I need to go make sure Mike leaves the shop on time. He promised me a nice romantic dinner. I aim to collect."

"Awesome." Bailey smiled. She couldn't be happier for her friends. Cindy and Mike were proof that love did indeed triumph. "I'm gonna head back to Mama's and see if she needs help. Or at least chill out for a while." She hugged Cindy. "Call me when you want to set something up at the school."

"Will do. Thanks, Bailey."

BAILEY WAS BOTH pleased and rattled by the day's turn of events. She loved and missed her cousins. They had all grown up together. In fact, Mike, Liz, and Bailey were only weeks apart. Mike was the oldest twin by seven minutes. Bailey was born barely two weeks later. They'd been inseparable, a trio of trouble until they started school. Then it didn't take long for their trio to grow to six with the addition of Beth, Diana and Cindy. They'd all remained friends from elementary school through college and beyond. The four of them, Cindy, Beth, Bailey and Liz had remained close despite Mike's issues and Diana's death. It wasn't until Bailey dropped out of college and left for LA that any distance grew between them, the most between Beth and Bailey. They patched it up eventually, but it was something Bailey still struggled to keep from happening again.

After Bailey got back to the house, she let Elvis outside and watched as he sniffed around a lot before taking care of business and coming back inside. She could hear the jukebox from the bar and decided she really didn't want to see if her mother needed help. She knew the woman didn't. Fiona had been running that bar since before Bailey was born. She had a few waitresses and a bartender, but she ran most of the show herself.

Bailey sighed and sat down on the couch. She pulled off her boots and then waited. It didn't take long before Elvis was attempting to remove her socks. For some strange reason, the dog would allow her to be barefoot or have shoes on, but he couldn't stand socks. Bailey understood. She wasn't a big fan of them either.

Elvis had just succeeded in removing the second one when they heard the knock at the door. Not expecting anything, except maybe a delivery of her stuff from LA, she ambled to the door. She almost decided to pretend she wasn't at home when she saw Beth's silhouette through the curtains.

"Hi," she said, but didn't open the screen door.

"Hi." Beth waited on the very edge of the porch. "Can I come in?"

"Yeah, I suppose." Bailey kicked at the door with a bare foot. It swung open. "Come in." This was awkward.

"Thanks." Beth shut the door behind her. "I'm sorry about lunch. I really wasn't expecting to see you."

"It's okay. I'm sure I deserved it." She raised an eyebrow.

"That's kinda loaded."

"Sorry. I don't really do the whole passive aggressive martyr thing well." She answered. That was true. Bailey was usually blunt and to the point.

"I know. You never have. I'd hoped you would have given as good as you got. You normally do." Beth said.

"Are you saying you wanted to pick a fight with me?" Bailey said. That seemed out of character.

"Yeah. And I'm sorry." Beth took a seat on the very edge of the couch as if she were afraid of getting comfortable. "Would you believe that I still have anger?"

"Yes." Bailey sat down as well. "I'm sorry. I guess I never really apologized for how I behaved at your wedding."

"Well, you certainly lived up to your reputation as the bad girl of rock and roll. But that's not why I'm angry with you." Beth sighed. "Jerry abandoned us, you know. He took off with some tramp and fled the country, after he'd embezzled a ton of money from his clients."

"He what?" This was news. She wondered for a brief moment why no one had told her. "Bastard."

"It wasn't a complete shock when the end happened. It was more the manner in which it happened." Beth said.

"I'm sorry." Bailey could not think of anything else to say, at least not anything that wouldn't cause more problems than they already had. Bailey may have always been blunt, but she had learned tact.

"I don't believe you are. You never liked Jerry," Beth countered.

"Is that why you're mad at me?" It seemed unlikely, but Bailey wouldn't take anything for granted. "Because I never liked your husband?" She hated granting him that title. It stuck in her throat.

"Sort of." Beth looked down at her hands. "Bailey, that was one of the three toughest times of my life and you weren't here for it. I had to go through all of that without my best friend. I feel like I've had to go through the last fifteen years without you. I mean sure, you've been here for this or that, and there's always our trips for your birthday, but damn, Bailey. You emotionally disappeared on me. Even when you moved to LA, after things got settled, I could call and we would talk for hours about any problem I had, or thought I had. Then suddenly you're gone. Poof. Add that to the worry of whether or not I'd see lurid details about you slapped all over the press and it's a lot of rage. For fuck's sake, you're notorious. Every time I saw your name in the paper or on the web, my heart would freeze because I knew it was bad news."

"Beth, oh man, I am so sorry." Bailey moved closer and pulled her into an embrace. She had no other response to that. "I've got you," she whispered as Beth began to cry into her shoulder.

It took everything she had to keep from breaking down herself. She'd never really paused to think how her actions would affect her friends. She never thought about how her intentional absence from Beth's company would affect Beth. She'd been more concerned with her own feelings and desires. She never gave a second thought to how they would feel about her carefully cultivated image. Most of all, Bailey had never realized just how selfish she'd been by withholding the one thing Beth wanted from her, her friendship, because she was mad that Beth had chosen to marry Jerry.

"Ouch." It was more of a rough push than a slap. Bailey felt the sting in her arm down to her fingers.

"You always leave when I need you. Why?" Beth pulled back and looked at her.

"Because I'm a selfish bitch." It was the only answer she could produce, and while it wasn't the whole answer, it was enough to start. "I chose a music career over my friends. I suck. I'm sorry."

It felt odd to be accepting all the blame. After Beth's wedding and the subsequent fallout from that, Bailey had made the attempt to be more present in her friends' lives. She had even been present at the birth of Beth's children. It was just so hard to remain present in Beth's life. There was more baggage there than with the others. Jerry hadn't helped matters. They had loathed one another almost on sight.

"I know. I've missed you." Beth sighed and stood. "I'm sorry. I didn't mean to come over here and dump all over you. I wanted to apologize and well, the rest kinda just happened." She looked sheepishly down at Bailey.

"Next time will be better, right?" Bailey stood, realizing that the visit had come to an end. "I'll be here for a while. If you need to dump again, I'll be here."

"Promise?" Beth held out the pinky finger of her right hand.

"I promise." Bailey hooked their fingers together. "Go take care of your kids. I have to go see if Mama's eaten anything other than the garnish on her drinks."

"Later, Bailey."

"Bye." Bailey watched until Beth had gotten in her car before shutting the door. It was true, there was no place like home.

Chapter Three

WHILE SHE WAS no stranger to hospitals, Bailey had never spent much time at the local hospital. Her mother had surprisingly not been accident prone when drinking and no one in her immediate family had ever been admitted for more than a night or two. Mostly her childhood experience with the hospital had been the occasional emergency room visit when she had broken her arm or when Mike, Liz or Scott had done something equally stupid and damaging.

It smelled too clean in the building. She knew that was universal. Every hospital she'd ever been in had that same over clean smell. Under the smell of bleach, she could pick up traces of the cafeteria and the faint hint of illness. At least she imagined she could smell that last. Hospitals didn't precisely scare her, but they didn't inspire comfort either.

She'd parked at the front of the building and followed her mother's directions through the long deserted hallways. She shook her head. The hospital was laid out a lot like an airport that had grown too fast. It was oddly spaced and hard to get anywhere quickly.

Finally, she found her uncle's room on the third floor. She paused for a moment outside the closed door to gather herself. She had never seen her uncle in a weakened condition. She knew it would be a shock and didn't want to let it register on her face. Dwight may have been her uncle, but she'd spent as much time at his house with Mike and Liz as she had at her own.

"I heard someone was playing sick?" She said as she opened the door.

"I just did it to get you home." Dwight was sitting up in bed reading a paper. He put it down and smiled at her. He almost looked healthy, until she noticed the oxygen tube at his nose, the weight loss and the pallor of someone who hadn't seen the outside in a long time.

"That's what I heard." Bailey said and closed the door behind her. "Where's Aunt Ellen?"

"At work. I think she needs the distraction and I don't need to be watched every minute of the day. Of course, I say that and I'm in a hospital where I'm watched all day and night." He chuckled a little and then coughed.

"You okay?" Bailey handed him the water sitting on the table next to his bed.

"Yeah. I'll be okay. I'm just tired of being poked, prodded, bled and force fed. I just want to go home and watch basketball in my underwear." He sighed. "The oxygen treatments are every four hours, but I'm not sure what good they're doing. I just want to watch TV in peace for once."

"You can do that here. Not sure the nurses will like it if you sit around in your underwear, but you can." Bailey didn't have anything to say about oxygen treatments or anything, so she ignored it.

"My TV is bigger at home," he grumbled.

"I know. Seriously though, you need anything?" She asked.

"Bailey, please don't ask me that. If it's not Mike in here looking at me all teary eyed and reproachful I have Liz pretending nothing's wrong. My wife, the rest of my kids and friends all tiptoeing around my bed as if breathing heavy will knock me dead. Please. Just act normal. I need that." He sounded tired and frustrated.

"Why haven't you said anything to them?" She asked, amazed. He was usually as blunt as every other Cooper.

"Because I'm sick. It's not convenient for them. They don't know how to handle it," he said honestly. "I can understand that, but it gets frustrating sometimes trying to be strong for them."

"So why tell me?" she asked. They'd been close, but it had always been an adult/child relationship. He had never confided in her like an equal before. It was disconcerting.

"Because like your grandfather, you don't usually stand on convention. You also seem to let people be who they want to be. You did that with Mike," he said. "You have this habit of accepting people for who they are."

"Yeah, well, growing up around a bunch of drunks will do that." Bailey searched for something else to talk about. She didn't want it to get emotional. "So, when are you and Ellen taking the bikes across the country?"

"Soon as I finish kicking this cancer's ass." Dwight said. "It's not taking me out. Doctor said this morning my lungs are clear. As soon as the respiratory guy gives me the all clear, I'm out of here and back to fighting the good fight."

"You mean I flew all this way for nothing?"

"Not for nothing. You got to see me." He smiled wide. "I'm worth the trip."

"That is true." She had to laugh. Something about the

Coopers gave them arrogance and swagger that almost always got them into trouble. "Cindy wants me to come play for her class and Mike asked me to be his best man. Is that okay with you?"

"I don't mind if you play for her class," Dwight joked. "Mike and I have a very rocky relationship, I know. It's not easy. I don't expect you to understand. And it's not because you're not a parent or because you're whatever. It's because, like I said before, you and your grandfather are a lot alike. When I get out of here, I'll try to make it up to him. I made a lot of mistakes where he's concerned. I'm just glad it's not too late."

"That's not really my concern, if you know what I mean. It's between you guys. I was just curious if you were okay with not being his best man." She shrugged it off, not wanting to get too personal. It was making her uncomfortable, seeing and hearing him speak so honestly and openly. It had been hard trying to maintain a relationship with both Dwight and Mike during the more turbulent times.

"Yeah. You've earned it." He looked sad and introspective.

"Excuse me, dear." A nurse poked her head around the door. "I'm sorry, Mr. Cooper it's time to take your vitals."

"Guess that's my cue." Bailey stood. "I'll come back tomorrow and see you, if you're still here."

"Your mom will know where to find me, I'm sure." He waited until she was at the door before calling back out. "Bailey, thanks for coming. This stays between us, right?"

"Of course." She winked at him and walked out.

It didn't take as much time for her to find the truck as it did for her to find Uncle Dwight's room. She had no real plans for the rest of the day so decided to go pick up Elvis and go visit Scott at his tattoo studio. She didn't want him to feel left out.

THERE WAS ALREADY a good-sized crowd at the bar when she pulled in the driveway. She ignored that and walked over to the house. Elvis was happy to see her, especially since she said the magic words. It didn't take long to get him buckled in the sidecar and drive to Scott's new tattoo studio. Liz had described it for her, but Bailey wanted to see the place for herself. Her younger cousin was a gifted artist and she was glad he was getting popular.

Bailey parked the motorcycle in front, unbuckled Elvis and snapped his leash to his harness. She didn't know if having a dog in a tattoo parlor was a health code violation, but she was willing to risk it. After all, she wouldn't be taking him behind the counter around the machines.

"You can't bring a dog in here," a large fake blonde woman with multiple facial piercings said when she walked inside.

"A dog?" Scott Cooper stood up and looked over the counter. "That's Elvis. Bailey. How the hell are you?"

"Pretty good, cousin. I was told you wanted to see me."

"Always." Scott grinned. He used a gloved hand to wave before brushing his long blond hair back from his eyes with his wrist. "Give me a minute. We're almost done. Keep Elvis in front of the counter though."

"No worries." Bailey sat down on one of the plush couches and picked up one of the portfolios lining the low table beside it.

"I am so sorry. I had no idea. I mean Scott said you're his cousin, but I didn't know if that was just bullshit. I mean there's a lot of Coopers in the world and a lot of people have blonde hair. You do kinda look like him though. I mean, your hair is purple now, but I've seen it blonde. The eyes are the same shade of blue."

"It's okay. Breathe," Bailey said. She was worried for a moment the poor woman would pass out from lack of oxygen. "Seriously, it's okay. Do you have a name?"

"Most people around here call me Dolly," She answered. "I do the piercings. Do you need anything?"

"No, I'm good. I already set off metal detectors. I don't need any more."

"Did you want to gauge any? I mean I've never seen you gauge your ears."

"I never did." Bailey flipped through the portfolio. "This is neat. Who did this?"

"That's Dev's. He's new too." Scott answered as he came around the counter. He was wearing a tartan kilt, skater style shoes, and a white dress shirt with the sleeves rolled up almost to his elbows. Unlike his brother Mike, Scott was clean shaven.

"Look at you, attracting talent and stuff." She said as he engulfed her in a hug.

"I wouldn't be if it wasn't for Mike. Half the people who go to the store see that tattoo on his arm and he sends them here. Of course your interview in the tattoo magazine a few years back didn't hurt either." He took a seat next to her on the couch.

"I just told the truth. You are my favorite tattoo artist." She shrugged. "What you got for me? Liz said you had an idea."

"Well you know how we've been wanting to find something

to tie everything together on your left arm to finish the sleeve? You've got a whole group of different tats up and down your arm and nothing to tie them together. I think I've discovered it."

"What did you have in mind?" She asked.

"Well, we can go with music notes or verses, quotes, flowers or this based on the old illuminated manuscripts the Celts used. What do you think?" He grabbed a notebook off the table and flipped to a page to show her what he was talking about.

"That's gorgeous and a hell of a lot better than flowers or music notes. But it looks very involved." She examined it closely.

"It is. You're not scared of the pain, are you?" He asked. His smile was wide and his eyes twinkled a little.

"No. I just think maybe the Book of Kells is a little too highbrow for me. What else you got?" She rolled her eyes at him. She could tell he enjoyed teasing her.

"All right I'll leave the Book of Kells for my sister, if she ever decides to get a tattoo. Other than the one she already has. I've got this. It's Van Gogh's sky. Kind of a Van Gogh clouds inspired theme."

"I've got to say, Scott, that's one of the most gorgeous things I've seen in a very long time. We can go with that one." She looked at the drawing in awe.

"Sweet. When do you want to start?" He glanced at the clock. "I have another appointment in a few minutes, but we can schedule something."

"I don't know. When do you have time? I'm pretty much free whenever. Well, I do have to play for your future sister-in-law's class in a few days. Other than that, I have no plans."

Scott tossed his notebook back on the low table in front of the couch. "Mike said he asked you to be in the wedding."

"Yeah. You gonna be in it?"

"Groomsman. Paul flat out refused, pompous ass that he is. You know, the man has never forgiven him. And because Liz and I are okay with it, he's mad at us too."

"Paul always did have pretensions. It was like he was always looking down his nose at us." Paul was the oldest of the Cooper children. "What about Jordan?"

"Jordan is still deployed. He said he's trying to make it home, but he's also trying to keep the time open if something happens with Dad. And Heath is just the usual hippy weirdo. He's said he'll be an usher, but he's not wearing a tux, and he's not cutting his hair."

"There are too many of you sometimes." She shook her head.

She was closest to Mike, Liz and Scott mainly because they were the closest in age. Scott was only eighteen months younger than they were. He had even been a grade behind in school. Paul was five years older than Bailey and never forgot that fact.

"Six. With you, we're seven." He grinned. "Come on, you know you're practically one of us anyway. And look, we have the whole gamut. Artist, musician, dirty hippy, therapist, small business owner, army dude and asshole."

"That is true. What is Heath doing for a living now days? Last I heard he had built a yurt and was trying to be a goat farmer." Heath was the youngest Cooper and was vying for the title of strangest.

"Add growing organic soybeans to that and you have my wayward brother. You know he walks into town to use the payphone. Won't have a phone at his place and won't dare use a cellphone." Scott shook his head. "I don't get it."

"And I thought I did too many drugs once upon a time." Bailey said. Her cousins always kept life interesting if nothing else. "I won't keep you. Give me a shout when you want to meet up and get started on that epicness."

"Sure. Give me your new cell number. Aunt Fiona said you changed the last one." He picked up his notebook again and rummaged on the table until he found a pen.

"Dude, I've had the same number for almost twenty years, I think. I haven't changed it." She was slightly confused by that. "She was probably drunk." It was the go to excuse and was usually the correct one.

"Give it to me again though. I think I deleted it." He wrote it down as she stood and gathered the dog. "Thanks for bringing Elvis. He's so well behaved."

"True. If only we could keep his drooling under control." Bailey wiped the couch with a handkerchief she kept for just such occasions. "Thanks, Scott. Nice to meet you, Dolly."

"Have a great day," Dolly called.

"I'll call you. See ya, Bailey." Scott pulled the door closed behind her.

Chapter Four

"MAMA HAVE YOU seen my jacket?" Bailey asked as she searched through her suitcase again. She hadn't unpacked really. She was as accustomed to living out of bags as she was having clothes hanging in a closet.

"What jacket?" Fiona stood at the door, a glass of orange juice in her hand. Her blue eyes were bleary from too much alcohol and too little sleep.

"My motorcycle jacket. I can't seem to find it."

"Maybe you left it over at one of your friend's houses." Fiona shrugged and walked back to the living room. Bailey followed.

"I don't think so. I don't remember wearing it since I got home. Except on the motorcycle of course." She loved that jacket. It was one of her favorite things.

"I'm surprised you keep up with anything. You sure you didn't get wasted and leave it somewhere?" Fiona's tone was one of forced unconcern.

"Positive," Bailey answered in exasperation. "I don't drink, Mama. I haven't in several years."

"Oh yeah, you're an angel. I forgot. So we should forget all your bad behavior from previous years." Fiona seemed to take Bailey's sobriety as an affront.

"Mama, did you borrow my jacket?" Bailey ignored the rest of her mother's statements. It wasn't anything she hadn't heard before. It was the tone of her voice that made her suspicious.

"Why would you dare ask such things?" The outrage was obviously feigned.

"Because it's my fucking jacket. I love that thing." It wasn't often she stood her ground with her mother. They fought often and sometimes viciously, but Bailey usually backed down when pressed.

Fiona's eyes widened. "I would never."

"Mama, come on. It's missing. The last place I had it was here. Just tell me if you borrowed it. I want to wear it to the school today."

"Fine. I borrowed it. Big deal. I bet you let some of those sluts of yours wear it."

"Mama, there's a few things I don't like anyone to touch but me. That jacket is one of them." It was true. Bailey was very protective of her motorcycle, her motorcycle jacket and her oldest guitar. The jacket and guitar she had worked for while in high school. It took a long time for her to earn enough to pay for them.

"Whatever. It's in my closet." Her mother waved her hand in a dismissive motion and walked out the door.

Bailey sighed in resignation and walked to her mother's room. She remembered doing the same thing several times while in high school. Her mother always borrowed clothes without asking. It was something Bailey never understood. It wasn't as if Bailey wore typical girl clothes either. Mostly she'd worn jeans with various levels of holes, rips and gashes, and either overly large men's dress shirts or T-shirts. They were hand me downs from her cousins.

Her jacket was there. As was her favorite shirt, a pair of boots she hadn't seen in years and two pairs of jeans. She took everything but the boots back to her room. Everything else could be washed. She would deal with that later. She was going to be late for Cindy's class if she didn't hurry.

BAILEY LOOKED AROUND the entranceway of her old elementary school. It looked almost exactly the same, except maybe a little smaller than she remembered. Signing in had been fun. The secretary had looked at her askance, triple checked that she was on the approved visitor's list and then called down to Cindy's classroom to make sure again. Bailey was highly amused when the secretary had politely asked her to wait for an escort. Several of the other ladies in the office peeked around doors and through tiny windows to take a look. Had she been there for any other reason, she may have decided to shock them. But Cindy had asked, and since her friend had to continue to work there, Bailey decided to behave.

A short, blonde woman appeared around the corner. "Ms. Cooper?"

"Yes?" Bailey was, as always, surprised to be addressed so politely.

"I'm Donna Clark, the principal here. If you come with me, I'll escort you to Ms. Arnoux's class." The principal had short, graying hair and a no-nonsense look. She also kept looking at Bailey like Bailey was about to go on a rampage.

"Thank you." Bailey shouldered her guitar case and followed, wondering how she managed to get an escort from the principal herself.

"So, you went here, didn't you?" Ms. Clark asked.

"Yes. I believe I spent a lot of time in your office." Bailey chuckled a little in memory. At least she hadn't been in there by herself. Mike and Liz usually accompanied her.

"Bailey!" A small voice echoed down the hallway right before a weight hit her legs and thin arms wrapped around her.

"Bailey?" A second small body hit her.

"Whoa, guys." She staggered a bit under their combined weight.

"Rebecca, Sarah," Ms. Clark interrupted. "What are you two doing out of line?"

"But this is my Bailey." Sarah put her hands on her hips and looked sternly at her principal before she turned and favored Bailey with an even sterner look. "Mom said she brought you from the airport, but you didn't come see me."

"You haven't seen me either." Rebecca, Beth's oldest child, looked at her severely.

"Sorry, girls. I will though. Now get back to class. I'm here to see Aunt Cindy."

"Then you'll see Jacob," Rebecca pouted.

"I'll make it up to you both, I promise. We'll all go get ice cream or something. Now go before we all end up in the principal's office." She shooed them back to the lines of children crowding along each side of the hallway.

"Ah." Ms. Clark seemed stunned.

The look on her face bothered Bailey. "What? You think I eat children? You read too many tabloids." Bailey did appreciate one thing about her reputation. She could usually say whatever she wanted and most people didn't act surprised. "Can we go see Cindy now?"

"I would never have believed it," Ms. Clark finally admitted. "I mean you hear stories. I thought Arnoux was crazy, but you—"

"Are human? Have family?" She expected more from people in her hometown sometimes. After all, her family had deep roots in the community. She may have not been the most behaved person growing up, but she felt locals should know better than to believe all her press. It never failed though. The principal and Cindy's mom were proof of that.

"I made an assumption. I apologize." Ms. Clark paled. "I should have known better. Ms. Arnoux's class is right down that hallway, the second door on the left. I think you'll be fine on your own."

"Thank you." Bailey was caught between humor and

exasperation. Humor won when she realized just how embarrassed Ms. Clark had been. She vowed to buy Sarah and Rebecca the largest ice cream cones she could find in return.

The door to Cindy's classroom was closed. Bailey took a moment to look in the window before knocking. Now that she was here, she felt a little nervous. These were kindergarteners, tiny impressionable humans, a room full of them and they outnumbered the adults. Bailey took a deep breath, knowing it could not possibly be worse than some of the bars she'd played in the early days.

"And here's our guest." Cindy opened the door as her assistant motioned for the kids to sit in a circle on a multicolored rug. "Class, this is my friend, Bailey Cooper. She's a musician and I believe she brought her guitar with her."

"I did." Bailey smiled at the crowd of children.

She spent the next hour playing children's songs, taking requests and answering questions. Beth's son, Jacob, was very glad she remembered his name. All his friends were impressed that he knew the visitor. They had no idea who she was, her band played songs a lot harder than most kindergarten students should listen to, but they loved the idea of having her visit anyway.

When it was time to leave, she got a hug from each one. She was slightly concerned at what parents would say, but there was no denying twenty-five insistent five-year-old children. She only made it through the door after they had elicited a promise to return. Cindy giggled the whole time. Her teaching assistant did as well. They'd even recorded a lot of it and taken pictures for the class scrapbook.

Chapter Five

AFTER BAILEY MANAGED to make it out of the school, she decided to pick up lunch and meet Liz at her office. If she knew her cousin, she would eat between appointments, if she remembered to do so. She picked up a couple of hamburgers and headed over to Liz's office.

Only Liz's car was in the parking area. That didn't surprise her. Liz often stayed while the office staff left for lunch. She and her colleagues shut the clinic down for an hour and a half every afternoon. If they didn't, Liz swore they would never be able to leave the building. Fortunately for Bailey, someone had left the side door unlocked.

"Knock, knock." Bailey stood outside Liz's office door and held up the food and drinks. "Can I buy you lunch?"

Liz looked up over her glasses. "Looks like you already did. Come in. Did you go to Cindy's class already?"

"Yep. It was surreal. I haven't been touched that much since the last time I went crowd surfing." Bailey handed out the food. "It was fun though. I think."

"I'm sure you had a good time." Liz unwrapped her burger. "You're amazing. You remembered no onions." She sighed in happiness. "Did you meet anyone?"

"I met the principal. She didn't trust me at first." Bailey recounted the exchange with the shorter woman. "In the end she left me alone."

"I don't think she's from here," Liz said by way of explanation. "Of course, most people hear lesbian rock star and freak out."

"I can't help it. When we started there were already a few, and all of them had nice reputations. The PR guys thought with our music I shouldn't. Besides, it was so much fun making it." She played with a loose thread in the knee of her jeans. "I mean our family has never been the type to pull punches but getting to say whatever I think when I think it was pretty amazing."

"I know. And I know it was fun for you. Is it now?" Liz never really stopped being a psychiatrist.

"Yeah, I suppose." Bailey shrugged. "So how come you guys didn't tell me Beth and Jerry got a divorce, and that the bastard abandoned them? She came over the other day after lunch. I suppose Cindy told you what happened?" When Liz nodded, she continued. "So why didn't you guys say anything?"

"Dammit, Bailey." Liz ran her hands through her hair. It was a sign that things were about to get serious. Bailey regretted asking, but it was too late now. "Why on earth should we have told you? I mean, yeah, Cindy was all for it. In fact, getting you here so early was her idea."

"But not yours?" Now that they were talking about it, Bailey decided to talk about all of it. She'd learned the hard way it was much healthier in the long run.

"Nope. For fuck's sake, what would you have done? Ride up on your motorcycle and rescue her from a nasty separation and divorce? Offer her the choice you didn't the first time?"

Bailey went cold. "What choice, Liz? What are you talking about?"

"Bailey, for someone with a vagina you sure as shit know zilch about women." Liz leaned back in her chair and stared at the ceiling. "Do you not realize that you could have stopped the wedding had you been anything other than a cracked out petulant cocksucker?"

"Ouch." Bailey felt that almost as a physical blow. "Liz, could you please calm down and explain this to me? Because I honestly have no fucking clue what you're talking about. Beth's never been attracted to me."

"Wrong." Liz shook her head. "Oh so wrong. Oh, Bailey." She stopped after taking a good look at Bailey. "Oh, honey."

"And um, maybe no insults this time, okay? I thought we were way past that. I get enough of those from Mama."

"You know it's what I do. At least when I do it, it's productive. Hell, cussing you out all the way from here to LA got you into rehab, didn't it?"

"Yeah, but I deserved it then."

"Okay. True. You just act the part when you need to, but you've grown up a lot lately. I'm sorry, but you two are going to drive me crazy, you know?"

"Me and Beth?"

"Yes, Bailey. You are the sun that makes Beth's rose grow. You always have been. Look I don't know exactly what happened between you two in college, but you know why she married Jerry don't you?"

"I assumed she loved the bastard."

"No. At least not enough, I think." Liz took a large sip of her drink. "I thought I told you all this on the plane after the wedding. You probably don't remember. Anyway, Beth was pregnant. She ended up miscarrying not long after. And no, nothing you did, nothing you said, nothing caused it or could have prevented it."

"Shit." Bailey dropped her head in her hands. "That didn't mean she had to marry the bastard." Jerry didn't have a name as far as she was concerned. Bastard was his title and all she could bring herself to call him.

"You know I love you dearly. You're like the sister Mike could have been had he…well, been a girl I guess." Liz shrugged. "But you came out while in the cradle pretty much. Beth's bi, southern and her mother is so very different from yours. She was practically living with him anyway. After the test came back positive, she said yes when he proposed. Remember, sweetheart, Beth has always wanted a family. Besides, at that time, you couldn't have gotten married even if you both hadn't been so fucking blind."

"That still doesn't answer my question," Bailey said.

"True. I didn't tell you because Beth didn't need you to come rescue her. She needed to deal with the mess they made on her own before you were reintroduced as adults."

"We've known one another forever, we are adults."

Liz shook her head. "No, Bailey. I've seen you at the worst moment of your life. You survived, came back and matured. You're so much more level-headed and responsible now, but you've never given up the pure joy you find in life and the love you have in music, which is amazing considering all the self-hate your mother nurtured in you. But again, you've grown beyond that. Beth hasn't had that chance. She had to get herself through her adversity and be a whole person. I couldn't let you come home and do what you've always wanted to do and court her and woo her and have her be dependent on you. It would have dragged you both down. Plus, you've dealt with you, but you haven't dealt with your mother. Shit. There's just way too much dealing and not dealing."

"Do you ever stop working?" Bailey was amazed. Liz put so much thought into everything she did it was a wonder she slept.

"Not where you guys are concerned. I started studying psychiatry because of Mike, but you all keep me going. I should write papers on each of you." Liz sighed and leaned back in her chair. "I'm really glad you're going to be his best man. I don't think he'd be here if it weren't for you."

"Nah, he's a strong man." Bailey didn't want to think about Mike as he'd been when he'd shown up at her door in LA, almost broken and desperate. "All I did was give him a place to stay."

"I know better." Liz looked at her seriously. "We should probably finish this before my next patient gets here."

"Good idea. He's happy? The two of them?" Bailey asked.

"Yeah. I never would have pegged those two, but they seem to be over the moon for one another."

"Awesome." Bailey wadded up her burger wrapper and tossed it in the bag.

"You ready to run back to LA?" Liz asked.

"No. In fact, this last stint there was the longest I'd been there sober. It's not a fun place to be when you're sober. At least for me it's not." She shrugged. "I think that's why I was okay coming back. It's hard to meditate at Mama's, though. There's so much negative energy."

"I don't know about energy, but there's a lot of negativity around your mother. Promise me something, Bailey." Liz cleared away her mess and stood. It was the cue that lunch was over. "Don't let her send you back down that road. She'll try."

"I know. I won't." Bailey stood too. "I can't let her unbalance me. Thanks for everything, Liz. I wouldn't have made it this far without you."

"Flatterer." Liz tossed the bag of trash at her. "Throw that away for me, please. And thanks for lunch."

"Anytime."

"NEXT TIME YOU'RE going to be gone all day, take that fucking dog with you." Fiona staggered inside from the porch. Her actions made both Elvis and Bailey jump. They had both been lying on the couch, snoozing slightly.

"Did he make a mess?" Bailey asked, astounded. She hadn't found anything amiss when she returned that afternoon.

"The fuck should I know? I was over at the bar. I just know you left him here. I heard him bark."

"Oh. Okay. I'll take him with me from now on." She knew her mother was lying. The house was too far away, and the bar too noisy, for her to hear anything that happened in the house. It was just a control issue.

Fiona nodded. "Damn right. My fucking head."

"You okay, Mama?" Bailey was out of practice. She used to know immediately whether to run or offer assistance when her mother came in wasted. She wasn't sure what she should do this time.

"Did you fucking listen? My goddamn head hurts."

"I heard you, Mama." She got up and poured her mother a glass of water and found a few aspirin. Fiona took both with shaking hands. "Need some help getting to bed?"

"How many times they pulled you off stage and you didn't know where you were? Then you went to rehab. Good thing you don't have a father. He'd have died of shame. Wonder why I haven't."

Bailey bit back her anger and unease. It was easy to believe her mother didn't mean any of it when Bailey could smell the alcohol from ten feet away. "Mama, let me help get you bed."

"I don't need help from the likes of you." Her actions belied her words as she stumbled and fell to her knees.

"Here, Mama." She helped her to her feet and then steered the older woman to her room.

Bailey managed to get her mother under the covers and tuck two pillows on either side of her. Her mom hated sleeping on her side, but Bailey wasn't yet ready to be an orphan. Besides, it was ingrained behavior.

Bailey walked outside as soon as she was sure her mother was asleep. The music from her mother's bar was still loud. Fortunately, it wasn't anything she had played. She hated hearing her own songs. She heard them enough after writing them, rehearsing them, recording them and then playing them on tour. Even the ones they did that she didn't write bothered her after a while.

It was nice to just sit outside for a while and exist. Even at night, LA always seemed like something was going on, like it was moving much too fast. It never felt like that on her mama's back deck, the only sane place in the house. It was peaceful, and apart from the bar next door it was quiet. But even with the slower pace and the solitude, she couldn't turn off her brain. It was one of the problems with visiting home. There were ghosts there.

Bailey thought back about what her mom said. Her mother didn't always get abusive when she was drunk, but it was often enough that Bailey had the routine down. She didn't often regret not having a father. She had a grandfather, a wonderful uncle and a few overprotective cousins. She didn't feel as if she'd missed out on the healthy male influence kids were supposed to have. She didn't even mind not knowing just who her dad was most of the time. She had suspicions, but she never followed up on them.

She knew that would only cause a lot of people pain.

It was the rehab comment that got her more than the comments about fathers. Bailey had never spoken to anyone about that except Liz. It was private and not something she was overly proud to admit. Granted it had been necessary, it just exposed two great weaknesses in what she thought of as her character. More importantly, it had scared her and almost ruined her friendships with Beth, Cindy and Liz.

Bailey had declined to be in Beth's wedding, citing her busy tour schedule. It made a convenient excuse. The last thing she wanted was to be there at all. But on that day, she was there, sitting by herself on the bride's side. It took a lot to get her there and not all of it was sheer nerve. A good portion of it was tequila, cocaine and prescription painkillers.

Even now, years later, Bailey only remembered bits and pieces of the ceremony and even less of the reception. She did remember threatening Jerry's life. In fact, she had vague memories of slamming him against the wall of the choir room where he was getting dressed before threatening him. She never asked anyone if that was true.

She also vaguely remembered waking up on a plane back in LA with a very upset Liz beside her. It was the next few hours she would never forget. It was hours of sobbing grief and stern talks. Liz had lectured and comforted. Together, they cobbled together a plan. Bailey checked herself into a rehab clinic and Liz went home to smooth things over. Bailey did manage to thank her for that.

She sent gifts as signs of contrition. She was out of communication range for three months anyway. The gifts, and Liz's glib turn of phrase, seemed to help. She did know that Beth had redeemed the all-expense paid vacation to Barcelona, but they had talked even less after that.

She wished she could have blamed the estrangement between them on that one incident, but she knew it was more. They were inseparable in high school, all four of them, holding strong after Diana's death and Mike's estrangement. They had chosen the same college. Bailey hadn't stayed though. She left mid-way through their freshman year for LA. She and Beth had an argument about something. Bailey was out and proud. Beth was unsure about anything. They were only friends.

Bailey had surrounded herself with an aura of indestructibleness she fueled with alcohol and one-night stands, even in high school. It continued in college. She always watched

Beth, wishing she could say something, give words to her feelings, but she was scared. She never admitted it to anyone, but she was scared of Beth and the love she felt for her. Bailey had been knocked down so far by her mother, and yet raised up so far by the rest of her family, that she was in a constant war with herself over confidence and self-esteem. She didn't win that struggle for certain until she was out of rehab. But it was in college that it all went wrong.

Free from her very conservative mother's gaze, Beth dated. So did Bailey. She was a musician. She had her pick of one-night stands. And then one fateful night it all fell apart between them. It happened at a fraternity party. A guy who'd been after Beth for weeks had her cornered. Under the guise of help, Bailey intervened, though really she was jealous. Beth was pissed. They both said things Bailey wished she could forget. Essentially Beth reprimanded her loudly, and publicly, for always trying to protect her. She asked why Bailey felt the need to do that. Bailey didn't have an answer.

Two weeks later Bailey was on a bus to LA, having sold most everything she owned except for the truck, a jacket and two guitars. Four years after that she was on the radio. They remained cordial since they were both friends with Cindy and Liz. They were so involved in each other's lives that Bailey and Beth couldn't completely avoid one another.

After Bailey and her band released their first album, and the others had graduated college, they began getting together at least once a year. They usually rented a house and the four of them would get together. They had been to Venice, Vienna, Oslo, and Aspen just to name a few. Every year a different person picked a different place. Bailey often picked up the tab if someone needed help.

Things had begun to heal between them. They were almost back to their old comfort level in Oslo until Beth announced her engagement. Bailey had been proud of herself. She hid her feelings very well, with the aid of some pharmaceuticals. A few months later at the wedding it came to a head. The last ten years were as tense as the period during college. But they'd never been as close again. Jerry discouraged Bailey's inclusion in their lives, and for a long time she'd allowed him to keep her away. They both had. And then two years ago they were in Vienna and life changed again.

Now she wasn't sure just what Beth wanted. She knew, though, what she wanted in life. She wondered if maybe there was something between them after all. Bailey looked back on everything and felt as if her biggest mistake was assuming things would just fall into place. She knew better now. She knew that getting anything took an awful lot of work. She'd never done that work with Beth. She'd never attempted to date or court her. Perhaps it was, as Liz had suggested, time to try. She would never know otherwise. She just didn't know how she would handle possible rejection. It could mean the end of her friendship with Beth completely. She needed a little more information first.

Chapter Six

BAILEY WAS THE first to arrive at the restaurant. She had practiced being late so much that she had it down to an art form. But this time she wanted to be there when the others arrived. She needed every minute she could get with Beth so she could analyze the other woman's feelings. It wasn't long before Beth and Liz arrived at the same time. The three of them got a table and waited on the bride-to-be. It was very out of character. Cindy was usually first for everything.

"I heard you impressed the hell out of Cindy's kindergarten class," Beth said. She smiled at Bailey, as they got comfortable around the table. "And that Sarah and Rebecca had some choice words for you."

Bailey pinched the bridge of her nose. "Yeah. Sarah's still a little spitfire. You should have seen the principal's face."

"I bet Ms. Clark didn't know what to do with you." Beth seemed more relaxed and in a much better mood than the last time they'd met at a restaurant.

"I don't think she did." Bailey laughed harder as she remembered the abashed look on the principal's face when the girls had run up to hug Bailey. "They, the girls, decided that I owe them since I didn't see them immediately after arriving here."

"Rebecca didn't tell me that." Beth smiled again. It reached her eyes and Bailey had to remember how to breathe. "Jacob's a little taken with you. He gushed over the whole experience."

"Nah, he just liked that all his friends were impressed that I knew him by name," Bailey replied. She was getting slightly uncomfortable with the praise. "And even then I was just some stranger with a guitar."

"What did you play for them?" Liz finally joined the conversation. "Sarah only said that she was pissed you didn't get to play for her class."

"Just a couple of children's songs and a request or two. Cindy told me what to expect, so I learned a few the other night." Bailey found herself distracted by the twinkle in Beth's eyes.

A young waitress stopped at the table. "Are we expecting another?" Beth nodded and the waitress handed them each a menu. "Can I get you anything while I'm...you're waiting?" She blushed.

"A glass of wine," Beth said.

Liz looked over the menu. "Same here. Bailey?"

"Ice tea please. Sweet if you have it," Bailey said.

"I'll, uh, be right back." The waitress hurried away.

"She didn't ask what type of wine you wanted," Bailey said.

Liz shook her head. "I think she was a bit distracted. You did it again."

"Please. She's twelve," Beth scoffed.

"Come on, she's cute," Liz said.

"Ladies, I'm right here, you know," Bailey pointed out. She was amused at their reactions, at least Beth's reaction. It was promising.

"We know," Liz answered. "But it's up to you to fix our orders if she gets them wrong."

"Okay," Bailey said. "Anyway, Jacob's a cutie."

"Thanks." Beth's good humor returned. "You haven't seen them since the annual Christmas video chat."

"Nope. I was surprised they remembered me." She didn't want to qualify that statement or explain. So far the evening was going well and the self-deprecation was an attempt to keep that flow going.

"What's up with you being humble?" Liz asked. "I think it's pretty safe to say you're unforgettable. Especially with the presents you give them."

"Was that a compliment, Liz?" Bailey wanted to change the subject. "Where's our blushing bride-to-be anyway?"

"She's supposed to be here already." Liz looked at her watch.

"She was going by her mother's first," Beth answered. "Her mom is giving her a really hard time about the wedding."

"Why?" Bailey was honestly confused.

Liz looked at her seriously. "You know why." It didn't take a lot of thought before the reason clicked.

"Heifer." She changed the epitaph as the waitress reappeared carrying a tray full of glasses. Cindy was right behind her.

"Sorry I'm late." She slid into the booth next to Bailey, causing Bailey to slide over in front of Beth.

"Okay, ladies." The waitress placed the tray on a holder and began placing two wine glasses in front of each person. "I brought some samples of our most requested red and most requested white for you all to sample. Let me know which you would like to order." She efficiently poured half a glass of each for everyone.

"Thanks," Cindy said, relief in her voice.

"My name is Amanda. I'll be right back to take your orders."

She let a light hand squeeze Bailey's shoulder as she finished pouring the wine.

"What the hell?" Cindy said when the waitress was gone.

"Bailey." It was all Liz had to say to explain.

"Oh." The three of them looked at Bailey who shrugged.

"Yeah, yeah. I didn't do anything this time." Bailey flagged down a bus boy and requested a glass of water. The waitress had forgotten her tea.

"Sorry I'm late."

"No worries." Bailey moved the wine glasses away from her plate and took a grateful sip of water.

"So, was it that bad?" Beth asked.

Cindy looked ready to cry. "The woman is relentless. She's really grasping at straws to get this wedding canceled."

"Well, let's talk of other things." Bailey hated seeing women cry, especially if that woman was her friend.

"You know, all the other teachers are jealous and have demanded that I ask you to perform for the school. The music teacher was quite insistent. And my wonderful son has decided that if you're going to perform for the school, he's playing drums for you," Cindy announced.

"Wow. And Ms. Clark is okay with all that? The front office people kept looking at me like I was a Viking about to start a rampage," Bailey said. "We'll see what comes of it I guess."

"You big softie," Beth teased.

"Hey, we agreed never to bring that up. It'll ruin my reputation as despoiler of maidens, eater of babies and goddess of rock." The world had narrowed. She almost forgot about everyone else. "You wouldn't want to ruin my reputation, would you?" She arched a brow and dropped her voice an octave.

"No," Beth said softly. "We certainly can't have that."

"Good." Bailey smiled inwardly as she watched Beth gulp a glass of wine. She caught Liz's eye and winked. This, she decided, was going to be fun. Beth had given just enough indication of interest that Bailey felt the risk was worth it. "I suppose we should take it easy on the poor girl and have our orders ready when she gets here. What's good?"

"Most everything on the menu," Liz answered. "Take a gamble. It's not like you can't send it back or trade if you don't like something."

Bailey mock saluted. "Yes, overly analytical one."

"Well, Eric has decided that he's upset with you as well," Cindy said. "According to him, not seeing your godson is a major sin and he's only going to absolve you of it if you take him to some movie he's dying to see."

Bailey waved it away. "Not a problem." She really loved spending time with Eric.

"Do those people you hang out with in LA know you have a cult following all under the age of sixteen?" Beth asked.

"The band knows and mostly that's who I hang out with now." She shrugged. "I think I drove Quan crazy with that video Ian sent me of Sarah's dance recital," She said to Liz.

"She insisted," Liz answered.

"Thought you were worried about your reputation?" Beth teased.

"Guess I'll have to find someone to make headlines with to make up for it." Bailey caught Beth's eye and kept her gaze. "Know of anyone like that, Ms. Forsyth?"

"Yeah, the waitress," Beth said blandly. The other two laughed, but Bailey watched her target closely. Beth's cheeks reddened a bit.

"Nah, too young and innocent." Bailey leaned back. "So, Cindy, what can we do for you?"

"Well I need to take Liz, Beth and the girls to pick out bridesmaids dresses. I don't suppose you want to come with us, do you?" Bailey thought she heard a little doubt creep into Cindy's tone.

"That's up to you. I have very few plans, and I wear dresses. I can do that whole femme chic thing, you know."

"We know. It was part of your third album stunt," Liz said dryly. "Not sure the look is going to be the same."

"What...the all-black prom dresses torn and artfully sprinkled with neon paint won't work for weddings?" Bailey teased. "I know. And I'm not the least bit insulted, Cindy."

"I'm glad. Mike said you wouldn't be, but I wanted to make sure. You mean the world to both of us, but I have these two and he has you," Cindy gushed.

Beth pointed at Bailey's cheeks. "I think you just blushed. You did!"

"Didn't. Whatever," Bailey scoffed, grateful for the change of topic. "We need to order. I'm famished."

"Well, go find your fan and get us food," Liz said.

"Why do I have to do everything?" Bailey mock whined.

"Because you're special," Beth answered.

"Never mind. I have her." Cindy waved the young woman over.

They ordered and spent the rest of the time going over wedding plans.

Bailey knew that Cindy had eloped with Roger, Eric's father, and always regretted not having a large wedding. She was using this time to make up for the past. It was clear that Beth and Liz were fully in line with that thought. Bailey saw no harm in joining them. She was ridiculously pleased for Mike and Cindy and pledged her support to the matrimonial cause.

In the end, plans were made. The check was paid. And the quartet drifted apart like always. Bailey made it home to find her mother still at the bar and Elvis ready to be walked before bed. She obliged him, knowing she had broken her word to take him with her.

She waited on the porch while Elvis found the perfect spot, and thought about the evening. She was encouraged after her flirting with Beth. Liz had seemed pretty normal. It was Cindy she was worried about. The woman's mother was causing a lot of stress in Cindy's life and Bailey wished she knew a way to stop it.

When Elvis was finished, he ran back in the house. Bailey took that as a cue for bed. She was tired, despite not having done much during the day. The two of them settled on her full bed and were soon snoring. She never even woke up to hear her mother come inside.

Chapter Seven

BAILEY STOPPED THE old truck in front of Liz's house and thought again how best to phrase her request. She wasn't given much time before four feet of unrestrained energy bounced outside her car door.

"Bailey! Hey. You're here. Is it time for ice cream? Can we get Rebecca too? Please? Hey, you haven't seen the way Dad painted my room. Come see." Sarah said in a rush as they walked to the front door. Sarah opened it and left it open as if she assumed blithely that Bailey was right behind her.

"Breathe, Sarah," Bailey said. "Okay. Show me your room."

"Hey, Bailey. What's up?" Ian asked as Sarah pulled Bailey down the hall by the hand.

"Bailey's here to see my room," Sarah said.

"Looks like I'm getting the grand tour," Bailey called back.

Sarah's room was a complete wreck. Nothing was in place. Clothes were everywhere. Books were on the floor and shoes were on the bed. It was the opposite of Liz's room as a child. Perversely, Bailey found it hilarious.

"Nice colors, pipsqueak." The turquoise paint with pink stripes was a little eye blinding, but someone had managed to tame it with a neutral grey accent wall. "Mind if I go talk with your mom and dad for a minute?"

"Maybe later we can play a game or something? I have a lot of them."

"Definitely," Bailey promised. "I'll be back in a minute, okay?"

"Were you able to see the floor?" Liz asked as Bailey walked into the kitchen.

"Parts of it," she said. "You don't go in there much, do you?"

"Nope. I used to try and to get her to keep it clean and organized, but she appears to do better when it's a mess. So I let it go. She's not allowed to leave any other room in the house a mess though. That's one of the rules we stick with."

"Very cool. So, I actually came over here to see if I could borrow Sarah."

"You know that sounds a bit weird, right?" Ian commented mildly.

"Yeah, I know. But I promised the girls ice cream and it'll

look better if I show up with one kid already," Bailey said. And it was true that she was close to Sarah. She saw Liz and Sarah several times a year. Sometimes Ian even accompanied them.

"So you're using my daughter to pick up chicks? Didn't you try that once with Eric?" Liz crossed her arms and leaned against the counter.

"Yes and yes. Different chick this time. What do you say? Can I take Sarah for ice cream?"

Liz glanced at Ian quickly before answering. "Of course. Thank you for asking. Honestly, though, I think you're her third favorite human ever. And that changes depending on whether she's mad at me for correcting her or not."

"I can't help it. She knows awesome when she sees it." Bailey struck a pose.

"And it has nothing to do with you taking her and her mother everywhere on the planet, does it?" Ian said. "Or the fact that she has you twisted around her finger. Or that you—"

"Okay, you got me. It's been my long-term secret plan to travel the globe with my cousin because she needs a break and I'm single and occasionally like company. And during that time to work really hard to win a small child's affections by showing her things like the Parthenon." Bailey looked down at him. "Really, Ian. That's what you got?"

"No. Not really." He sighed.

"It's okay, man. I do get it." And she did. Ian made a nice living as a real estate agent, but he never would have been able to afford sending his wife and daughter on a two-week cruise of the Aegean Sea. "I promise I'll try to reign it in. But ice cream?" She gave him her best charming smile.

"Yeah, it's fine." He shook his head. "I'm just glad you and Liz are cousins. It must have been hell on Jerry to compete with you."

"Wait. What?" Both Bailey and Liz looked at him.

"Nothing. I'm sure he imagined it." Ian got up quickly and went to find Sarah. They could hear him telling her the plan from the other room.

"What?" She asked Liz.

"I'll find out and let you know," Liz promised. "Hey, pumpkin. You listen to Bailey, okay?"

"Yes, ma'am." Sarah was bouncing on her toes. "Come on, Bailey."

"Okay. You want to stop by and pick up Rebecca? I did promise you both." Bailey asked innocently.

"Yeah," Sarah said, as if that was one of the dumbest questions in the world.

"I'll have her home before dawn," Bailey promised.

"Just call if you're going to miss dinner," Liz called as they climbed in the truck.

"BAILEY? WHAT'S GOING on?" Beth asked after she answered the door.

"I thought I'd take the kids for ice cream," Bailey said, suddenly unsure if this was a good idea or not. "I mean I did promise."

"Can they come, please?" Sarah asked. The nine-year old had wiggled between Bailey and the door.

"Yeah, okay." Beth opened the door wider. "Come on in."

"I guess I should have called first."

"It's okay. It's just a madhouse around here on the weekends."

"Do you want to come with? Or would you rather...?" Bailey let the question hang. She wanted to appear casual and slightly aloof. It was important to rebuild the friendship first before she threw in the rest.

"Sure. Let me throw on some clothes. Sarah, Rebecca is supposed to be cleaning her room. If you want to go in and help her get ready, I would certainly appreciate it." She looked at Bailey. "Make yourself comfortable. I'll be back in a minute or five."

"Take your time."

Bailey took a moment to look around. School pictures and artwork adorned the walls. There were no pictures of Jerry to be seen. She wondered how long Beth had waited before removing them. She wondered too if the kids had any in their rooms. She imagined they did. Beth wasn't that cold-hearted and vindictive.

Jacob came running down the hallway and jumped in her arms. "Bailey! Mom said you're taking us for ice cream? All of us?"

"Yep, all 14,000 of you."

He looked confused. "But there's only three of us."

"What? Only three? Guess I'll have to make do with the three of you then. Sarah's coming too, though, okay?" Bailey leaned in to whisper in his ear. "You don't mind being with a bunch of girls, do you?"

"Not for ice cream," he said seriously.

"Good answer, young man." She squeezed him once and then let him get back down onto his own feet. "Let's go, people. Ice cream awaits."

"Then what are we waiting for?" A fully dressed Beth asked as she shooed the two girls out the door. "Come on, sluggard."

The ice cream parlor was only a few blocks from Beth's house. It was an easy walk. Sarah and Rebecca walked together for the most part. Jacob insisted on holding both Bailey's and his mother's hands on the way there. It was quite the scene.

"Here we are folks." Bailey held the door open for them. "Whatever you want. The check's on Jacob."

"Hey," he protested. He placed his hands on his hips and gave her a look so reminiscent of Beth that she couldn't help laughing.

"Relax, sport. I got this." She ruffled his hair and steered him to the display. "Now pick something out."

"Hey, Bailey, this one's the color of your hair." Sarah pointed at a purple sherbet filled with some sort of candy.

"Nice color," Bailey said. "What do you want, Beth?"

Beth waived away the offer. "Oh no, just the kids."

"Seriously? Beth, come on. It's ice cream. What flavor do you want? Tell me now or I'll order for you."

"C'mon, Mom. You love ice cream," Rebecca said.

"It's okay," Bailey told the kids. "Seriously. I'd never talk your mother into doing something she didn't want to do."

Beth looked at her. "Since when? I can't decide between mint chocolate chip and chocolate chip."

"Get both. Live a little," Bailey said. "Give in to self-indulgence for once."

"Self-indulgence? What's that?" Jacob asked.

"Well, it's basically, ah." Bailey looked to Beth for help. Beth was trying very hard to hide a smile. She was obviously not going to be of any assistance. "Well it means in this case, to give in to something you really want to do but know you shouldn't, like if you were on a diet but you really wanted a piece of cake so you ate it."

"Good answer." The person behind the counter said. "We have an excellent self-indulgent chocolate and chocolate chip with mocha chunks if you're interested."

"I just want strawberry, please," Jacob said. "Is that okay?"

"Certainly. Tell the lady what y'all want." Bailey turned to Beth. "You were no help."

"I figured you had that." The cool green eyes were still

amused. "It really was a good answer. But I expected that from you. You're good with words."

"Not really. A few verses and an angry chorus? Please."

"That's your mother's view. It's not reality." Beth rolled her eyes. "Come on, we should order and get a table."

The kids ordered and were quickly given their ice cream cones. Beth sent them off to claim a table while the adults ordered. It seemed a line had formed behind them. The ice cream parlor had been open as long as Bailey could remember. It was obviously still a big draw.

"So, Bailey, what brings you back here?" Beth asked when they sat down with their orders. The kids were playing one of the games the owners left on the tables for entertainment.

"I figured it was obvious. Cindy called me a week or so ago and asked me to come home. Told me she was getting married. Tiny is still deciding if he wants to stay part of Creature Feature or retire. We didn't have anything to take the studio. Kat's in Japan and Alejandro is taking his husband on a cruise for their anniversary. So..." She shrugged.

"You figured you didn't have anything else to do so you came home?" Beth finished for her.

"Kinda. I kinda missed you guys too." She watched the kids spin the wheel to see what happened next in the game. "I figured I could work on new stuff on Mama's couch as easily as I could out there. So I didn't ask. What are you doing these days? Still at the bank, right?"

"I am. I handle some of the business accounts." The pride in her voice was audible.

"No kidding? That's awesome." It was and she was proud of Beth.

"Thank you. Did you guys want to stay for dinner?"

"I have to get Sarah back home." Bailey was glad the kids weren't listening. She didn't want to overstay her welcome and knew Sarah would protest the excuse to leave.

"Okay. Maybe some other time. Those two are inseparable. They kinda remind me of us when we were that age."

"That's funny." Bailey tried not to choke on her ice cream. "I see them more as you and Cindy."

"Maybe. Still, I'm glad Rebecca has such a good friend. I know they'll be together at least through high school. Hopefully Jacob will find one as well."

"You worry about them, don't you?" There was more she wanted to ask, but she didn't know how.

"Of course I do. And about more than I ever imagined."

"Like what?"

"Grades obviously, though so far they've both been getting pretty good grades."

"Kindergarteners get grades?" Bailey couldn't remember getting grades at that age.

"Yes, believe it or not. It's not like a percentage out of 100 or anything. But it is a pass/fail or satisfactory/needs work system."

"What else do you worry about?" Bailey asked.

"Honestly? Being a good parent. Raising strong, happy people. Scarring them for life. Whether they have friends. It's a never-ending cycle of concerns, I can promise you." Beth looked down at the table. "I double checked with Liz. It's considered pretty normal."

"I figured it would be. So they seem well behaved and unlikely to cause too much harm intentionally," Bailey teased.

"That's what I'm going for." Beth stood. "Speaking of, if you're going to get Sarah home for dinner, and if I'm going to feed these two monsters, we should head back."

"Oh yeah. Come on, monsters. It's time to head back." Bailey had been expecting disagreement and wasn't disappointed.

"Please, Bailey. We're not done with the game," Sarah said.

"Mom, can't we stay a little longer?" Rebecca asked.

"I don't want to go yet," Jacob said.

"Nope. C'mon. It's time to go." Bailey stood and looked down at them. She fought back a smile as they pouted.

"But we just got here and you never hang out with us." Sarah crossed her arms and looked ready for a real fight.

"Sarah, I promised your mother you would be home for dinner."

"Rebecca, Jacob. Come on, you heard Bailey. It's time to go home."

"Can we do this again?" Rebecca asked as they cleaned up their mess.

"I don't see why not," Bailey said. "Next time we'll do this in the right order and eat dinner first. Sound good?"

"Yeah," the three of them said in unison.

"Good. Let's go." She held the door open for them. There would certainly be a next time. That she knew.

Chapter Eight

BAILEY PARKED OUTSIDE the skating rink and sighed. She hated skating. She never really learned how when they were kids. She'd been more interested in modes of transportation with two wheels. She, Mike and Scott had raced motorbikes in school. Liz had as well, at least until she discovered boys.

Sighing a little in resignation, she got out of the car, grabbed the present and walked to the door. It opened before she reached it. Beth's dad grinned broadly and held the door open for her.

"Wonderful to see you, Bailey." He'd always been nice to her. He was one of her favorite people.

"And you as well, Mr. Forsyth. Am I late?" For a moment she felt a little panicked, which was odd. She didn't normally care when she arrived as long as she was there. It was habit and part of her carefully cultivated image.

"Not at all. We just got here to set up. Go on in. Beth is in the party room with her mother. I'm sure they could use a cool head in there. Parties for children are not for the faint of heart, you know."

"Not sure how good I'll be at diffusing tension, but I can certainly help," she said.

Bailey walked through the second set of doors and into the skating rink proper. It was loud. The carpet was old and multicolored. The walls were painted black and covered in glow in the dark murals. It wasn't brightly lit and she was grateful. She wasn't sure she wanted to see what the place looked like with the lights on, she could imagine it well enough. She had played in worse places, but she hadn't always been sober and noticed just how foul they were.

"Hiya. Are you here for a party?" A bubbly teenager asked.

"Yes." Bailey hesitated. She had a deep distrust for people who used the word *hiya* and it took a minute to get beyond it. "The Ellzey party."

"Awesome. It's just down the hall there. Last room on the left."

"Thanks." Bailey walked down the hallway to the party room. The door was open and she paused a moment to look in the room. Beth was standing on a chair trying to hang a banner on the wall while her mother was putting plates on the table. She put the present on one of the seats and walked to where Beth was standing. "Need some help?"

Beth dropped the banner. "Shit, Bailey. Warn someone next time."

"Relax. I wouldn't have let you fall," Bailey said. "Need some help?"

"Yes, please." Beth gratefully stepped down from the chair. "Can you?"

"Of course." Bailey took over the hanging of the banners. "Where are the kids?"

"Jerry's parents are bringing them," Beth answered. Her mother made a disparaging noise. "Relax, Mom. They came in for the party. They'll leave after it. I think it's great they came to see the kids."

Bailey attempted to tune out the bickering behind her. Such family matters were way out of her realm of experience, and while she agreed with Beth's mom that letting the kids be alone with Jerry's parents could be trouble, she refused to enter into that conversation. She knew better. So she hung banners and posters of Jacob's favorite superhero, making sure that the walls at least were festive enough for a birthday party.

One by one kids arrived, dropped off presents and ran to get on skates. They had an hour or so before it was time for cake and presents. Everyone left the room to either skate or watch. Bailey took up a position at the railing to watch.

"Not a big skater, eh?" Ian asked as he joined her at the rails.

"No. I never took the time to learn. You?" She said idly.

"Me either. Look at those two though. You'd think they were born with skates on their feet." He pointed at Beth and Liz. The two women were very much at ease on roller skates.

"I don't get it." Bailey shrugged. While she didn't understand the allure of skating, she certainly appreciated watching. Beth displayed a natural grace on wheels. "I can't move like that on anything."

"C'mon let's sit." Ian steered her over to a bench. "It's fun to watch, though, isn't it?"

"It is at that." It was an amazing display of beauty and grace. And yet it was somehow almost sensual. "Sarah said she was going to be a flower girl in Mike and Cindy's wedding."

"Yeah, she's excited. I can't believe they want something big, but what do I know about weddings. Liz keeps saying no." His smile disappeared.

"She's as tied to you as she can be, you know. Not everyone

needs a piece of paper," Bailey reminded him.

"Oh I know. And it usually doesn't bother me, it's just Mike's upcoming wedding has everyone asking all the old questions." He shrugged. "It's annoying."

"I can imagine." She looked up when a pair of skates landed in front of her. "What's that?"

"Put them on. You're going skating." Beth looked down at her.

"Come on, Beth. I can't skate." Bailey pushed the skates away.

"I'll help. You'll be fine," she cajoled. "Take those boots off and put on the skates."

"You do know we've reached the age where falling hurts, don't you?" Bailey looked into those green eyes and thought for a moment how true that statement was. She had fallen a long time ago and it had hurt a lot.

"I'll do my best to keep you from falling," Beth promised. "Come on, chicken. You're wasting time."

"Chicken?" Bailey used the indignation at the childish insult as a way to blow off the tension she felt. It was hard keeping her feelings to herself. "We'll see just who's a chicken."

The skates were heavy, much heavier than the boots Bailey had been wearing. She laced them tight and tried not to think about just how many feet may have worn them over the years. It was one problem she had with both skating and bowling. She hated wearing other people's shoes.

As soon as she stood she was in trouble. It was so very easy to forget lessons that were never learned well. Bailey grabbed on to the table for support until she got her balance. Unfortunately, after she was balanced she had to move. With a resigned sigh and a moment of irritation directed at Beth, she slowly made her way to the skating rink floor.

The lights had dimmed again. Multi-colored spotlights and a disco ball were turned on as the music slowed to an older R&B remix. Bailey would have been completely disgusted if Beth hadn't taken her hand and pulled her further onto the floor.

They made two rounds of the skate floor like that, Beth pulling one hand and Bailey using the other to balance by lightly holding the handrail. She tried, but every time it felt as if her feet were going in opposite directions, she panicked and stopped, which made matters worse. Finally, Beth turned around, took both of her hands and pulled.

"Bailey, look at me. Don't look anywhere else. Just keep

looking at me, okay?"

"You're going to get us both killed," Bailey said.

"Do you trust me?"

It was dark on the skate floor, but Bailey knew instantly the earnest look Beth would have on her face. "I do. Yes." It was true. She trusted few people in her life and most of them were her old friends.

"Then look at me. Watch me. Concentrate on the flow. It's a bit like a dance, okay? Match what I do and watch up here. Okay?"

"Okay." Bailey sighed and surrendered to Beth's commands. Soon she was shakily able to make it around the floor holding on to only Beth's hands.

"And the Ellzey party. It's time to head to the party room," the deejay announced.

"Hey, look at you. You made it all the way without the wall." Beth smiled. "Come on, trooper. Let's go get some cake and ice cream. I'd like to see my son blow out his candles."

"Lead the way, but lend me a hand, okay?" For a moment it felt strange to ask for assistance. It was a ghost of things past. She had never asked for help as a kid. She had learned that lesson well.

"Anytime."

Once off the skate floor, Bailey stopped at one of the low benches that ran around the carpeted area by the party rooms. She pulled the skates off and just walked around in her socks. She felt more confident that way.

The kids clamored around the table; most still had their skates on as they were allowed another hour to skate after the party. It was very quick. Jacob blushed a little as they sang to him and then managed to blow out all six of his candles. Beth had opted to have him open his presents later as the kids wanted to play more than see what toys he had gotten.

"Wow." Before Bailey knew what was happening, they were all back out either skating or playing video games. "I feel like I just watched a nature special on piranha and cows."

"Kids are amazing, and they usually are amazing at creating a mess," Mr. Forsyth commented. "Bailey, help an old man collect the trash, would you?"

"Of course." She grabbed one of the large black bags that he was holding and began to clear the tables.

"The only part that really sucks is we have to clear up after ourselves," Beth said. "At some other places they charge cleaning as part of the fee. They don't here, which is one reason it's so much cheaper."

"It's not that bad," Liz told her. "I mean you went plastic on everything. All we have to do is toss it all."

"Still, it would take a lot longer without your help. Thanks, guys," Beth said as she began pulling down decorations.

"Anytime," Bailey said.

"Okay. I think we got all this taken care of. Bailey, you should find your shoes. Need some help?" Mr. Forsyth asked as he manhandled one of the trash bags.

"I remember where they are, but I'll help take the trash out if we can stop by and pick them up," she said.

"Good plan." He waited until she had the other trash bags in hand before walking out the door. "Tell me where."

"Over there at the tables," she told him. She saw him nod and followed not far behind him as he led the way.

"So. How long you going to be in town?" he asked as they found the table she had shared with Ian.

"I don't know," Bailey answered honestly as she pulled on her boots. "At least through the wedding. Maybe longer. I haven't really decided yet."

"You doing okay, money-wise?"

She looked up at him. "You'd know that better than I would, but my checking account is flush. I think I've been living cheaper than I have in a long time recently."

"I noticed. You've been pretty under budget for the last few years. Everything all right?" the older man asked.

"Yeah. Everything's great. I guess I'm just getting old." She shrugged.

"Please." He waved off her comment. "If you're getting old than I'm getting ancient. Let me be old and you stay relatively youthful, okay?"

"Sure." Bailey laughed as she picked back up the garbage bags. "Let's get this trash outside so we can watch the kids play."

"So Beth can give you skating lessons again, you mean." He arched his eyebrow. "You don't fool me, Bailey Ray."

"I never intended to try." She felt the flush start at the base of her neck and was glad no one else was around to see it.

BAILEY WAS LYING on the couch with Elvis at her feet when her phone vibrated in her pocket. She pulled it out and smiled when she saw the name flash on the screen. She sat up to answer it, much to Elvis's dismay.

"What's up, Beth?"

"Can I ask you a favor? I really hate to ask, but it's Mom and Dad's anniversary so they have plans. Liz and Ian have plans and Cindy can't do it either," Beth said in a rush.

"Do what?" Bailey's interest was piqued. Beth sounded desperate.

"My babysitter came down with something. I've got a Chamber thing tonight. It's too late to cancel and, well, I'm kinda stuck." She sighed deeply. Bailey heard it through the phone as if Beth was standing beside her.

"Beth, you're babbling. What do you need? Just ask."

"Can you watch the kids tonight, please? I really wouldn't ask but there's really no one else I trust." Bailey heard the desperation in Beth's voice.

"Sure. Want me to head over and pick up a pizza?" As always, it amazed her when she was included in something vaguely domestic. She loved the kids, though, so it wasn't an imposition. It did amuse her to wonder what people who only knew her reputation would think of Bailey Cooper, lead guitar and singer of Creature Feature, babysitting.

"That would be wonderful. Thank you. You're awesome. I have to leave in like half an hour. Can you make it?"

"Yes." Bailey chuckled as she searched the floor for her socks and shoes. "You know, there's not many people who would think to trust me with their kids, even if I wasn't in the top five you considered."

"Bullshit, Bailey. You know all of us would in a heartbeat. Quit believing your own press," Beth snapped.

"Yes, ma'am." Bailey could tell Beth wasn't in the mood to play. "I'm leaving now."

"Good. Thanks."

Bailey was true to her word. She and Elvis picked up two pizzas and were parked in Beth's driveway before the other woman was ready to leave. The smile of relief on Beth's face was almost reward enough.

"I come bearing food," she said when the kids opened the door.

Jacob was very excited. "Yay! Pizza."

"Elvis! Bailey! Are you our babysitter?" Rebecca asked as she bathed the dog in attention.

"Looks that way. So we up for a movie or two and a lot of carbs?" Bailey asked as she took the food into the kitchen. "Your mom ready?"

"Yes. Thank so much, Bailey. You're a lifesaver." Beth sighed in relief. She stepped into the kitchen and pulled her blouse straight. "Just don't let them juggle knives. Everything else, I trust you to manage."

"Which one of them keeps trying to toss steel about?" Bailey looked at them both. "Come on, which of you likes to throw sharp things in the air?"

"Jacob, actually," Beth answered. "I'm just kidding, sweetheart." She soothed her son after his burst of righteous indignation. "Seriously, I'll be home in an hour or two. I'm sure the three of you can concoct a lot of trouble in that time frame. Kids, be good. Bailey, just be you. Bye."

"Have fun." Bailey called after her before turning to the kids. "So, pizza and a movie, or did you guys have other ideas?"

"Sounds good to me. Elvis can sit by me." Rebecca threw two pieces of pizza on her plate and took off for the living room.

"We can watch Captain Warrior and Space Elf," Jacob said excitedly. "I can show you my Elfin Warrior Sword."

"She got you the Elfin Warrior Sword, dummy," Rebecca called.

"Hey, don't call people dummy," Bailey said. "I'll watch whatever you guys want to watch, sport."

"Hey, how did you get my Elfin Warrior Sword, Bailey?" He asked.

"I challenged the Ninja Monk of Kridang for it," she answered as she put food on plates for both of them.

"Really?" His eyes went wide.

"No. I know the Captain Warrior and her Elfin sidekick. I just asked." She grinned at the look on his face. It was a great mixture of disappointment and awe.

"Cool." He took his plate and ran to join his sister. "C'mon."

"He watches this movie all the time," Rebecca said in a very patronizing tone.

"You don't watch it with him?"

"I have to. We just have the one TV. Mom won't let us have one in our rooms yet. We have to take turns." Her rolled eyes gave a clear indication of what she thought about that idea.

"Is it his turn?" Bailey asked.

"Yes. We just watched Power Princess Python," Jacob said.

"Okay then. It's Captain Warrior. Play it, my good man."

They finished dinner and the movie before Beth returned. Bailey was unsure about bedtimes, and reluctant to make them go to bed anyway. Instead she lost a game of cartoon racing to Jacob and then attempted to help Rebecca find the mystical key in a game she was playing. Jacob, of course, provided plenty of not so helpful tips during this time, much to the annoyance of his sister. Bailey had to remind her more than once that Rebecca had done the same thing on the previous game.

"Who won?" Beth asked as she came inside. They hadn't heard her enter since she had used the garage door.

"Mom, I beat Bailey at racing," Jacob said proudly.

"He did. And I can't seem to find this key thing." She sat the controller down in disgust. "Sorry, Rebecca. We'll have to try again next time."

"It's okay, Bailey. Thanks for your help."

"Wow. They must have had a great time. Past bedtime and they're still polite. I'm impressed." Beth put her purse and keys down by the door. "I'm going to go change. Kids, you need to head to bed."

"Bailey?" Jacob asked as soon as his mom left the room.

"What's up, sport?"

"Do you think my..." The young boy seemed nervous. "Do you want to come see my play? I'm gonna be a firefly. My mom is making the costume."

"Are you really?" Bailey grinned down at him. It was amazing to see how much he looked like his mother. "I think I can squeeze that in."

"Oh right, because you're so busy," Rebecca chimed in.

"Got me. I'll be there, Jacob. Don't worry."

"Promise?" He looked so serious that Bailey felt her heart melt.

"I promise." She meant it.

"Good." He sighed hugely. "Good night, Bailey."

"Goodnight, Jacob." She waited until he left the room before turning to Rebecca. "How do you know I'm not busy?"

"Because you're always over here," she said, as if it were the most obvious thing in the world. "How long are you staying?"

"Staying where, Rebecca?" That question confused her. "What do you mean?"

"Nothing." Rebecca looked almost frightened. "Good night, Bailey." She ran out of the room right before her mother entered.

"Your kids are something else," Bailey said when she heard Rebecca's door close.

"My kids have fallen in love with you."

"Is that going to be an issue?" Bailey knew instinctively that this was uncertain ground. She certainly didn't want to overstep boundaries, but those two kids were part of Beth. She couldn't ignore that.

"No. I trust you not to break their hearts."

"Why do you say it like that?" Alarms went off in Bailey's mind. This was dangerous ground. She didn't know where such a conversation would lead and didn't want to know. It was too soon. There was still too much to be healed between them.

"Because." Beth looked away. "Because their dad did."

"Um. Okay." Bailey wasn't sure how that factored into anything but was willing to let it go with that, even though she knew that wasn't everything Beth meant to say.

"So, do you want to watch a movie or something?"

"You've got a game system here. It's already set up. Do you play?" Bailey asked. She hadn't yet set up her game system at her mother's house. She wasn't looking forward to that argument.

"Not in a long time," Beth said.

"Then it's about time to jump back in. You've given up too much. It's not healthy." Bailey offered the other controller. "How was your Chamber thing?"

"Not bad." Beth waited until the game screen came on.

"What's up? You've been a bit off since you called and begged me to watch your kids. I mean I was really trying to joke with you and that's not working. Don't make me resort to tickle torture." She tried to think of something to break Beth out of the funk.

"I'm allowed bad moods, you know," Beth snapped.

"I know. Trust me, I'm not doing the whole you're too pretty not to smile bullshit. I was just trying to get you to tell or scream or laugh. I thought that would help you get through whatever it is that's bothering you. It used to." She wondered for a moment if she had misjudged.

"You're right. I used to do a lot of things. When did we grow up, Bailey?"

"I'm not sure. I'm not sure any of us have. I mean there's adult things we do like pay bills and so forth, but aside from a little more responsibility, aren't we pretty much the same people when it comes down to it?" It had been a long time since they'd talked like this.

"I wish. I remember having no cares. Life was simple then, wasn't it?"

"Not really." Bailey hated to do it, but she felt it was important. Nostalgia could kill a person. She'd seen it happen.

"Look, think back to when we were in high school. Remember the pressure? Good grades for you. Overbearing teachers. Bored cops following us around whenever we were out late. Boys. Girls. Hormones. Memorizing shows and steps and music. Finals. Getting into college. My mother. Mike. Cindy's parents and their epic fights. Remember all that?"

"Wow. Now that you mention it, it wasn't all that calm and peaceful." She put the controller down and turned to face Bailey.

"Nope. I bet college wasn't either. It wasn't fun and games for the two seconds I was there, and the first few years in LA certainly weren't either," Bailey said honestly.

"I'm surprised you think that. You certainly didn't do any studying." Beth leaned back against the couch. "I feel old, Bailey. And look at you, always youthful. You don't look like you've had a rough life."

"Thanks. I think. You certainly don't look old. What makes you feel that way?"

"I don't know." Tears started but Beth seemed unaware of them. "I just wish..."

"You wish what?" Bailey whispered, putting her arm around Beth's shoulders.

"I wish I knew what was going on." She dissolved into sobs.

Bailey wrapped her arms around Beth and held her close, the sob causing her body to shudder. It was surreal. She'd held Beth many times before, but this was different. Bailey could tell that Beth was holding on by a thread.

"It's okay. Let it all out." She rubbed Beth's back. Beth snuggled closer and buried her face in Bailey's shoulder.

It was tough. She was holding the woman she loved in her arms and yet it wasn't the time to say or do anything about it. They had a long history of friendship to rebuild. The last thing Beth needed was a complication, and the last thing Bailey needed was to lose the relationship between them completely.

Bailey broke the silence instead of breaking her resolve. "Anything you want to talk about?"

"I don't know how my kids are handling this. I don't know if they'll ever see their father again. I took all the pictures of them and him and put them in their rooms. I couldn't keep them in here. Can I tell you something?"

"Anything."

"I burned most of my wedding pictures. I kept a few in case Rebecca or Jacob want them later. I kept all the ones of my family and friends though."

"That's understandable," Bailey said.

"I just got notice that the lien against the house has been lifted." It was several minutes before Beth spoke again. "And now that I'm single and had my year of mourning or whatever, all the eligible bachelors think it's okay to try to worm their way into my bed. Tonight was miserable. It's been a long time since I felt like a bleeding otter in a pool of sharks."

"Anyone you need me to talk to?" Bailey tried to keep her tone light and teasing, but she felt her protective instincts stir.

"No. It's just getting old. Kyle and Elijah are the worst, but nothing I can't handle."

"I thought this was a Chamber thing? Shouldn't it have been a bit boring like talking about how to drive business to downtown and plans for festivals?"

"I suppose for someone with a much more color..." She stopped. "I'm sorry. I was about to take it all out on you. Yes, it is generally boring. Although, it's not always looking at pie charts and reports. Usually there's food and alcohol. Lots of brown nosing. And of course, the obligatory small-town bed hopping. It was my first meeting after the divorce. My boss thought it was time."

"You sure you don't want me to go talk to a few of those guys?"

"Yeah I'm sure. Thanks for listening." Beth sat up and straightened her clothes.

"It's what I'm here for."

"How long are you here for?"

"As long as I need to be." It was as close to committing as Bailey felt comfortable. "So you ready to get beat down?"

"Please. I can take you any day of the week."

"Prove it." Bailey held the game controller out but this time as a challenge.

"You're on."

Chapter Nine

"I CAN'T BELIEVE you're actually going to one of those school plays. Didn't you think the birthday party was bad enough?" Fiona asked as she stood in the kitchen mixing concentrated orange juice with vodka.

"The birthday party was a lot of fun," Bailey said as she laced her boots. "Jacob loved his presents and they seemed to have a great time skating."

"You trying to buy that boy's affection in the hopes it'll land you his mother?" Fiona asked. She didn't look as if she'd slept for long, if at all.

"No." The very idea was disgusting. "Not at all."

"What did you get him?" Fiona was done mixing the concoction and poured a glass. "Orange juice?"

"No thanks." Bailey made a mental note to only drink what she brought into the house. "He's really into this superhero movie. I know one of the actresses. She autographed a prop for him."

"Old fuck?" Her mother asked without looking up from pouring a large glass of juice and vodka.

"What? No." She rubbed her head. "I'm going to be late."

"I wouldn't worry about it, if I were you. School plays are horrible. The music's bad. Everything is badly acted. And all the parents are there judging everyone else's costume making skills, who's fucking who, and what kid is passing. It's a fucking nightmare."

"That why you never went to mine, Mama?" Bailey asked. She wasn't sure she wanted to know the answer.

"You think the bar would run itself?" Her mother shot back instead of answering the question.

"Yep. Pretty sure you have employees."

"Who rob me blind when I'm not around."

"Whatever, Mama. I'm going to be late. I'll see you when I get home, maybe."

"Have fun," Fiona called sarcastically behind her.

Bailey tried to put the whole conversation from her mind as she drove the truck to the school. It was difficult. It explained so much and reopened wounds she'd thought long since healed. She turned up the sound and sang along with the radio. It helped ease the ache. She wanted to be in a good mood when she got there.

The parking lot of the school was packed with cars. It looked as if everyone in the city had turned out for the kindergarten play. While impossible, it did take Bailey aback to see it so full. It seemed as if this play was a big deal.

She managed to find a spot on the front lawn behind several other cars. She joined the mass of people headed to the entranceway. There was a jam at the sign in desk. Fortunately, she was saved from the line.

"Bailey, I've already signed you in." Beth approached her and put a sticker on Bailey's shirt. "See? Ready to go."

"Excellent. Thanks." That was a relief. She'd been worried she would miss the performance.

"Liz and Ian have seats saved for us." She linked her arm through Bailey's and directed her to the auditorium.

"Why are Liz and Ian here?" She asked without thinking.

"It's what we do," Beth answered simply. Bailey understood. It was just how close they were.

"Yeah, it is," Bailey answered.

The auditorium doubled as the cafeteria. One side was dedicated to a decent-sized stage while the other was a full commercial kitchen. The tables had been moved and folding chairs were lined against the walls and in rows several feet from the stage. A large, clear area was left in the middle. She was about to ask what that was for when teachers started leading children in to sit on the floor.

"This is different." Bailey looked around. It looked nothing like she remembered.

"It's new. The hurricane a few years ago uprooted the oak that used to be in the courtyard. This is where it landed," Liz said.

"What's the deal with the stage in the cafeteria then?" It seemed odd to Bailey. It certainly was different than how she remembered.

"Well it gives the kids a place to have their plays. If you remember, we didn't. We had to go to the high school," Liz explained.

"You know; I really don't remember that," Bailey said. That didn't surprise her. "In fact there is very little of elementary school I do remember."

The principal walked over to them; intent it seemed, to make up for her previous faux paus. "Ms. Cooper. It's great to see you again."

Bailey didn't feel the need to stand. "Ms. Clark."

The principal took a deep breath and then braved on. "Apparently the rest of the school is up in arms that you didn't perform for them. I've been asked to see if you would be interested in playing for the whole school. Our music teacher is beside himself."

"That is a lovely offer, Ms. Clark." Bailey tried not to wince as Beth's elbow met her ribs. "I'll certainly consider it."

"Okay. Just let me know." The principal bounced off before it got too awkward.

"Thank you for being polite," Beth said.

"Well I do have manners. I use them just enough to keep them from getting rusty." Bailey leaned back in her chair and tried to get comfortable.

It was an amusing look into the regular lives of "normal" people, Bailey soon discovered. It wasn't all that different really from a gathering in LA. The same archetypes were present, just on a smaller scale. Several people kept walking up to say hello to one of her friends. A few smiled and nodded politely at her as well. Most she didn't recognize, but occasionally one or two would tease her memory.

"Bailey, you remember Kyle Jordan, right?" Beth asked as one of the vaguely familiar faces walked up to them. He was tall and handsome, just beginning to gray.

"Bailey Cooper, sitting with our Beth. This is a pleasant surprise." He said politely, quickly looking them over. His gaze stopped for a moment on the arm Bailey had draped on the back of Beth's chair.

"Kyle. It's been a long time." She remembered him clearly as soon as she heard his voice. She had to work to keep the disgust from her face. She glanced at Liz and saw Liz's warning look.

"Be nice," Beth whispered. "What type of bug is your son?" she asked him. All the kids in the play were different insects.

"A spider. He gets to scare the ladybugs," he said smugly.

"You must be so proud." Bailey couldn't bite back the comment. Kyle was one of the many rich and popular kids who tormented both Bailey and her cousins.

"Now, Bailey, shouldn't we let old grudges die? How about the three of us get some lunch and talk about how things change? Beth, you up for it?"

"Things haven't changed in that department, Kyle. Sorry," Bailey said before Beth could say anything. She promised herself she would not growl at him. She almost kept it.

"Well I'll see you around then. Beth, it was a pleasure as always." He quickly retraced his steps.

"Staking claim in public?" Liz leaned over and whispered in her ear as Beth turned to speak with someone else. "That was a bit much, don't you think?"

"He's an unmitigated, unrepentant douchebag," Bailey whispered back. "I have zero regrets."

"It's about to start," Beth said, and brought their attention back to the reason they were there. "Jacob was so nervous this morning. He went over his line so many times Rebecca and I know it too."

"I'm sure he'll be great," Bailey reassured her. "If he gets it from you, he'll be a natural."

Beth waived it off. "Please. It was one play."

"It was one play in college. All the plays in high school and two community theatre ones," Bailey said, unaware of the amazement on Beth's face and the smile on Liz's.

"How do you remember this stuff?" Beth asked.

Bailey shrugged. "I don't know. You'd think with all the amplifiers I've been around my memory would be shot and my brain would be mush."

Further comment was saved as a jumpy young man crossed the stage and waved for everyone's attention. He was very animated as he begged their patience and introduced the play. Bailey realized he must be the music teacher. She had to admire him. He directed the lines of nervous, excited children while remaining calm in the organized chaos. Soon, everyone was in his or her place, the adults were seated and all the students sitting on the floor were still and quiet. At least everyone was as still and quiet as possible.

The play was a simple one and Bailey tried her hardest to enjoy it. It was difficult. The music system wasn't well balanced, the microphones had feedback and half the children who used one held it too close and muffled their words. Still, the costumes were cute. Jacob remembered his line and said it proudly. Only one kid froze completely. When it was time for the final bow, the music teacher looked relieved.

Bailey stood up with the rest of the adults and clapped. Beth and Ian were taking pictures. As soon as the other students left, parents swarmed the stage to see the actors and actresses. Bailey followed along behind the others.

Beth quickly found Jacob and gave him a big hug. "You did great, sweetheart."

"Thanks, Mommy." He wrapped his arms around her and smiled as Ian took pictures. "Bailey, did you see? I didn't forget my line."

"I saw that, Jacob. You were awesome," she said and he practically jumped into her arms. "That was a great play and you were the best firefly up there."

"Thanks, Bailey." He squirmed down. "I gotta get back. We're having a cast party now in the music room. I don't wanna miss the cupcakes."

"Go ahead, sweetheart." Beth hugged him again. He then turned and ran back to his class.

Cindy walked over. She looked a little down. "Hey, guys. Guess if Perrins is taking them to his room I have a few minutes."

"You okay?" Liz asked.

"Yeah, I'm fine. Can't wait for the weekend. This play has been driving the kids mad. And then there's Mom." Cindy sighed. "Oh well. I need to go get my room ready for the rest of the day. Maybe they'll calm down a little after this."

"Good luck," Beth told her. "I have to get back to work."

"What? No one wants to go to lunch with me?" Bailey asked.

"Can't. Sorry. I have a patient I absolutely can't reschedule," Liz said.

"And I've got a showing in twenty minutes," Ian said. "Sorry, Bailey." He did at least appear apologetic.

"I swapped lunch to be here. I packed. Sorry." Beth reached out and rubbed her arm. "Maybe some other time, okay?"

"Fine." Bailey sighed in mock exasperation. "At least I'm good company. See y'all later."

BAILEY CLIMBED BACK in the truck and headed over to Arnoux's café. She didn't mind eating by herself. She had a book on her phone and a notebook in the car if she had a stroke of inspiration. She took both and settled at a place on the counter and waited for a server. She didn't expect Ms. Arnoux herself.

"Bailey, I'm so glad to see you." Ms. Arnoux placed a hand on her arm and took a seat next to her at the counter.

"Really? I must say that's a first. I was under the impression you didn't like me much." Bailey tried to keep from crossing the line into full smart-ass mode. It was difficult.

"I'm sure that was all a youthful misunderstanding." Ms. Arnoux waved over a server and requested tea. "Were you eating?"

"I was going to get a roast beef po'boy and a glass of tea, but I haven't ordered yet."

"Make that happen, please, Jazz. Thanks." The older woman shooed off the server.

"Can I help you with something, Ms. Arnoux?" Bailed ask as politely as she could. Cindy's mother was already getting on her nerves.

"Actually, yes. I could certainly use your help." Ms. Arnoux practically pounced on the opening. "I would have assumed you would be against this travesty of a wedding my daughter is planning."

Bailey was bewildered. "Why would I want to oppose it?"

"I just thought that your kind of people didn't approve of that either. I mean it's odd and can't be at all productive."

"My kind of people?" Bailey's ears burned. "Musicians?" She played dumb.

"No dear, gays. I mean you pick a side and don't deviate from it. Cindy has always been straight."

"Cindy is still straight. So is Mike. Straight woman. Straight man. No problem for most." The line between wanting to educate and wanting to brutalize had never been finer.

"But it's not natural. They can't have children."

"Ms. Arnoux, you have seven grandchildren. Cindy has given you one of those. Not everyone wants kids and not everyone can have kids. They love one another. They want to spend their lives together. I support that."

"Would you feel the same way if it was your sister?" Ms. Arnoux challenged.

"Liz is my cousin, not my sister. She's Mike's sister though. Perhaps that's where you got confused." Bailey was in a quandary. The server had just delivered her food. On one hand she wanted to walk out. On the other she was just handed a roast beef po'boy. "Look, Ms. Arnoux. I get it. I get why you oppose the wedding. I get why you don't like me or those of my kind. We don't fit in your box, the one you put everyone and everything that makes you comfortable in. Here's the thing, though. There are more of us outside that box then there are in it. Furthermore, we're not leaving. We've got lives and rights and all that good stuff. We're not going to peacefully and meekly feel ashamed because you won't share your box with us. Now I love Cindy to death and Mike's as much a brother as he is a cousin. You're tearing your daughter apart. Roger was a class A asshole. Mike's hard working, steady, decent and worships the air she breathes.

Let them be happy. If you can't, at least fake it and take some pressure off them."

"Well, I..." She stood and took a long moment smoothing her blouse. "You've given me something to think about. Enjoy your meal. It's on the house." And with that, the older woman left, leaving Bailey staring after her in wonder.

Chapter Ten

IT TOOK LONGER than Bailey planned to remove the sidecar. She was going to be late, but there really was no help for it. She didn't want to give Beth a choice between the back of the bike or the sidecar, so it had to be removed. She texted Liz an updated time and then hurriedly washed up and changed clothes. It had proven to be messier than she'd expected as well.

By the time she made it to the road Beth lived on, Liz's car was pulling out of the driveway. Bailey wanted to wait a few minutes to make it seem more coincidence and less conspiracy so she parked the motorcycle a few houses away and turned off the engine. It wasn't long before her phone rang.

"Hey, Liz just came by to take the kids to some paint party." It was Beth.

"That sounds cool. You didn't go?"

"Nope. I wasn't invited. From what I was told, it's a kids-only thing." Beth said. "It's oddly quiet. Where are you?"

"Outside. I was about to go for a ride on the motorcycle and get something to eat. Wanna come with?"

"Yeah. How long before you can get here?"

"I'm actually about a block away," Bailey replied sheepishly. "I was kinda headed over that way anyway."

"Awesome. I'll meet you outside."

As she promised, Beth was waiting on the porch when Bailey pulled into the driveway. Bailey handed Beth the extra helmet and waited until Beth found her balance before starting to drive. They didn't talk. Bailey for one didn't want to do so. She loved driving the motorcycle down the highway along the beach. Beth's arms were loosely around her waist and it was a very surreal experience. The last time they'd ridden like that had been their senior year in high school.

However, the ride was over too quickly for Bailey. She was hungry and her chosen restaurant wasn't far from where Beth lived. She parked the motorcycle and helped Beth down. They didn't have to wait for a table long after entering the restaurant. The hostess showed them to a table, handed them menus and left without much fuss.

"So what happened with Elaine? I liked her," Beth asked, breaking the comfortable silence.

"No you didn't." Bailey didn't look up from her menu.

"Okay, I didn't. She was a bitch. I did like that other one though. Cassie?"

"KC. Close. Yeah."

"So what happened? There's no reason you should be single."

Bailey glanced up. "There are lots of reasons."

"Well, what happened with Elaine?" Beth persisted.

"It's complicated." Bailey sighed. She owed Beth the truth, she knew that. Beth was the one person in the world to whom she couldn't lie. "I guess the short story is that I didn't want a repeat trip through rehab and she did. She wanted to party."

"Rehab?" Beth coughed. "Sorry, but what?"

"Damnit, Liz," Bailey swore. "Guessing you didn't know about that?"

"No idea. When?"

"The day after your wedding." Now there was a topic of conversation. Bailey silently pleaded Beth to turn away from that line of questioning.

Beth looked thoughtful. "That explains a lot."

"Explains what?"

"Why you went off the grid afterwards. I tried to call. Left a few messages."

"I'm sorry. I'm sorry for making an ass out of myself then too. It wasn't a good time in my life, that whole period."

"What, if you don't mind my asking, was it? What got you? I always thought you were impervious."

Bailey was relieved. She heard no recrimination in Beth's tone, only concerned interest. "I'm certainly not impervious. And you can ask me anything." Bailey took a long drink of water. "Are you sure you want to hear this? It's not pretty."

"It's part of you, part of your history. I wasn't there the first time. Let me be there now."

Bailey got the feeling Beth was regretting the distance between them just as much. "Okay. Cocaine. That was my downfall. You'd think with an alcoholic mother I'd have known better, been more careful." Bailey hung her head and looked down. She couldn't meet Beth's eyes.

"Tell me about it. How did it happen?" Beth leaned across and placed a gentle hand on Bailey's own. She seemed genuinely interested and empathetic.

"After I left college, I went to LA. That much you know. I worked my ass off doing whatever I could for money. I lived in the slums for a while, but kept working, you know? I tended bar, was a drink runner and a bouncer. Hell I even worked a few strip clubs doing security and cleaning shit. I kept responding to ads looking for a guitarist, hoping for a spot. I met Kat through a job. She was a drummer in need of a band. We decided to look together. Now we had half a band."

"I think I saw all this on that DVD special," Beth said.

"Yeah, the sanitized version." Bailey rolled her eyes at that. She took a deep, steadying breath and then continued quickly and as impersonally as she could. "The real one was much more gritty. We would work until sun up, try to get some sleep in this roach infested hell hole we paid too much in rent for, and then rehearse and meet with other musicians until it was time to work again. It seemed a never-ending cycle. I couldn't afford to call home, so I wrote when I had time. Hell we couldn't afford food half the time. I think I subsisted on popcorn, bar nuts, orange slices and cherries for months. Anyway, we finally get Kris and then DJ. And it all finally starts to come together. We're playing gigs and getting known locally. I managed to quit one job and keep the other. I'm dating KC. Things are moving along and then we get signed. It felt like it took so long that the signing seemed anticlimactic."

"I remember. You sent us all a copy of the demo. It was really good. We were so proud of you," Beth said. "We still are."

"Thanks." Bailey ginned. "After that came the recording sessions and then the tours and the rewrites and the meetings with the PR people. They just gave up and let us stay a rock band. They were going to try to mold us into something else, but it was hopeless. We would be in the studio for hours on end and then they'd take us to parties to meet people. We'd do gigs here and there. It was crazy mad. If I had thought I was tired before, it wasn't anything to how tired I was after. Some things changed. We had better places to stay. We played at better places. And we had food. And then they brought out the higher class of drugs."

"Go on," Beth prompted gently as the silence lengthened.

"The first time. We're in the studio, having just played a gig for the label and getting our name out there. I'm exhausted. I don't feel well. Kat's dragging. She can't keep the beat to save a life. Our manager storms in, yells at us for several minutes and then leaves. A few minutes later this guy we've never seen before comes in. Everything about it set off my hinky meter, you know? Anyway, he starts passing around drinks, offering pick me ups to us. What the fuck, right? At that point, I'd smoked pot and maybe dropped acid once or twice. We were all using caffeine pills like crazy and here we are, exhausted, giddy from nerves, no sleep, promises of fame and fortune and this guy just offers this for free. We took him up on his offer. And that's all it was at first for all of us. Just a way to get through one last recording session. Then it became a way to perk up and get through a performance. Then it was how I got through any number of things. I learned when to add alcohol and when not to do so, and what to take later when I wanted to sleep. It became my crutch, my everything for a few years. Kris' too. That's why KC left me, and Kris left the band. Rock bottom was your wedding. I'm sorry. So very sorry. Liz got me out of there. She took me home and helped me get into a place. I gave her power of attorney so they could force me to stay if something happened."

"That's why she had to leave so quickly to get to you when you collapsed in Rome?" Beth asked.

"Yeah. I never rescinded it. And I'll tell you that Roman pneumonia was a bitch. And no, it wasn't a relapse. It really was pneumonia."

"I believe you." Beth squeezed Bailey's hand. "Why didn't you tell me any of it?"

"I was ashamed. And like I said, it's not pretty." Beth felt like a weight had been lifted, though. "After all that, I don't do much. When we're not touring or in the studio, I travel, read and play a lot of games."

"So what happened at the awards show?"

"You would ask about that." Bailey surprised her by laughing. At least that had been an enjoyable experience. "Heather is a friend. She's in another group and they needed a little publicity. So we manufactured it, the argument, the champagne, all of it. I only agreed since she promised not to toss red wine on me."

"Are you serious?" Beth's eyebrows raised. "You set that up?"

"Yeah. Did wonders for her. She got a few interviews and interest in her band spiked."

"How do you stand it, Bailey?" Beth's tone was gentle.

"Stand what?" She was confused by the question.

"Pretending to be something you're not? The loneliness? I know you get lonely." Beth still hadn't removed her hand.

"I have friends. Elvis. I'm pretty comfortable by myself." Bailey began to absently stroke Beth's hand with her thumb. "I may not be the full person my reputation claims I am, but a lot of it is pure me. I am impatient with idiots. I do judge people quickly. I have no filter. I'm tattooed and pierced and dye my hair whatever color I want. I've had women try to get me to stop playing video games or riding a motorcycle or one wanted me to get a cat and get rid of the dog. I just don't deal with it anymore. I'm old and stubborn."

"Stubborn? Yes. Not old, though. And you have a very strange sense of humor and very little in the way of shame. I know. But you're also very good with kids. You're extremely loyal and protective of your friends. You body slam people into walls for them." She smirked. "He told me."

"Bastard." Bailey was suddenly embarrassed. "What did he say?"

"Just that you threatened to disembowel him if he did what he did." Beth didn't look angry. "How did you know?"

"I didn't. I just didn't want you to end up like Cindy. Roger was a bastard to her. I mean yeah, she got Eric out of it and eventually Mike came into the picture, but she had to go through a lot for that. I wanted better for you."

"Why?" It the loaded question Bailey wasn't yet ready to answer. She wasn't confident enough in the outcome.

"I hadn't anything to go on, but honestly I just didn't like the guy." She attempted to avoid the real question. "He seemed very possessive. I was worried. You know how I feel about my family. Bastard was coming into it with attitude. It set my hackles up."

"Oh." Beth slowly pulled her hand back and then picked up her menu. "Hey, I got two wonderful kids out of it."

Bailey smiled. "I know. Your kids are awesome."

"They think you are too." Beth looked around. "Is it just me or have we not ordered yet?"

"No, we haven't." Bailey looked around as well. "It's not that crowded. You think they're avoiding us?"

"I think someone's coming over," Beth said.

The young waitress did come over and take their order. Of course, no explanation for her delay was given, but Bailey was fine with that. It had given them a chance to get the serious parts of the discussion over without fear of someone choking on anything. They made small talk while they ate. It was nice and comfortable and very reassuring.

"You want to go for a ride along the beach or are you ready to head back?" Bailey asked as they left the restaurant.

"It's later than I thought. I'm sure Liz has my kids back. We should probably go home." Beth sounded reluctant.

"Not a problem." Bailey was a bit disappointed, but remembered the last ride had ended somewhat the same. That time though, they'd only stopped for gas and had the misfortune to pull in next to Beth's parents. Beth's mom flipped out at seeing her daughter on the back of a motorcycle and took her home in the family car.

Liz's car was in the driveway when they got back to the house. The kids heard the motorcycle and all ran out of the house, eager to show off their artwork. Liz just looked bemused from the doorway.

"All right, everyone back in the house," Beth hollered as she accepted Bailey's help to get off the motorcycle. "Thank you for dinner."

"It was my pleasure." So close. She was so close to leaning over and kissing her, but three elementary school children surrounded them, each one wanting to be heard, each begging for a ride. "Okay. After I put the sidecar back on, each one of you can have a ride."

"With helmets," Beth clarified. "Now come on, let's let Bailey go home. She can see your artwork later. It's past bedtimes."

"Goodnight," Bailey said softly as she watched them grudgingly turn and go back in the house.

Beth stood next to Liz on the porch. "Goodnight, Bailey. Drive safe."

It was a dismissal, and she knew it. So Bailey did what was expected and left. She took the long way home, trying not be discouraged by the progress they had made so far.

THE PARKING LOT around the bar was packed as usual. She could hear the jukebox over the sound of the engine as she pulled the motorcycle into the garage. After stowing her helmet and jacket in the sidecar, she did something she normally didn't do. She locked the garage with a padlock to which only she had a key. Things had been too strange around the house lately and she no longer trusted her mother to keep her hands off anything.

"Well, well. If it isn't Bailey, the wonder dyke. You come to do some trolling around here?" The familiar voice pierced the darkness and made her turn around.

"As you know, dickhead, this is my mother's bar. It's astounding to see someone of your perceived social status hanging out here. Get kicked out of all the high dollar places?" That was one thing about being back for any length of time. The opportunity to run into the unsavory memories grew exponentially the longer one was home.

"I only come here when all the other spots in town are dead. Nothing wrong with a little beer goggle noodling." He walked closer and she noticed he wasn't too steady on his feet.

"You've just never grown up, have you, Kyle?" she asked.

"You gonna play all holier than me? Dyke bitch. Busted up my plan to get cozy with Beth at the school." She smelled the alcohol from his breath despite the distance between them.

"She has much better taste and more brains than to fall for your scheme." That made her angry. She'd always hated Kyle, and he knew it.

"Oh, I forgot how upset you get when someone makes a move on one of your people," he taunted, stepping closer. The smell of alcohol mixed with too much cologne was nauseating.

"You didn't make a move on Mike, you damn near raped him. And if I remember correctly, aren't your front two teeth fake? I'm sure I managed to kick them out of your head. Or was that Will? No, I think it was you." She slowly moved her left leg back and lowered her center of balance. She hadn't gotten where she was in life without learning how to bar fight. She doubted Kyle knew that she took a lot of fitness classes to maintain the stamina to do a multi-country tour.

"Bitch! Damn freak had tits even though it tried to hide them. Maybe a little dick would have straightened it out, you think? Maybe it'd straighten you out as well." He took another step closer, a grotesque sneer on his face.

"Kyle. Back the fuck up. I don't have the patience for this bullshit. Either find a way to get your sorry ass out of my yard or I'll beat the shit out of you again and let the cops get you home."

"This ain't your yard. Your mama don't mind me around here. Hell she's even let me ride that bike of yours. It's a beauty. Bet it makes you feel all hot and powerful when you're riding, doesn't it? Oh, you didn't know that, did you? Everyone your mother wants has ridden that beast. Sometimes she even dresses like you. Now I haven't had her like that, but a lot of these fellows have."

"I'm not telling you again, Kyle. Get the fuck out of here." Bailey felt her control slipping. She really didn't want to have to hit him. She didn't want to get sued, and she knew he would do his best to make her life miserable just because he could.

"Oh, did I tell you something you didn't want to know? Poor little Bailey. Half orphan, all trash." He smirked.

She refused to turn her back on him and slowly made her way to the porch as he just stood there staring at her, smiling that grotesque smile. Finally, she made it inside and locked the door. It wasn't the first time in her life that she had heard such accusations. It wasn't even the first time she'd been upset by them. However, it was the first time she'd heard the other parts. The first time she'd been, however indirectly, included, and it make her stomach churn.

"What's going on out there?" Fiona asked as she came around from the kitchen and looked at Bailey. "Were you fighting?"

"No. Mama, have you let anyone ride my motorcycle?" She knew the truth. She knew her mother would lie about it as well.

"Why on earth would I do that?"

"You did, didn't you?" Bailey shook her head in disgust. "Damn it, Mama. I trusted you and left it here for safe keeping. What kinda losers have you let ride it? Do you know what could happen if someone had wrecked while on it? I'd have been sued for everything I have. And you know what? They would have won. Doesn't that bother you?"

"No one would sue you," her mother scoffed.

"Yeah, Mama, they would. So what? You use my motorcycle as an enticement to your bed?"

"How dare you say that to me," Fiona raged. "You have no idea what you're talking about."

"I don't want to know anymore. I know too much as it is. You need help, Mama."

"Get the fuck out of my house, you fucking hypocrite. You don't know what it took to raise an ungrateful bitch like you. No one would date a woman with a child. I should never have kept you."

"But you did. And you made damn sure no one else got a chance to get close to me, didn't you? You need help, Mama. I'm sorry you didn't accept my offer before. But you need to do something before you find yourself a sad, bitter lonely old woman with severe kidney and liver issues."

"I don't need you. Didn't I tell you to get the fuck out of my house? And take that fucking dog with you." She kicked at Elvis but missed.

"Fine. Come on, boy. Let's go for a ride." Bailey grabbed a bag and threw a few of her clothes into it. She debated taking the motorcycle, but opted for the truck instead. She threw her guitar and a few other possessions into the back, the dog into the front and left.

Chapter Eleven

BAILEY WASN'T SURE where to go after she left her mother's house. She drove along the beach and fought back tears and rage. She parked for a moment and watched the moon, trying to even her breathing. She knew she had to get herself under control before she could make any decisions. Finally she felt centered and pulled out her phone.

"Hello?" Mike answered on the first ring.

"Can I stay over there tonight? You at home or Cindy's?" She asked. Her head was still ringing with both her mother's and Kyle's voices, but she could breathe and her heart was no longer racing.

"Cindy's. C'mon over. Everyone's asleep already, but I'm up watching the game. Bring the dog? My larder's pretty bare."

"I already ate. Haven't you?"

"Yeah, but pizza goes great with ballgames."

"Order the pizza." She told him. It still amused her how much Mike could eat. "I'll pay for it when I get there."

"Done. Drive safe." Mike disconnected.

She made it to Cindy's right before the pizza. She left the dog in the truck and paid the young man. Mike came out and took over the food while she grabbed the stuff out of the back. Cindy lived in a nice neighborhood, but she wasn't going to lose her prized guitar out of carelessness.

"So what happened to make you want to stay here?" Mike asked when both Bailey and the dog collapsed on the couch.

"My mother." Quickly, and with many shudders, she told him about the conversation with Fiona. She told him parts of it anyway. She saw no need to reopen old wounds for him, so she skipped the conversation with Kyle.

"I think I need a mental shower now," he said. "Question is: do you believe her?" Mike asked as he grabbed a few paper plates.

"No." She accepted the slice of pizza he handed her. She wasn't really hungry, but it was something to do. "Makes sense in a way. I mean, every time I leave, I always seem to be missing clothes. I asked her the other day if she had my motorcycle jacket. She lied at first, but then it was there. Hanging in her closet like she fucking owned it."

"She had your jacket? The leather one you found in that thrift store in Pensacola? Your signature jacket?" He seemed surprised. "I didn't think anyone was allowed to touch that."

"Yep. I need to disinfect it. I have a feeling I don't want to know why she borrowed it. Mike, what the fuck is wrong with her?" Bailey put her head in her hands and stared at the floor.

"You'd have to ask Liz, but I would hazard a guess that your mother is a narcissist who is insanely jealous of you."

"Dude." Bailey didn't know if she should be offended or impressed. "You got all that from Liz, didn't you?"

"Actually yes. We've talked about your mother quite a bit. I mean, yeah she is your mom, but she's our aunt and she's toxic as hell."

"I'm slowly beginning to realize that." She pulled out her phone and texted Ian. "Guess I can start looking for houses now. Damn woman finally kicked me out. I lasted longer there this time than I thought I would."

"So you're staying?"

"I don't know yet." She added to forestall questions. "If nothing else it'll give me a place to stay when I'm here. Kat's not ready to give up the rock star life, however abbreviated it is these days. I'm honestly not sure if I am or not. I love playing. I love music. And face it, Mike, it's the only thing I'm good at."

"That's your mother talking. Bailey, you are an awesome musician. But you know as well as I do that it's not all you are. Remember all those talks you gave me when I first came to LA, and then after when Cindy and I came out to see my doctors? Bailey, you are beyond all this."

"I know you're right, but it's just Fiona was so nasty. And she's borrowing, no, stealing my clothes. It's like she wants to be me. It disgusts me, Mike and I don't know what to do about it." The very thought made her feel sick.

"Have Ian show you some houses," Cindy suggested from the doorway. "Sorry, Bailey. I was asleep but the call of nature and your voice kinda steered me in here."

"Sorry about that."

"No worries. We're friends. If you can't impose upon us in your hour of need, how can we possibly hope to do the same to you?" Cindy teased. "Seriously though, look at houses. It can't hurt."

"Right. And cut off your mom until she stops acting like she does," Mike said. "Talk to Liz or your therapist. And in there somewhere is organize my bachelor party, get fitted for a tux, help me settle the great band or deejay debate and spend time with your family and friends. Did I leave anything out?" He looked at Cindy.

"Talk to Beth about your feelings," Cindy said.

Bailey ignored the comment about Beth. "I need to decide what to do next with the band." She had too much other stuff on her mind at that moment. "Do you think Mama knows who my father was?"

"Yes," they both answered. Mike continued. "I think her refusal to tell you is part of her control. Do you really want to talk about this? You never have before."

"Maybe. I've only talked about it with my therapist. Not Liz. Not my sponsor." Bailey paused a moment. "On my birth certificate it says unknown."

"I'm sure it does. If she did know, and again, I think she does, she wouldn't want to put down someone who could cause trouble or take you away. So I would bet it was someone either married or politically connected. Either one would have been a scandal," Mike said.

"That's a good point," Cindy said. "You know how this town can be."

"True. I always figured she knew because she wouldn't tell me that she didn't know. But then maybe she didn't want to admit that she had no idea. Damn woman. Nothing about her makes sense."

"That's good," Mike replied. "It means you won't turn out like her. I figured you were worried."

"Sometimes, yeah. Thanks." That reassurance made her feel a lot better.

"No problem."

"Have you and Beth talked about what happened in Vienna?" Cindy asked as Mike excused himself for a moment.

"What are you talking about?" Bailey said. "Nothing happened in Vienna."

Cindy smirked. "I saw you kissing."

"Hey, she kissed me," Bailey protested. She refused to close her eyes and get lost in the memory. It didn't work. She could feel that soft hand on her shoulder. She remembered turning to look at Beth, the look in her eyes and how soft her lips were. Bailey shook her head to clear it of the image.

"And you were responsible and stopped it before anything could happen. That almost killed you, didn't it?" Cindy asked.

"It did. It really did. Then to not have her remember a thing the next morning? Man that was awful." It felt good to talk to someone about it. She'd never admitted it had happened before.

"She was so drunk though. It really was the right thing you did," Cindy told her. "Even though it was hard."

"Thanks," Bailey said. "Although that pretty much made me realize a bunch of stuff. Like just how much I loved her. Let me ask you something." She paused as Mike rejoined Cindy on the couch. "The two of you met as kids when everything was different. Hell, Mike, you weren't even Mike yet. What made you realize you were in love with one another?"

"It's different with us, Bailey. I was never in love with, well I hate to use the dead name, but I was never in love with your cousin Michelle. I'd honestly never considered the possibility. After Mike came back from California, I didn't recognize him as Liz's twin. He was such a different person, and not just because of the physical changes. He was happy. He smiled. He laughed. It was amazing."

"No, you're amazing." Mike attempted to deflect the attention. It didn't work.

"He was a completely different person," Bailey agreed.

"Exactly. So I went into the parts store one day and didn't recognize the adorable guy behind the counter. He of course recognized me and wouldn't tell me his name. Ass that he was. I thought it was just another one of your endless stream of cousins." She elbowed him gently in the ribs. He grinned. "It was funny to him, still is. I didn't put it together until I saw him at the cafe with Liz. I'll be honest it was a bit weird I guess; I hate saying that, but it was."

"You really had no idea who he was?"

"No, and even Liz thought it was hilarious. After that though it took a while. We talked. We hung out. Eventually we realized we were dating. I fell for him. And now here we are. So are you going to tell her?" Cindy looked at Bailey expectantly.

Bailey ran a hand through her hair. "I don't know. Right now, I'm not really sure about anything."

"It's okay. Do you want to sleep on the couch, or do you want to make up the spare room?" Cindy asked. "I'll warn you that Eric is up and out of here fairly early. I'm not sure he wouldn't take a moment to wake you up and ask you a million questions."

"He's fifteen. It'd be two questions and one of those would be a request for a ride to school," Mike corrected.

"True. I forgot boys stopped talking shortly after puberty." Cindy shook her head. "So, what will it be?"

"The couch is fine. I'll get a hotel room tomorrow. Thanks, guys. I appreciate it." Bailey stifled a yawn.

"Here." Mike held out a blanket. "I've fallen asleep on this thing a few times. It's actually comfortable. In the morning, if you want, we can go get all the rest of your stuff and put it out at my place. I'm sure it'll be safe there."

"Thanks, Mike." She lay down as Elvis got comfortable on the end of the couch.

"Goodnight, Bailey." Cindy turned out the light and went to bed. Mike was a step behind.

"AUNT BAILEY?" ERIC gently tapped her on the shoulder. "You okay?"

"Well I was." She yawned and rubbed the sleep out of her eyes. "What's up?"

"Nothing. It's just you're sleeping on our couch. That's kinda odd. Everything okay?" His long brown hair hung in his face and almost obscured his hazel eyes. She fought the urge to tell him to get a haircut.

"You know, you're a good kid, Eric. Is it time for you to go to school or something?" She sat up. "How much longer do you have left of the school year anyway?"

"A week and a half. I should catch the bus in a few minutes." He looked at her imploringly.

"Shit. Really? What time does school start?" She looked at her watch and was shocked at how early it was. She was also very glad she'd slept in her clothes.

"Ten after eight. We have to share buses, so I ride with the middle school kids too. They start earlier than we do."

"High school sucks, man." She shook her head. "Okay. Can you let Elvis out and I'll give you a ride to school?"

"Sure." He dropped his bag and called the dog. His face lit up like it was his birthday. "Aren't you on the motorcycle?"

"Nope. Not today. I'm in the truck, but if you want I'll stop before we get to the school and you can ride in the back." She remembered all too well how she'd jumped at the chance to show off the least little bit. She assumed Eric was the same.

"Excellent." He said and opened the back door for Elvis, walking outside right after.

"Eric? Shouldn't you be getting on the bus?" Cindy called from the hallway. "Oh. Did he wake you?" She asked when she entered the living room.

"Nope. I told him I'd give him a ride. I need to get stuff from Mama's before she tosses it all out on the lawn, but I need breakfast first. Any place you know where I can take a four-legged guest?"

"The café. Mom's not usually there in the morning and if you eat outside, they won't mind. Lots of people do it now for lunch. It's part of the city's new plan to make it a walking community," Cindy explained.

"Very cool. Mind if I take Eric with me?" Bailey asked.

"Not at all. Knowing him he grabbed a toaster pastry thing and planned on eating it on the bus. Mike said to ask you if you need help getting stuff from your mom's house. He wants to help."

"Thanks, Cindy. And thanks again for the couch last night. I'm going to call and book a room today. If I remember correctly the ones attached to the casinos would let me bring a pet." She shook her head, folded up the blanket she'd used and placed it on the end of the couch.

"You're very welcome. Are you sure you don't want to stay here? Or Mike's?" Cindy asked.

"Nah. Thanks though. I thought about staying at the grandparent's house, but all the other cousins still seem touchy about who gets what. And Mike taking great granddad's cottage in the back just pisses them off more. Why start a war when I can easily get a room?"

"Families suck," Eric said when he came back inside. "Not you guys, of course."

"Of course not," Bailey said in amusement.

"We better not," Cindy cautioned.

"Cindy, that didn't make any sense," Bailey said. "And as I've learned, you are the master of your own suckage. Either you suck or you don't. It's up to you." Bailey winked at her.

"Take my kid to breakfast. I'll see you later." Cindy grabbed a pre-made lunch bag from the refrigerator and a thermos of coffee.

"Yes, ma'am. We'll be right behind you. Eric, grab your bag." She clipped Elvis' leash on him and they followed Cindy out the door.

"When are you guys going to record a new album?" Eric asked as he climbed in the truck. Bailey took a moment to make sure Elvis was in the middle and not drooling on anything important.

"I don't know. I haven't written anything for us in a while. I feel kinda blocked. What about you?" She asked. "You come up with anything good on your drums?"

"Not really. I can't practice the cool stuff at school. We have to keep with the stuff the band director picks out. And at home, well, it's not the same."

"I understand. You know, if I do end up buying a house here, I'll have to find one with a space I can turn into a studio. You'd be way more inspired in a space that's tuned, and of course soundproofed."

"That would be awesome. You'd really let me play there?" He asked. His eyes lit up.

"Of course. Kat let you play her drums once, right?"

"I'll never forget that," Eric said solemnly. His crush on Kat was only outmatched by his desire for her drum set. "I can't believe she let me play it. I'm so glad someone took a picture too. No one would believe me otherwise."

"All right, kid. We have enough time for breakfast before getting you to school," she said as she parked the car in front of the café. "You know what you want already?"

"Yes, ma'am. I love the breakfast here. Grandma can be a bit hard on Mom sometimes, but." The young man shrugged as he closed the door to the truck.

"I understand." She helped Elvis out and grabbed his leash. She did understand. Family relationships were complicated.

"Wow. That's a big puppy," the hostess said as they approached. "Outdoor seating? Straight through to the patio and pick a table. I'll send someone out to you in a moment."

"Thanks." Bailey grinned at her. The young woman continued to look at Elvis. "You can pet him. He likes to be scratched behind his ears."

"Thanks." She bent down immediately. Elvis sniffed her hand and then let her pet him. He seemed content. "I love bulldogs."

"Me too," Bailey told her.

"Thanks. Um, sorry. Go ahead and I'll send someone out right away."

"Do you get that a lot?" Eric asked as they picked a table.

"Actually, I do. Elvis is a bigger hit than Freddy, but not as big as Bowie was." Bailey had never been allowed pets as a child. She made up for that as soon as she could. Bowie was her first attempt with a dog, after a disastrous first attempt with a cat. She quickly learned that cats are not compatible with touring. Hers had been much happier at home.

"I think I remember Bowie. He was the Lab, right?"

"Yes. I've got a picture of you trying to ride him." She said.

A waitress soon brought them menus. Eric had grown up eating at Arnoux's Café and knew what he wanted. Bailey took a moment and decided on an omelet with coffee. Even Elvis got breakfast. The hostess made sure he had his own bowl of cheese grits.

Eric was a good breakfast companion. He wasn't overly talkative, but he did have the ability to keep a conversation going, as long as it was about music or video games. Since those were two areas near and dear to Bailey's heart, they didn't lack for things to discuss.

Bailey paid the bill and they got back in the truck. She didn't want Eric to be late. They only had a little time left and she knew most of that time would be reviewing for exams.

As she promised, Bailey stopped two blocks from the school and allowed Eric to climb in the back of the truck. He slumped down below the sides when they passed the crossing guard but was back up as soon as she turned into the school. She smiled as he did his best to look cool jumping out of the back with his bag over his shoulder. It reminded her of how she would have done the same thing.

Chapter Twelve

THE BAND USUALLY had someone make arrangements for them when they toured, and Bailey used the same person when she traveled. This time she called and made the reservations herself as she drove back to Cindy's house.

Mike's truck was gone when Bailey pulled in the driveway. She was exhausted. Check-in time was hours away and she didn't have a key to Cindy's house. With a groan of frustration, she put the truck in reverse and decided to head to the store. It was important to get her stuff from her mother's house as soon as possible. She didn't trust her mother not to throw it all out in the yard.

Unfortunately, Mike wasn't at the store either. She pulled in and decided to use the cell phone she paid so much for instead of driving around aimlessly. She found Mike on the road to New Orleans in search of an order of parts that never arrived. He did promise to go rescue her motorcycle that night. Bailey didn't want to leave it there long. She called Ian hoping for a distraction in the form of house hunting. Ian was willing to set up a time for viewing houses, but he was unable to fit her in for a couple of days.

After a drive through meal eaten at the local harbor, Bailey called the hotel and requested an early check-in time. As luck would have it they had a room available. She headed there next, ready for some sleep. It didn't take long to check in and within twenty minutes she was laying on a bed attempting to nap.

She'd just managed to drift off when there was a knock at the door. Elvis continued to snore, but Bailey hadn't counted on him answering it anyway. She got up and stumbled to the door, not bothering to look through the peephole before opening it.

"Ms. Cooper. I'm Don Reince, the front desk manager here at the hotel. I would like to apologize on behalf of my staff and our organization for this unfortunate incident," a young man, in an ill-fitting suit, said when she opened the door.

"What?" She wasn't even half awake as a bellhop pulled a cart into her room and began putting her stuff on it. "Mistake?"

"Yes, ma'am. I believe you were mistakenly told that we could not put you in a suite when you called. I'm here to rectify that mistake. Walter and I will assist you and escort you to your new accommodations."

"Okay." While Bailey didn't mind the standard king room she'd been given, she knew, from personal experience, that a one room suite would be easier to spend more than a week in. Besides, she was still half asleep and in no mood to argue.

"Thank you, ma'am. Is there anything else?" The manager asked. They both looked around the room. The bellhop had gotten most everything on the cart.

"No." She clipped Elvis's collar and leash on him, grateful that she hadn't unpacked. Bailey shouldered her guitar case. That she entrusted to no one.

"Then if you'll follow us, please." The manager waved the bellhop ahead and then closed the door behind Bailey. "I'm sure you'll find this suite much more to your liking."

"This room was fine," Bailey said, vaguely aware that someone was going to get in trouble for this mistake.

"I'm sure you'll find the new room more to your liking," the manager said smugly. The bellhop pressed the call button for the elevator, but didn't say anything.

"I'm sure," she said.

The elevator arrived much sooner than she expected, though not quite soon enough. The manager bounced a little on his toes. It was an irritating habit and it was driving Bailey crazy. She couldn't wait to be rid of him and able to go back to sleep.

Mr. Reince used his card to get the elevator to stop at the top floor. He held the doors and waved Bailey through. The bellhop followed quietly. Elvis of course padded softly beside her.

"Here you go, Ms. Cooper." The manager gestured to one of the four doors leading off the hallway. "This is the suite we've picked out for you. I hope you enjoy it." He unlocked the door.

"Nice." It was. It wasn't the nicest place she'd ever stayed, but it was much nicer than she would have guessed for being a hotel near her hometown.

She let Elvis loose and walked down the short hallway. There was a kitchen of sorts, more for entertaining than cooking, a living room with plush rugs, leather furniture and colorful drapes. The one bedroom had two complete bathrooms, one with a tub and one with a shower. There was an additional bathroom near the kitchen area. It was a pretty big suite. She wouldn't go stir crazy there.

"This room comes with a private cabana at each pool. There are two. One is more family oriented. The other elevator goes straight down to our VIP lounge. If you wish to gamble, there is a high roller area not far from it. We also have snacks, private concierge service and other services available there."

"It's very impressive," she told him.

"We're not quite Las Vegas, Ms. Cooper, but we do know how to treat our VIPs." He smiled stiffly. "Is there anything else we can assist you with today?"

"Do I have to call for use of the cabana or can I just show up?" She asked. None of her friends had a pool. She knew they would love the opportunity to use one.

"You can just show up. Any time from when the pool opens at eight in the morning until it closes at ten each night. The pool attendants will get you set up. Of course, there are pool bars up there as well."

"Thanks." She accepted an envelope with her keys and a menu of the hotel's amenities. "Here." She tipped the bellhop. She wondered for a moment if she should tip the manager but thought better of it. He didn't have to lug around heavy bags all day.

"Thank you, ma'am." The bellhop grinned at her. He pocketed the bill and pushed the cart outside.

"I'll leave you to your rest." The manager executed a half bow and left. She bolted the door behind them.

AN HOUR AFTER settling in, Bailey escorted Mike, Cindy and Eric to the suite. She'd decided to share the luxury instead of resting. They were suitably impressed, but eager for the pool. While they changed, Bailey called the pool attendant and had everything set up for them. It was a great way to show gratitude for couch space the night before.

"This is nice." Cindy reclined in one of the lounge chairs. "It's always so great traveling with you, Bailey."

"We didn't travel this time," Bailey said. She looked around, approving of the accommodations. "This is kinda nice. Even in Vegas the cabana was separate. This time they threw it in with the room."

"Guess it was to cover for their embarrassment after they put you in a regular room," Mike said as he opened a beer. "Drinks and food and shade all at a pretty nice pool. Very cool."

"Yep. And it's too much for just me, so I thought I'd share."

"Are you inviting Beth and kids over?" Cindy asked.

"Of course. I already did." Bailey grinned. "They'll be over in about an hour. I think we'll order down burgers or something when they get here."

"Aren't you paying for this?" Eric asked. "I mean they don't give all this to you for free, do they?"

"Nope. Well, some places will if you play there, but I'm paying for all this," she said.

"That's a lot." Eric looked around doubtfully.

"It's relative. Besides, you think Elvis appreciates this? Please." She laughed to lighten the tension. She knew money was a concern in their household since Mike came in to the picture. Roger, Eric's dad, never paid child support unless forced. Cindy's mom had stopped, or delayed, the payments from the Arnoux trust and neither Cindy nor Mike made all that much on their own. And weddings were expensive.

"Well, son, when you get rich and famous, you can pay for it," Mike teased. "Now aren't we here to swim?"

"I believe we are." Bailey pulled her swimsuit cover off and jumped in the pool. Mike and Eric followed.

It was a nice day. The sky was clear, the air was warm, and the pool was heated just enough to make the water feel warm and smooth as silk. Bailey, Mike and Eric played with childish abandon as Cindy sat on the side of the pool and worked on her tan. It wasn't crowded. Only two other families were there, and they stayed on the other side of the pool, away from the cabanas.

Cindy interrupted a spirited game of keep away by calling out, "Bailey?"

"What?" Bailey asked as she watched Mike erupt, sputtering, with the ball they were using.

"Beth called and asked to reschedule," Cindy said. "She had something come up."

"Is everything okay?" Bailey swam over to the edge and looked up at her friend.

"Yes. She said it was a work thing and that she wouldn't be able to be here tonight," Cindy answered. "But she did ask what you were wearing."

"She didn't," Bailey protested. She couldn't imagine such a thing. "Did she?" For a moment she was back in high school trying to find out if someone had asked about her at lunch.

"Yes, Ms. Cooper, she did. Now go play. You can call her later." Cindy held the phone out of reach in case Bailey decided to exit the pool.

"Fine." Bailey mock groaned. "We'll still have a great time, just the four of us. Go ahead and order dinner if you want. We can eat it here."

She had debated inviting Liz, Ian, and Sarah, but decided against it. She would have them over a different evening. She wanted to spend time just with Mike, Cindy and Eric. They were all great people and she loved them dearly. She also knew life was harder on them than it was on the others most of the time. She was glad she was able to alleviate their stress, if only for an afternoon.

Chapter Thirteen

"SO WHAT DO you think?" Ian asked as he unlocked the door.

"Dude, we haven't even gone inside yet," Bailey said. She was tired of looking at houses. So far nothing was perfect.

"Nice front yard," Liz said. "Never thought you'd have a rose trellis though."

"That and the fairy garden would have to go," Bailey commented.

"Okay, so the front's a little froufrou. Wait until you see the rest," Ian said. He opened the front door and ushered them inside.

Bailey stared at the living room walls in distaste. "I think I've seen this wallpaper in horror movies."

"Definitely," Liz agreed. "Early modern ax murder décor."

"You two have to think about the bones of a place," Ian said. "This house is solid wood. Good location with a decent sized yard."

"Bones, huh? You spent a lot of time with your dad at construction sites as a child, didn't you?" Bailey teased.

"Every summer. Paid for a car and all sorts of stuff." he answered.

"This house needs major updating, despite the bones of it," Liz said. "The kitchen alone looks like you need heels and pearls just to cook in there."

"What?" Ian looked at her askance as Bailey roared with laughter.

"TV mom old, dear. Try to keep up." She stuck her tongue out at him. "I think they filmed forties or fifties comedies in here."

"Okay, the last one was too new and impersonal. At least look at all of this one," Ian pleaded. "We're Goldilocksing it here. Too small, too big, too neat, too —"

"Crime scene," Bailey finished for him.

"Does Beth know you're looking at houses? Liz asked.

"No. I haven't said anything. Why?" She actually hadn't spoken to Beth in two days. Whatever was going on at the bank was keeping her busy.

"Just wondering what she had to say about it." Liz turned

away from examining the old sink.

"I don't know. We haven't really discussed it.

"Have y'all done more than just discuss things?" Liz asked.

"Nope," Bailey said. "Taking things slow."

"Slow? Bailey you've waited for decades. And knowing you, slow is glacial. Have you at least talked to her about the two of you?"

"You mean have I declared my undying love for her?" Bailey turned to face her. "No. I have not."

"No of course you haven't." Liz sounded exasperated.

"Again, no. I'm not sure I want to." Bailey peered into the pantry. "How many rooms is this?"

"Three plus a bath and a half," Ian called from the other room. He was wisely staying out of any conversation that didn't include real estate.

"Why haven't you told her? And why wouldn't you?" Liz prodded.

"Liz, I'm trying to decide if I like the house or not."

"You don't," Liz answered. "There's no dishwasher, the laundry room is outside, and the backyard is not conducive to outdoor activities, like entertaining and giving dogs space."

"Okay then. Good enough. Next, please," Bailey called.

Ian sighed. "Fine. The next house is around the corner. Want to walk?"

"Sounds good to me," Bailey said. "Lead the way."

"So why are you thinking about not talking to Beth?" Liz asked as they walked slightly behind Ian.

Bailey shrugged. "I just don't know if it's a good idea."

"You're scared you mean." Liz knew her too well.

"A little," Bailey answered honestly.

"Why? What scares you?"

"Gee. What doesn't is more accurate."

"Amazing, seeing you scared." Liz's voice held a note of wonder beneath the teasing tone. "What are you scared of though? Itemize. It'll help."

"Itemize? Sheesh." Bailey paused for a moment. "Kids. Responsibility. Rejection. Intensity. Disappointment. Boredom."

"Okay, we can deal with these. First. The kids. Rebecca and Jacob love you. You can handle the responsibility or not. That's up to Beth, really, and how involved she wants you in the day-to-day parenting. I'm betting she wants a full partner, so you'll be a stepparent with shared duties. Boredom I can understand. You're used to picking up and leaving when you want, doing whatever you please then touring, recording, the parties, the clubs all whenever you want it. You'd be saying goodbye to a lot of that. Is that something you're willing to sacrifice? I think it is or we wouldn't be searching for houses. So, rejection? Intensity? Disappointment? Explain in detail."

"Speaking of looking at houses, isn't that what we're supposed to be doing?" Bailey grumbled. Sometimes she hated that Liz was a psychologist

"Yes, but it's also a convenient time for me to meddle in your affairs." Liz rubbed her hands together like a cartoon villain and cackled.

Bailey shook her head. "You know, sometimes I suspect you of sadism."

Liz ignored the other comment. "Rejection?"

"What if she says no?"

"What makes you think she will?" Liz countered.

"She never gave any indication before." Bailey stuffed her hands in her pockets and shrugged.

"You are so blind. She did. She hung on your every word. She had to sit or stand right next to you all through high school. Wherever you were, there was Beth. But you were too intent on proving something to all sorts of imaginary foes, and chasing cheerleaders. Then in college when you came on a bit too strong, and she was ready to play the field, you sulked, left and became a rock star. Bit of an overcompensation I must say."

Bailey was impressed. "That's quite a summation."

"I'm gifted. What was next? Disappointment?"

"I think I said intensity before disappointment," Bailey corrected.

"Yeah but I want to explore this one first. So, disappointment?"

"Fine." Bailey sighed and stopped walking. Ian had already gone ahead. "What if we talk and we decide and then it sucks. Like the sex is awful or we try and it doesn't last? People preach on that friendship thing about how it's so worth it and how they don't want to fuck it up. Hell, I was thinking that the other night, myself. I understand that, but that's not all of it. What if I admit it tonight? She's down with it and then reality pops that bubble? What if she needs more than I can give? What if she says no? I can't be just friends after that." She found the crux of the matter. "Is having Beth in my life like this better than not having her at all if she says no?"

"Wow. You really are worried, aren't you?" Liz dropped the

slightly mocking tone she always had when not with a patient.

"Yes I am," Bailey answered honestly. "I've had two long term relationships and several very short ones. Both the long ones ended in disaster and the short ones, well one could be a horror movie. I travel a lot. I've been single and alone for a very long time. Well, not always alone. It's hard to be alone on tour, but seriously who could possibly believe taking a chance with a forty-two-year-old punk/metal guitarist would be a good idea?"

"Beth would," Liz answered simply. "You forget we know you. We remember who you were and know who you are now. And we all love you regardless."

"But is that enough?" It was enough to make her want to pull her hair out in frustration and confusion.

"Bailey, I love you like a sister. So does Cindy. So does Mike. Beth loves you as a woman. Talk to her. Forget disappointment. Forget fearing the intensity of your feelings. She can handle it. Quit with the bullshit excuses and tell the woman before someone else asks her out and she gives up on you again."

Bailey threw her hands up in defeat. "Okay. Fuck. I'll talk to her. Now can we go check out this house before your baby daddy busts a gut? He's already like half a block away. Let's just go."

"After you." Liz made a sweeping motion with her hand and smirked. Bailey had to bite back the growl.

THE HOUSE WAS an older wooden two-story craftsman. It was painted white with black shutters and a green door. The part that impressed Bailey the most was the wrap around porch on the front. She was tempted to put in an offer before she saw the rest of it.

"Like it?" Ian asked from the porch.

"So far," Bailey answered honestly.

"I can't believe this house is for sale." Liz was in awe. "I've dreamt of this house for years."

"I think the owner passed away and the kids couldn't decide who got it. Notice the different paint jobs." He pointed out the various shades of colors on the porch and façade. "Anyway, it's supposed to go on the market tomorrow."

"But we can see it today, right?" Bailey asked.

"One way or the other, we'll see this house," Liz promised.

"I can show it to you today. There's no need to plan break in viewings, dear," he teased. It was something Liz was well known for doing. "My boss seems to consider you a preferred client, and one of the few who would pay the asking price without blinking."

"In other words, he prefers my bank accounts."

"Something like that," he said dryly.

"Well show us already. I've always wanted to see the inside of this house," Liz demanded.

"Me too," Bailey agreed.

"I've seen it before." Ian stuck his tongue out at them but then grew serious at the look on Liz's face. "Okay. Okay. Let me unlock it."

Bailey waited on the porch while Ian unlocked the door. It was solid wood with an ornate door knocker and transoms on either side. The door opened onto a hallway with polished wood floors. As soon as she stepped inside, Bailey knew she wanted the house. She grabbed a flier and read the highlights. The whole downstairs had wood floors. It had a large eat in kitchen, a living area, a formal living room, study and a dining room all downstairs. It had a yard with a huge oak tree, four bedrooms and two and a half baths. The detached garage even had an apartment over it. It was perfect.

"Submit the offer tomorrow," Bailey said. "Asking price is fine."

"You don't know what they're asking and you haven't seen more than the foyer," he said.

"I think she's made up her mind," Liz told him. She ran her hand along the banister. "This would be so much fun to redecorate."

"Seriously, Bailey, look around. Examine every inch of the place and then negotiate," Ian advised.

"Fine. We'll examine every inch." Bailey made a great show of walking around and looking at everything. "Seriously, it's a solid wood house, it's got termite protection, so your flier says, and I certainly want a thorough inspection. But I want it. Asking price is fine."

"It's worth it," Liz called from the half bath downstairs. "A lot of this stuff looks original, but it's been updated and made to look like it came with the house."

"How do you know these things?" Bailey asked.

"I'm addicted to the house shows," Liz admitted.

"She is," Ian said. "Okay. Are you completely serious about this? You don't want to negotiate?"

"No. But I do want an expedited closing. Asking price. Cash. Two weeks. Can you make that happen?"

He looked a little shocked. "I'll do my best."

"Don't worry, sweetheart. She's a Cooper. You should know by now how we are when we want something." Liz rubber her hand down his arm.

"I remember very well." He smiled at some shared memory. "Okay. First thing tomorrow we buy us a house. It's too bad I'm not the listing and selling agent."

"It's okay. That's still a good deal of commission." Bailey patted his shoulder. "Sweet. So now what?"

"Decide how you're going to furnish it," Liz suggested. "And which room Sarah and I get."

"None of them. You'll be over here often enough anyway," Bailey said.

"True. Come on, we can go eat lunch while our upright and honest realtor gets back to work."

"Thanks, sweetheart." Ian managed to keep most of the sarcasm from his tone. "Do I need to give you a ride back to your cars?"

"I don't think so," Bailey answered. "The café is just over there. It's all easy walking distance wise."

"Then I shall lock up and take my leave." Ian kissed each of them on the cheek. "I'll call you tomorrow, Bailey."

"Thanks, Ian."

Chapter Fourteen

"IT'S BEEN A pleasure, Ms. Cooper." The closing attorney stood. "Enjoy your new home."

"Thanks." Bailey picked up the folder containing copies of the closing documents. "It has been a pleasure."

"I'm sure most of your neighbors will be happy to meet you," the selling agent commented dryly.

"What's that supposed to mean?" She looked at Ian for explanation.

"One of your new neighbors got wind that you were buying the house. He called his good buddy the mayor and asked him to stop you by injunction or something."

"Huh." Bailey shrugged. "Guess that didn't work."

"No, it didn't," he said.

"It would be wise to remember that although we cannot pass an injunction against who buys property, this is not Los Angeles. Not all behaviors accepted there will be tolerated here," the other agent told her.

"Well damn. I guess I'll have to cancel the naked mud wrestling and move the sacrifices to the backyard." She pocketed the house keys. "Ian, thank you, man. I have to go call my manager and get the ball rolling on the other house. I'll take you and Liz out to dinner one night."

"No problem." He was obviously biting back a laugh.

She pulled her cell phone out and called the band's manager as soon as she was outside the attorney's office. "Hey, Brian. What's up?"

"Nothing much. You still at home or you back in LA?"

"I'm at home. Actually, I just bought a house here."

"Oh no. You're not leaving us are you?" Brian sounded worried.

"No. I'd just rather live here than in LA So I was hoping your wife's friend was still a real estate agent."

"She is. But she's small. Not anyone who's used to handling multimillion dollar homes."

"Doesn't matter. I'd rather give commission to people who need it, or deserve it. So if you could do me the hugest favor please? Can you get her to sell the house? I don't want most of the furniture, but I'd like to have all the books and pictures and equipment and shit."

"Bailey, sweetheart, you know Nancy and I would do anything for you and Kat. Hell, I wouldn't have a career if it wasn't for the two of you. Done. I'll get the kids to help. We'll get you packed up and have everything shipped out to you. What about your car?"

"Can you send it too? I kinda like it."

"Not a problem. Guess all you have out there is that motorcycle," he said.

"I have a truck too, but it would be nice to have something I can use to take more than one other person with me."

"That would be a bit difficult to do on your motorcycle. Okay. Consider it done. We'll get it handled."

"Any news from Tiny yet?" She asked. She wasn't yet ready to make a full decision on the band's future, but she did want to know if one was immediately forthcoming.

"As far as I know he still hasn't decided. Maybe when Kat gets back we all could do a group call. Get his decision then," Brian suggested.

"That's a good idea. Thanks, Brian. I appreciate it. I just literally signed the papers so I'm going to take possession now."

"You're welcome, Bailey. Send us pics of the place. Talk to you soon."

"Bailey. Congratulations." Beth's dad clapped her on the back as soon as she put the phone back in her pocket. "Glad you'll officially be closer."

"Thank you, Mr. Forsythe."

"You gonna tell Beth at lunch? You two have been hanging out a lot lately. It's almost like old times. Are you going to make it official this time and ask my daughter out?"

"Yes, sir. That's the plan. I'm trying to rebuild our relationship before we add that extra dimension. That doesn't bother you, does it?"

"I think you know better than that, young lady." He looked at her over his glasses. "I admit it was a shock we had to deal with when we realized what was between you two back in high school. It was kinda hard not to see it to be honest. We love both our kids for who they are, which makes accepting them very easy. The wife and I love you too, Bailey. You're more than welcome in our family. And seriously, it's about damn time."

"Thank you, sir." She ducked her head in embarrassment.

"Now that's something I've only seen once before." He roared with laughter. "Enjoy the new home, Bailey. I'll see you later."

"Yes, sir."

Bailey tossed the folder in the saddlebag and texted Mike before pulling on her helmet. It was time to go get her stuff and the dog. Then they had to get the rest of her stuff from her mother's house. She really hoped Fiona wasn't at home. She had been putting it off just for that reason. She did have to admit that the pool at the hotel was another consideration. It had been so relaxing. She was going to miss that.

"Congrats." Mike grinned widely when he saw her pull in to the driveway. He was already parked and leaning against his own truck. "Glad you're back."

"Thanks. I think. Goober."

"Your mother here?"

"Beats me. Let's just get what we can this trip. I shouldn't have a lot to move. Brian's sending the rest of my stuff straight to the house."

"Got it. You just tell me what to get and I'll haul it." She shook her head as he flexed his muscles.

"Thanks, buddy."

THEY MANAGED TO load Mike's truck with the unopened shipping boxes from California Bailey had sent herself, her high school memorabilia, and all the other stuff she had habitually left at home. They were almost finished when her mother made an appearance. Mike made a quick exit, but Bailey stayed. She was frozen in place.

"So you're moving out? Giving up?" Fiona Cooper staggered down the hall. Her voice was raspy and her hands shook. She was sober. It was almost as if she'd forgotten she threw Bailey out of the house in the first place.

"Giving up what?" Bailey asked. She knew better. She knew not to engage if her mother was sober. Fiona was usually at her worst when sober.

"Being a fucking rock star. Knew your voice wouldn't last."

"I'm not giving up, Mama. I'm just buying a house here."

"For a used woman and her kids? She turn gay for you now that she's alone with those kids? Guess she knows where to get her meal ticket." A sober Fiona was worse than a drunk one. Bailey fought the urge to make her mother a drink just to get her to calm down.

"Mama you need to stop. Just chill out."

"Who are you to tell me what to do? Fucking slut, chasing

girls in high school. Hanging out at that dyke bar." Fiona
staggered a little and leaned against the wall.

"Yeah, well, I guess the apple doesn't fall that far, does it?"
Bailey surprised herself by saying it.

"What did you just say to me?" Fiona straightened up and
looked as if Bailey had slapped her.

"I said the apple doesn't fall far from the tree. You tree. Me
apple." She was tired of the abuse and she realized her cousins
were right. Her mother was toxic. She couldn't hope to have a
relationship with anyone and not have it be poisoned by Fiona if
they remained in contact.

"You fucking bitch," Fiona screeched. She looked
frightening. Her blonde hair was thinning and brushed away
from her face. Her green eyes were popping and bloodshot. She
looked nothing like the woman Bailey remembered. "You're
lucky I didn't have you aborted."

"Really, Mama?" It wasn't the first time she'd been told that.
It stung every time. "You wouldn't have done so. You milked
being a single mother too much."

"She only wants you because you're rich. You're just a stupid
rich dyke who can pay for everything," Fiona yelled.

"I'm done here. I can't do this anymore, Mama. If there's
anything else here of mine, I don't need it." Bailey shouldered the
last bag she had packed.

"It'll be in the yard, you ungrateful asshole. You're just like
your fucking father."

"I don't have a father, remember? Anytime anyone you were
sleeping with got close to me you kicked them out. Hell, Ed gave
me my first guitar and taught me how to play. You kicked him
out and he dared to make sure I got lessons. So what did you do,
Mama?" Bailey could not disengage. She had held back for years
and couldn't do it any longer.

"I was trying to protect you," Fiona lied.

"You told him you'd have him arrested for trying to molest
me. Why would you do that? The man just wanted to be involved
in my life. Hell, he was practically a stepfather, he acts like it and
you go ballistic on him. And don't get me started on the fights I'd
hear between you and Uncle Dwight."

Fiona paled. "You don't know what you're talking about."

"Bullshit. Mama you were jealous of any guy who gave me
the slightest bit of attention until I started sleeping with girls."
Bailey shook her head. "I can't do this anymore, Mama. I've got
most of my stuff. You kicked me out once already. Anything left

you can stick it up your ass."

"Just get out of my house, you ungrateful bastard."

"With pleasure."

The only things left at her mother's house were a few clothes and dog toys she could live without if it came to that. She had the guitars, recording equipment and awards. Mike had already left with the crate from LA and of course the truck and Elvis were at Liz's house. There was no reason to stay there a second longer.

"YOU LOOK STRESSED," Beth said as she joined Bailey at the table.

"Yeah. I just had a huge fight with my mother. She said some pretty cruel things." Bailey waved the waitress over. She was tired, emotionally worn out and thirsty.

"Was she sober?" Beth asked as soon as the waitress took their drink order and departed.

"Yeah."

"Oh, Bailey. I'm sorry." She placed her hand on Bailey's. "Wanna talk about it?"

"How did I not remember how evil and mean she is?" Bailey asked after the waitress deposited two glasses of tea on their table.

"Selective memory." Beth shrugged. "Seriously, Bailey. I think it's easy to forget when you're not around it. Plus, there are times when your mother is charming and funny as hell."

"That's usually when she's drunk," Bailey said.

"Very true. And you have to keep that in mind when you deal with her."

"I'm not sure I want to deal with her anymore," Bailey said. "Mike is right. The woman is toxic."

"She must really have upset you."

"Yeah it was bad." Bailey put her head in her hands. "She called me a worthless bastard, or something similar. It was harsh."

"Oh, honey." Beth took her other hand. "You know, I'm amazed you turned out as well as you did, considering."

"Yeah I guess." She shrugged. "You know, I haven't even looked at the menu."

"Me either." Beth took her hands back and examined the menu. "The kids keep wanting to know when they can come visit you at the hotel and go swimming now that we have the time. The last few weeks have been crazy."

"Oh. Well, I was going to take you over later and see it, but I closed on the house today. So I won't be at the hotel anymore. I checked out this morning."

"I'm sorry. What?" She folded her menu, placed it carefully on the table and looked at Bailey as if she'd heard something serious.

"Ian showed me a few houses and I picked one. We closed today," Bailey said sheepishly. She found herself overly justifying her actions. "I was going to tell you, but you've been so busy at work and I needed to be out of Mama's. The couple of times we've talked I've just wanted to talk and not rehash everything that Mama said. So, I bought a house," she finished lamely.

Beth looked amazed. "Well y'all certainly kept that a secret."

"Yeah. Sorry. I kinda had to get out of there fast and hotel life isn't all it's cracked up to be. So I rushed them through everything. I need to paint and get furniture." Bailey closed her eyes to help her think of what else she might need. "Dishes and appliances and wow, I need a lot of stuff."

"I can help with that." Beth seemed excited. "Can I help with that?"

"Sure." Bailey shrugged. "I'll be sleeping on the floor tonight. I haven't put my futon back together from where Mike and I got it out of the house, but when do you want to go?"

"You are not sleeping on the floor tonight." Beth was indignant.

"I've slept on worse," Bailey said dryly.

"You could stay over at my place."

"Uh." That thought was tempting. Incredibly so. "I'm not a big fan of couches, and Elvis snores badly."

"Oh. Well the offer's there." She looked a little crestfallen as she picked her menu back up and opened it.

"Hey, thanks." Bailey felt as if she'd just done something wrong. They ordered in silent confusion. "Would you like to see the house? I mean since you're going to help me decorate and everything," she asked after the waitress left again.

"Yeah. Of course. When do you want to go look at furniture?"

"I'm pretty free whenever. So whenever you're good."

"Ah the life of the unemployed and loafing," Beth teased.

"It's pretty awesome." Bailey played along. "So? When are you free?"

"We can go after the kids get out of school if you want. Do you want them to come too?"

"Sure." Bailey smiled again. "I don't mind spending time with them. Unless you want a few kid-free, adult hours." The smile widened.

"Um." Beth blushed.

"You look cute when you're slightly embarrassed," Bailey teased. It was true. And it made her heart flutter. She hadn't felt that in years.

"Thanks. Aren't we too old to be cute?" Beth moved back as the waitress sat their plates in front of them.

"Some people are never too old," Bailey said seriously. "Speaking of being unemployed and loafing, there's a garage apartment I may turn into a studio."

Beth looked at her. "Are you going to hang out around here? Move back?"

"Yeah. I'm selling the house in LA." Bailey met her eyes and held the look.

"Why?" It was an easy question. It didn't have an easy answer.

"I'll tell you about it later," Bailey said. She changed the subject. "Aren't you at lunch?"

"Yes. This is so much better than a sack lunch." Beth sighed. "This audit they've been making us do was killing me. I'm so glad we're almost done. This beats eating at my desk by such a wide margin."

"I would hope so. Here's my new address." She slid a card with the new address across the table. "Come over when you're ready. I'll just be trying to put together a futon."

Chapter Fifteen

"HI. ARE YOU guys looking for anything in particular?" The saleslady looked them over and turned her question to Beth.

"My friend here just bought a house and needs furniture."

She perked up a bit. "How wonderful. For what room?"

"All of them," Bailey answered.

"Oh wow." The saleslady looked taken aback. "What room would you like to start with?"

"The bedroom," Beth answered. "I mean I doubt you want to sleep on the futon for very long," she added at Bailey's amused glance.

"Well I do think my futon sleeping days are over, but it is better than the floor." Bailey shrugged.

"Do we get to pick out stuff too?" Rebecca asked excitedly.

"This isn't our house, sweetheart," Beth said gently.

"You two can help pick out the couches and stuff," Bailey said. "Plus I'll need game chairs and stuff."

"Awesome," Jacob said.

"And I suppose you can look for stuff for when we redo your room," Beth told Rebecca. "Now let's help Bailey. Okay?"

"Okay," they said in unison.

The saleslady led them around the store to where the bedroom furniture was located. She made small talk with Beth as they walked, leaving Bailey to walk with the kids. Bailey rolled her eyes at the situation. It was almost humorous.

"Oh, wow." Rebecca stopped in front of a girl's bedroom display. "Bailey, this is amazing. Don't you think so?"

"It's very nice," Bailey said. It was nice and she could see why appealed to Rebecca. It was white and looked like a cross between older girl and princess.

Jacob caught their attention. "Mom's way up there."

"Okay. Lets catch up." Bailey corralled the kids back on the path but took a quick picture of the furniture for future reference.

"What's up?" Beth asked as they caught up to her.

"Rebecca got distracted," Bailey said. "We find anything yet?"

"I assume you wanted a master bedroom set, right?" The saleslady asked.

"I had planned on it." She raised an eyebrow at the

saleslady's tone.

"What are you looking for? Wood? Metal? Contemporary?"

"I had some contemporary pieces in the house in LA, but I think sticking with a traditional Craftsman style would be better in this house."

"Oh, you lived in LA?" The sales lady seemed suddenly interested.

"I did. So do you have anything Craftsman-y?"

"No. But we have a large selection of contemporary sets."

"No thanks. We'll find our way out." Bailey steered the group toward the door.

"You sure you don't want to look at something else?" The saleslady asked.

"Quite. Look, here's a tip. The lady told you I bought the house and you've done nothing but kiss her ass. Now it's either because you find her attractive or you don't know how to deal with me. Next time focus on the one who's going to pay your commission, regardless of tattoos and hair color."

"I'm sorry, is there a problem here?" A large, older gentleman shuffled up to them.

"They were just leaving, Mr. Brown," the saleslady answered coolly.

"Mr. Brown?" Bailey offered her hand. "Bailey Cooper. My companion and I were looking for Craftsman style furniture to fill a house I just bought downtown. Your associate said you didn't have what we wanted."

"She also didn't pay any attention to Bailey but stayed right up my mom's butt." Rebecca added.

"Rebecca," Beth scolded.

"My apologies, Ms. Cooper." He shooed off the saleslady. "We don't have any here, but we have a large selection at our main store. If you'd like, I can call over there and let our sales manager know you're on your way. He knows our stock very well."

"We'd like that," Beth answered when Bailey shrugged.

"Good. Let me call him. Will you be going straight there?"

"Yes. Then dinner," Beth said.

"Guess so," Bailey said mildly. "Thank you, sir."

"You're quite welcome, Ms. Cooper."

"Where are we going for dinner?" Jacob asked as they left.

"I don't know, sport. What did you guys have in mind?"

"Pizza!" They hollered.

"Fine, but no place with puppets." Bailey put her foot down

on that.

Rebecca bounced in her seat. "Oh, we can go to Fortune's, then. They have karaoke."

"Sit down or the booster comes back," Beth warned. She bit back a smile when Rebecca blew a raspberry.

"Thanks for coming with me. Sorry it's not so easy," Bailey said.

"Hey, buying furniture is never easy. Besides, you're buying dinner. It seems a fair trade."

"You are a remarkably patient woman," Bailey said as she leaned back in the car seat. "Nice car in case I didn't say so earlier."

"How come you don't have a sports car? Don't rich people have sports cars?" Jacob asked.

"Some do. I drive a motorcycle. I figure that's reckless enough."

"Really, Bailey?" Rebecca said. "Why don't you have a sports car? You just have a beat-up old truck."

"I have a luxury car in LA. It's being shipped here as we speak. But, no, I don't have a sports car. I grew up racing motorcycles. I never had much interest in racing cars," she answered honestly. "And before you ask, I had a racing bike. I sold it a long time ago because I was too immature for it and could have very easily killed myself."

"How could you have killed yourself?" Rebecca asked.

"Why would you have killed yourself?" Jacob asked at the same time.

"Kids, this might be something Bailey doesn't want to talk about," Beth said.

Bailey shrugged. "It's okay with me if it's okay with you."

"I don't know." Beth said dubiously.

"Part then." When Beth nodded, she turned in her seat to look at them. "I'd go to a lot of parties. Sometimes it'd be late, I'd be tired, or I had a few drinks. It's not a good idea to drive in those conditions at all, much less drive a very expensive and touchy piece of machinery."

"Wow." Both kids looked at her. "Cool."

"How is that cool?" Beth asked.

"Bailey told us the truth," Rebecca said. "Dad would have made up some lame story."

"And hey look, we're at the store." Never in her life had Bailey been so relieved to be at a furniture store.

"Chicken," Beth commented as she put the car in park. They

laughed when Bailey imitated one.

A young man stood just inside the door and opened it for them. "Ms. Cooper?"

"I'm Bailey Cooper." She shook the young man's hand. "You must be the sales manager Mr. Brown told us about."

"I'm Donovan. I was told you're looking for something to go with a Craftsman style house?" He gestured at them to follow him but made sure he stayed right with Bailey.

"Yes. I just bought a house, closed on it this afternoon. I have no furniture."

"Not a problem. If you see something you like and we have it in stock, we can have it delivered tomorrow. Anything else we can order for you and have in about two weeks."

"Excellent." Bailey was impressed.

This store had a much bigger selection. After they exhausted the showroom, Donovan pulled out the catalogs. While she didn't find everything she wanted to put in the house there, though honestly Beth picked most of it out, they did manage to outfit the master bedroom, the living room, the breakfast area and two of the other bedrooms. One she managed to keep as a surprise. After receiving assurances that at least half of what she purchased would be delivered the next morning, she decided it was time to reward her shopping companions.

"Ready for dinner, guys?" She called as she signed the last piece of paperwork Donovan offered.

"I think they are," Beth said. "You sure you're okay with some of those choices?"

"Yeah. I told you furniture is not my thing. As long as everything is comfortable and easy to clean, I'm good." That was true. The only things she had really taken her time choosing, aside from the mattress, were the chairs for the video game area. As for the rest, as long as everything functioned as it should, matched, and didn't look beat to hell and back, she was content.

"Are we still going to Fortune's?" Rebecca asked as they climbed back into the car.

"That's what you guys requested. I guess that's where we're going," Bailey answered.

THE PREVIOUS OWNERS hadn't left much in the way of furniture or appliances. The one thing they did leave was the porch swing. Bailey could tell already that it was going to be one of her favorite places in the house. She sat in it, letting it rock gently while waiting for the furniture truck. Elvis was napping not far away.

"Can't believe they let the likes of you buy this house," a portly older gentleman said from the sidewalk. "Maybe kids'll egg your house from now on."

"Why Mr. Braddock. I'm honored you remember me," Bailey said lightly. Ian had told her that one of the neighbors had strongly objected to her presence in the neighborhood. Now she knew who it was.

"Hell raiser," he scoffed and continued to walk past.

"Don't mind him. He's just a bitter old man," a young woman called from across the street, once the old man was out of earshot.

"That he is," Bailey agreed easily. She stood up as she saw the truck turn on her road.

"This the Cooper house?" The driver of the truck asked as he pulled to a stop.

"It is. Come on in. Mind the dog. He doesn't run or bite, but I can't guarantee he won't lay right in your path."

"Duly noted." He opened the back of the truck. "Where do you want all this?"

"What you got there first?"

"Girl's room."

"This way." Bailey waited until they were close and then directed them upstairs to the room she had mentally assigned to Rebecca and Sarah. "Master is down here and this is the guest room. And if you happen to find the couch it goes downstairs."

"Not a problem," the driver assured her. "We're to put together just the one bed, right?"

"Right. I don't want to have to sleep on the floor again. Thanks, guys. I'll be outside if you need me."

It was a nice day. Since Bailey had no appliances, Mike had loaned her an ice chest. She grabbed a drink and headed back to the porch swing. Elvis was still lying under it, happy to be outside but shaded. She checked his water dish but it was still full. It wasn't that hot outside.

"You watching the moving show?" Mike asked as he got out his truck. She hadn't noticed him arrive.

"Yeah. Come have a seat and watch."

"Thanks. Got any more of that fancy bottled water?" he asked as he walked up the steps to the porch.

"Yeah. I'll go grab you one." She walked inside, dodged the furniture guys, grabbed another drink and rejoined Mike on the porch. "So what are you doing here?"

"I can't come to see my favorite cousin?" Mike asked in mock astonishment. "Okay, I thought you'd want to go get a fridge."

"Of course. You're awesome. As soon as these guys are done, I'll put some shoes on and we can go."

"Isn't that Mr. Braddock's house?" he asked with a laugh.

"It is. And he remembers me." She laughed. "Apparently he advocated pretty heavily against my buying the house."

"He's still an asshole." Mike shook his head.

"Yep. Most get worse with age too. It's gonna be a blast irritating him. I can't wait."

"Heard from your mom?" he asked gingerly.

"Oddly enough, no. She'll sulk for a while and then call. I'm not sure I'll talk to her though." Bailey shrugged. "Hey, I think they're done."

"Ms. Cooper?" The driver held out a clipboard. "If you're satisfied, please sign here and we're done."

She signed the form. "Thank you, sirs."

"You're welcome," the other man said. "I'm sure we'll see you again when the rest of your stuff comes in."

"Excellent. And thank you both again." She turned to Mike. "Take a look at what I got and I'll get on some footwear."

"Nice couch," Mike said. "What else you get?"

"It's upstairs. Go ahead."

"Bailey Ray! Is that a girl's bedroom suite?"

"It is. Just in case Sarah or Rebecca stay over," Bailey answered innocently. "Come on, man. Let's go."

"I don't believe you in the slightest, you know." He wagged a finger at her.

"Whatever. Man. I'm working on it," she said.

"Seriously? Okay then. Let's go get you some appliances. Let you get treated like a normal person for once."

"Wait. You and me are going shopping and you expect us to be treated like normal people? Please," she said. "Elvis. Go get on your bed. I'll be home soon."

As Mike drove them to the large home improvement store, Bailey filled him in on everything that had happened the night before. It didn't take long. Soon he was telling her the latest problems with Cindy's mother. That woman was rivaling Fiona for twisted tactics.

"So what are we looking for?" Mike asked as they walked inside the store.

"Everything." She laughed at his groan. "They left no appliances. I need it all. I don't know what to do with half of them, but I need them. From what I understand, normal people like to eat food they cooked themselves."

"Holy shit. All right. Let's start in kitchens. Get the basics out of the way."

"Can I help you?" a bored looking young woman asked as they entered the kitchen area.

"Yes. We need appliances," Mike told her. "All of them."

"What?" She looked at them suspiciously.

"I just bought a house and they left me with a naked kitchen. I need a dishwasher, fridge, stove, whatever else people have in there," Bailey said.

"You don't know what all you need?" The young woman's look didn't change.

"Look my mom's idea of cooking was opening a can of soup. So no, I don't know," Bailey answered.

"Okay. Well let's get you set up. We've got a few display kitchens set up. We'll start there. Then we can go through the rows if you don't find anything. Do you happen to know what style you're looking for?" she asked while tugging awkwardly on her uniform vest.

"I have pictures. I should have brought Beth. She cooks. She would know," Bailey groused while showing the associate pictures of her kitchen.

"Do you cook at all?" the sales lady asked.

"I do a bit. I boil water a lot." She shrugged. "Seriously, I know about what I want in a fridge and stove, but anything else kinda leaves me a little clueless."

"Well. Here are our sample kitchens. Let's see if we can find one that fits your layout. That's really going to be the big factor. You may want a commercial fridge, for example but if you don't have room for it..."

"Thanks." Bailey looked around while Mike wandered off to look at something else.

"So you and your..." The young woman's voice dropped off as if hoping Bailey would fill in the missing information.

"Cousin," Bailey answered.

"Oh. Is he single? He's cute," she said.

"He's engaged." Bailey smirked. "So this one looks kinda like my setup. I'm not fond of the colors, though. I'm not a big fan of anything other than stainless steel."

"Is your kitchen gas or electric?" the sales lady asked.

"The hook up for the stove is gas. Oh, I like that one." Before Mike wandered back over, they had picked out the stove, microwave, refrigerator and dishwasher.

"Got some of the other things you'll need," he told them, indicating the cart.

"In a hurry?" Bailey asked when she noticed a blender, vacuum cleaner and toaster oven.

"Well I thought maybe we could go play blackjack, if you didn't have any other plans." He shrugged like it wasn't a big deal, but she didn't buy it. He had a hopeful look in his eyes.

"Nah that sounds like fun. I just need a washer and dryer. I think. For this round anyway," she said.

"We have a great selection of both." The sales lady seemed overly chipper now that Bailey had proven herself to be a fairly easy customer.

Bailey did know how to do laundry. Her mother had made sure of that because Fiona hated doing it. It didn't take her long to choose one of each. What took the longest was finalizing the purchases and arranging delivery.

"It always feels pretty weird spending a large amount of money and leaving almost empty handed," Mike said as they left. "So. Blackjack? And if you're hungry, the casino has a pretty decent Pho bar."

"Okay. That works. I haven't played cards in ages." Bailey loaded the smaller items in the back seat of Mike's truck. "I don't think I've played since you met me in Vegas a few years ago."

"I'm sure you remember. Great-granddad loved cards." He shook his head in memory. "At least it kept us out of trouble sometimes."

"Right." She laughed. "How often do you go play cards, anyway?"

"A few times a year. I get two hundred dollars and a cigar and go every three months or so. It's a pretty harmless habit, I think. Cindy doesn't see the harm in it. She came with me a time or two, but she's not much of a gambler, at least with cards. She did pour some money down a slot machine though."

"I bet. How are you both doing since the old lady cut her off?" Bailey asked. She had her suspicions.

"You know she doesn't make much as a teacher." Mike sighed as he turned onto the Interstate. "She's got a mortgage, student loan payments, car payment and she pays for a lot of supplies out of her own salary. She hasn't seen child support from dickweed in years."

"What about you?"

"Honestly? This wedding is about killing me. I've got it. The shop makes a decent profit. It's not great, but for here it's a livable salary. I've been able to save some, but after all my medical bills it's not enough. It's never enough."

"Why don't you sell the shop? Tony's always telling me he wishes you would come back and be his assistant. You'd be running a sound booth before the year was over. There's a lot of money there," she said.

"I'm not LA material," he said as he pulled into the casino's parking garage. "And I know Cindy doesn't want to leave here. Besides we'd have to make five times as much to afford half of what we have."

"True. Oh well, if you ever change your mind." She let that drift off into silence for a moment. "Do you need a short term loan?"

"No," Mike said vehemently. "And I don't need you to take up part of the wedding either."

"Okay." His explosive conviction hurt. "You don't have to do everything alone, you know."

"I know. But you paid for most of my surgeries, you got me a job being a roadie and then helping out at the studio. Hell, Bailey, enough. Man. Don't you know we love you for you, not your money?"

"I know," she protested.

"I don't always think you do." He parked the truck and then turned to look at her. "Bailey, I know you feel guilty for leaving us. I know you feel guilty for something and you don't know what it is. But paying for everything you can doesn't assuage that guilt."

"I should have stopped him quicker," she said quietly. She still had nightmares about it. In most of them, she never made it there in time, but watched from a distance as Kyle beat Mike to death.

"You got him. I'll never forget the bastard spitting his teeth in his hand. And it's not your fault. Hell, it's not my fault. It's his. Let's go lose some money, smoke a cigar and judge the others from our lofty position as Mike and Bailey. What do you say?"

"Okay. Let's go." She said. She felt a little better. It helped that Mike was okay.

Chapter Sixteen

THE CASINO WAS going to be a fun diversion. Mike led the way to the blackjack tables and quickly found one with a five-dollar minimum. They cashed in at the table and sat down to play.

After a few hands, Bailey saw a familiar silhouette out of the corner of her eye. She shook her head, convinced she was seeing things. Still, she kept an eye out, paying more attention to the crowd and less to the game. Finally, she saw it again. This time she got a good view and recognized the drink server.

"Hey, I'll be back in a minute. That okay?" Bailey asked the dealer.

"Yeah I'll hold your spot." The dealer placed a clear plastic chip at her place.

"Maybe I'll play two hands while you're gone," Mike said. He had a pile of chips in front of him.

"You do that. I'll be right back." She leaned her chair against the table and turned away.

The casino floor was crowded with people and slot machines. It was hard to move though the madness in a straight line. Bailey kept her quarry in view as well as she was able. Finally she got a less crowded area and was able to approach.

"Aunt Ellen? What the hell?" Bailey grabbed her arm.

Ellen paled. "Oh shit. Bailey. What are you doing here?"

"Mike and I are playing blackjack. What are you doing here?" She asked, careful to look directly at her aunt's face. Those costumes were a bit revealing.

"Working. Some of us have to do that, you know. And grow up. You've seen me in a bikini," Ellen snapped.

"Well yeah, but damn, Aunt Ellen. Why are you working here?" She was confused. "You have a job already. You're working two? Why?"

"Because cancer isn't cheap," Ellen said. She shifted her stance to ease the tray she was carrying and looked at Bailey.

"Why didn't you ask me for help?" Bailey asked. She was certain no one had asked for anything. She would have remembered.

"You said no, remember?" Ellen arched a brow at her.

"You never asked me," Bailey said.

"Your mother said she asked and you said no, that you were broke."

"What? No. I never said that. She never asked. I didn't know about any of it until I got here. Bitch. Look, call me tomorrow. We'll talk. Does Mike know you work here?" Bailey said in frustration. She was even more upset at her mother.

Ellen shook her head. "No. None of my kids do."

"Then I would suggest staying away from the blackjack tables."

"Okay. Thank you, Bailey. I need to get back to work." Ellen turned away.

"Just don't forget to call me tomorrow, okay?" At her aunt's nod, she let her go.

Bailey went back to the blackjack table but had lost interest in the game. This wasn't the first time she'd heard that her mother had interceded on her behalf without letting Bailey know about it. It was irritating. She felt embarrassed as well. Mostly though she wondered what else she'd missed and how many other times people who wanted to rely on her were disappointed.

"Everything okay?" Mike asked when she returned.

"Yeah. Hey, have you ever asked my mother for anything, or has she ever offered to talk to me on your behalf?" She tapped the table for another card.

"Once or twice. Can't think of why though. What's up?"

"Nothing. Something a bit rotten seems to be going on. That's all." It was hard to keep her head in the game after that.

When Mike broke even for the fourth time he was ready to go. Bailey was surprised to find that she hadn't done badly and had only lost fifty dollars. She tipped the dealer and the drink server generously, hoping that the servers had to share, knowing the dealers did.

She drove his truck home since he'd drunk a few beers. Instead of sending him home, Bailey insisted he stay. Mike became the first overnight guest, although he had to make do on the couch. She hadn't yet bought sheets and things.

BAILEY KNOCKED ON the door and waited. She was unsure of her reception after the previous night's revelations. However she needed more information and Ellen was the person she needed to speak with first.

"Bailey? What's going on?" Ellen asked as she opened the door. "I was going to call you later."

"Hey, Aunt Ellen. Do you mind if we talk?" Bailey shifted awkwardly.

Ellen didn't open the door wider. "Is this about last night?"

"Among other things," Bailey said.

"Come on in." Ellen held the door open. "What's going on?"

"You said last night that you talked to Mama about me helping out with Dwight's bills. Could you tell me about it?" Bailey followed Ellen into the living room.

Ellen sat down on the couch. "Why?"

"Because I've noticed certain things recently. Mama." She paused, trying to think how to say it. "I've noticed more this trip that Mama has issues."

"Honey, your mother has always had issues."

"I know. I did grow up with the woman," Bailey said. "Let me put it this way. I didn't realize until I saw you last night that she was policing contact with me. And I'll be honest with you, I've never been happier that not only is someone else in charge of my finances, I've also put Liz in charge of everything else."

"Sounds like you knew something like this might happen." Ellen gestured to the chair. "Sit down. You make me nervous standing around like that."

Bailey sat as requested. "No. My financial manager did. So, can you tell me what's been going on, please?"

"Bailey, this is a can of worms you don't want to open."

"No, I want to know. I need to know." She felt that was correct. Liz was right. Bailey had never dealt with the issue of her mother.

"I can't go into all of it. I'd rather Dwight do it when he gets out. But I will tell you some. Your mother is very jealous of you and of our relationship with you. When Dwight was diagnosed, we asked her opinion on whether you would be able to help with fundraising or something. His golf club did a charity auction. She said no and that you were struggling and we shouldn't tell you." Ellen's hands were tightly clasped in her lap.

"Why on earth would she do that? And no offense meant at all, but why didn't you call me directly? You should all have my number." It still didn't make sense.

"You were in Germany for some festival and we didn't want to have you pay international fees," Ellen said.

"No. That's not why? It's not like I can't afford the calls. Hell, I call back to the states all the time when I travel. Liz and Mike could have told you so. I don't buy that excuse." She crossed her arms and leaned back in the chair.

"It's complicated, but your mother put herself at the point of contact for you and it just seemed easier to let her do it." Ellen rubbed her head as if it ached.

"I can't believe I didn't notice this. I can't believe it got to this." Bailey shook her head. "Regardless, I'm here now. What do you guys need?"

"They're doing another benefit auction if you could donate some stuff that would be great."

"Sure. I can make some calls and get a lot donated. What else? Do you guys need a check or cash or something? I know cancer can't be cheap."

"It's not. It's been so hard." Ellen started crying.

"You guys haven't asked your kids for anything, have you?" Bailey asked. "I know Liz would sell plasma for you."

"No, we haven't. Mike donated some stuff. Scott did too. Bailey, we don't want to ask for money. You know how proud your uncle is."

"I know. Family trait is pride and swagger." She sighed. "I'll talk to Dwight. And I'll get some stuff for the auction. When is it?"

"A few weeks after the wedding."

"I'll make sure you have something," she promised.

Ellen wiped her eyes. "Thank you, Bailey. We appreciate it."

"Not a problem." Bailey stood. "I'll see myself out." She was discouraged and disappointed.

AS SHE WAITED for the truck to start she dialed Liz's number. It went straight to voicemail. Liz was with a client. Bailey started the truck and headed in that direction anyway. It was almost lunchtime. With that in mind she stopped for food and waited to ambush Liz.

"Bailey? I'll be with you in moment." Liz was escorting a younger patient to the door.

"No problem." Bailey headed back to Liz's office and took a chair across from the desk.

"Wow. What brought that look on?" Liz asked when she entered the room.

"Our parents." Bailey handed over Liz's food. "Look, I really need some information and some help with what to do, okay?"

"Sure. Anything," Liz said.

"My mother supposedly told your parents that I was broke and couldn't give them anything for the auction."

"What? You're not broke, are you?"

"No," Bailey scoffed. "Why does that matter anyway? I can sign a guitar and donate that regardless of my financial situation."

"True. It's just that your mom told everyone you went bankrupt. I never mentioned it because it seemed like a private thing, and if you wanted to talk about it you would," Liz said delicately.

"Liz, how could I be bankrupt and still travel everywhere much less buy a house in downtown? Besides, I've had a self-appointed financial advisor since I was 19."

"True. And I should know better, but your mom is so convincing," Liz said. "I'm sorry, Bailey. You're mother is so charismatic she can make anyone believe just about anything, even when we know it's all bullshit."

"Yeah she can be. Especially when she's been drinking," Bailey said ruefully. It had taken a long time for her to understand this and realize that was one reason why no one believed Bailey's stories about her mother.

"So my parents asked you for donations?" Liz brought the subject away from Fiona and back to her own parents.

She nodded. "Aunt Ellen did today, yes."

"They ask you for money?" Liz's tone seemed strange.

"No. I asked if they needed cash but your mom never answered. Why?"

"Because she's been spending a very large amount of time at a casino. I wonder if she's trying to hit a jackpot. You know I'm worried that she's chasing one instead of asking for help." Bailey thought about telling her how she had seen Ellen working at the casino the night before but thought better of it.

"What makes you think she's been spending time at a casino?" Bailey asked. She didn't want to break confidence, but she didn't want Liz to worry needlessly either.

"Ian and I went to one of the restaurants a few weeks ago and mom's car was there. Then a few days later I went by her work and she looked exhausted and smelled like smoke. As you know, neither of them smoke. I've seen her like that a few other times too."

"Did you ask her?" Bailey tried to keep her voice even. She didn't want Liz to realize that she knew more about what was going on than Liz did.

"Yeah. She denied it at first and then snapped and said she was an adult and if she wanted to go play poker she would." Liz let out a long breath and leaned back in her chair.

"Well she is an adult," Bailey said. "So I guess this means I shouldn't give her money if she asks for it?"

"If you would please."

"Okay. I promise I won't give your mother money to go gambling with. Now what about my mother?"

"Maybe you need to take a break from her. Put her in a time out of sorts," Liz suggested. "She's toxic, Bailey. You've known that, but you've never had to deal with it too much."

"You should have heard what she said when I moved out." Bailey played with a hole in her jeans. Her lunch was still on Liz's desk untouched. She'd lost her appetite.

"I don't want to," Liz said. "I remember too many times hearing Mom cry after your mom would come get you." Liz wadded up her hamburger wrapper and put it in the bag.

"She cried? Why?"

"They never told you?"

"I asked your mother something but she said I didn't want to open that can of worms. But she wanted Uncle Dwight to tell me everything." Bailey shrugged. "How did I never notice how fucked up my family was?"

"You noticed. It's one reason you turned so easily to chemical dependency. It's also one reason why your sense of self-worth was always kinda fucked. But lately you've been working on making you better. So now that you've sorted out all the things you needed to sort out internally, including how you feel about Beth, you're ready to focus on other things."

"So I get to focus on this? Great," she said.

"It's time. Your mother is toxic."

"That's what Mike said." Bailey shook her head. "I can't have that or be around that. I guess the time out is a good idea. Fuck. I don't want her infecting those kids, or my not yet existent relationship with Beth. Sometimes I feel like I should have stayed in LA."

Liz pounced on the change of conversation. "So you're going to pursue one? A relationship with Beth?"

"Of course. I can't lie to anyone anymore. I love the woman. I thought for a moment that being back around her would temper it, but it doesn't. If she'll have me, I'm hers for as long as she wants."

"I'll be damned. I'm both pleased and shocked by this. So, what are you going to do?" Liz's eyes sparkled a little. Bailey suspected tears.

"Same as I have been doing. Spending time with her, and the kids of course, and then spending time with just her. I feel like I've got some assumptions and mistakes that I need, really, we need to work out. I spent too much time trying to impress. You're right. I should just be me, right?" At least she knew who that was this time.

"That's who she's in love with, not the guitar diva. You put on that mask in high school when you were afraid or insecure and it's only gotten more attached to you. Beth sees what I do, she sees under the mask and she loves you for it."

"Or despite it," Bailey said disparagingly. "Anyway, I'm going to head out of here. I should go home and spend some time online. I have the feeling there's a few usurpers after my crown and I need to go remind them not to fuck with me."

"I have no idea what you're talking about but have fun." Liz waved her to the door. "Go do whatever it is you do in those games and do it well."

"Thank you." Bailey stood. "I'll see you later."

Chapter Seventeen

BAILEY HAD JUST turned off the game console when Elvis started barking. She threw the controller down in disgust, having suffered a temporary setback in the quest and walked to the living room. The front door was open to let air in and Elvis was standing on his hind legs, tiny tail wagging in excitement.

"Bailey?" Jacob's voice came through the screen door. "Bailey?"

"Jacob, what are you doing here?" She opened the door to see both Jacob and his sister standing there. They were wearing bicycle helmets. "You guys rode all the way over here? That's gotta be a mile or more."

"We needed to talk to you," Rebecca said simply.

"We was real careful, too, Bailey. We watched for cars and stayed on the sidewalk and everything." Jacob looked so earnest. "Don't be mad, Bailey."

"I'm not mad, bud. Your mom is going to kill us all, though. Come in." She held the door open for them. "Take a seat and don't torment Elvis. I've got to go call your mom."

"But, Bailey—"

"But nothing. We can talk while we wait on her. She's got to be going nuts looking for you two."

Bailey left them sitting on the couch with the dog. She grabbed her phone off the counter and walked outside. She had no idea what Beth would say about this. Sighing a little, she hit Beth's number and waited. It was picked up on the first ring.

"Bailey, thank goodness. My mother just called and said the kids are missing."

"It's okay, Beth. They're over here," she said as quickly and loudly as she could without yelling.

"Their bikes are missing too and...what? Over where? Where are you and where are my kids? Are they okay?" Beth sounded scared to death.

"I'm at home. They decided to ride their bikes over here to talk to me about something. I swear I didn't ask them to." The whole situation made her feel defensive. She kept waiting for someone to call her a bad influence and she certainly didn't want this to adversely affect her relationship with their mother.

"You just keep them right there. I'll be there in a few. I may kill them both." The fear had left her voice. Bailey recognized the anger there.

"Beth, I know it's gotta be tough, but chill out for a moment." She wanted to calm her down, but she didn't want to overstep her bounds or make matters worse.

"Bailey Cooper, you don't tell me to chill out. Those are my kids. I decide how calm or not I should be. This is not a situation that calls for calm."

"Elizabeth Marie Forsyth," Bailey yelled into the phone. "They're fine. They're here and they obviously wanted to see me bad enough they risked death by mom. Now I can't tell you what to do. I know you're freaked. Hell, it freaked me out seeing them outside my door. But can you give us a few minutes before you unleash Armageddon on them? I don't mean wait an hour or so, but can you drive over and obey the speed limit? You wanted to know how they were coping with everything. Maybe this will tell us. If you trust me to talk to them, I mean. I don't know."

"Bailey, I don't know what's going on with my kids." Beth's voice was full of pain. "My life has been spiraling out of control for two years it seems. Talk to them. See what's going on in those small, stubborn brains. I'll calm down. I'll be there but a lot sooner than an hour, like if you can get them to talk you need to make them speed talk, got it? You do know that this goes against every mama bear instinct I have, don't you?"

"I imagine it does. Thank you, Beth. For what it's worth, I think you're a great mother." She peered around the corner and saw both kids sitting calmly on the sofa petting Elvis.

"Thanks, Bailey. That means a lot. See you soon."

Bailey grabbed a soda and two juices from the fridge before walking back to the living room. Jacob and Rebecca were still sitting on the couch. They looked up when she entered.

"So, what's going on?" She asked after they had each taken a juice. It had been a long bike ride.

"Bailey, are you gay?"

"What?" Jacob's question almost made her spit out her drink. "Where did you hear about that?"

"It's not a big deal. A couple of kids at school have two moms. And so does Derek," Rebecca said.

"Who is Derek?" Bailey asked.

"Derek Darling the Daring. It's a great show," Rebecca said.

"Oh. Okay. Next question. Who says?" Bailey wondered if she were in over her head on this one. Perhaps she should have waited for Beth.

"Everyone," Jacob answered. "When I told my friends that you were my mom's friend, they all thought it was cool. Then this bigger kid, Mark, called you a lesbian punker and the bus driver got mad at him. But even Ms. James agreed that you're a lesbian. That means you're gay, right? You date girls?"

"Yes." Beth was astounded at the maturity and knowledge. It was so casual and normal for them. It certainly wasn't like that when she was in elementary school. "Yes. I'm gay. Yes, I do date women." It was almost a relief. She'd half dreaded them telling her they'd made the neighbor's Chihuahua disappear.

"Are you dating our mom?" Rebecca asked.

"No. Your mom and I are just friends," she told them.

"Will you date our mom?" Rebecca asked.

Jacob raised his hand and bounced up and down. "Can you be our other mom?"

"Guys, a couple of things here." This was spinning out of control. "First. Your mom and I are not dating. We've been friends since we were Rebecca's age. Second. What in the world made you guys think that? And third. I am not a replacement for your father." She knew that last would sting, but she felt it needed to be said.

"We know that." Jacob waived her concerns away. "But will you?"

"Guys, doesn't your mom have some say in this? I mean it's not just up to us."

"But Dad always told Mom she'd like him better if he was you," Rebecca said. "And now you're here."

"Wait. What?" Bailey had to remind herself that Rebecca was only nine. She may have misheard or misunderstood what her parents had said.

"One time when it got really bad, Dad told Mom that he knew about you and her and that she'd like it better if he was you." Rebecca blushed. "He said a whole bunch of other mean things that made Mom cry before he hit her."

"Your father hit her?" The world went red. She felt the world spin.

"She said no, but we heard it." Rebecca seemed so much older than nine.

"I saw it once." Jacob looked as if he were about to cry.

"It's okay, Jacob. Cry if you need to. It's okay." Bailey put her arms around him. He snuggled into her embrace. Rebecca followed.

"Are you why he left? Why did he leave?" Now that was a

question Bailey didn't fully know the answer to.

"I don't know why he left, Rebecca. I hadn't seen or spoken to him in years. The last time I saw your mom was when we went to Vienna two years ago." She sighed. "I guess like everything else, sometimes love goes away. Maybe your dad couldn't love your mother anymore. That doesn't mean he doesn't love you. It just means that sometimes people grow apart and don't want the same things anymore. And sometimes, sometimes people do really stupid selfish things when they get their hearts broken, or when they're in pain. When love dies, it hurts like nothing else ever will. Your dad is probably in as much pain as you are." Bailey looked up and met Beth's eyes. She hadn't heard her come in.

"Hey." Beth sat down next to them. Jacob left Bailey's arms and crawled into his mother's embrace. "It's okay, baby. It's okay."

It wasn't long before Rebecca climbed over Bailey and joined her mother and brother. Bailey continued to sit there and watch. She was about to get up and give them some privacy when an arm snaked out and pulled her into the group hug.

"Well, that was something," Bailey said after the tears seemed to slow. "I've never been cried on by three people at one time."

"Cynic." Beth straightened up. "Come on, kids, let's get you home."

"Hey, after you get them home and settled, you want to go to dinner or something? I think your shock and nerves deserve a soother." Bailey winked at Jacob. He smiled broadly.

"You know, let me call mom. If I can drop them off there, we can go to dinner after." Beth walked to the screen door. "I'll need to make sure they're both okay several times before though, okay?"

"Go ahead. I'll keep the heathens company while you let your mom know what's going on." Bailey ruffled Jacob's hair.

"Thanks, Bailey." Beth walked outside on the porch to use the phone.

"So? Are you going to do it?" Rebecca asked excited.

"Yeah, but only because I want to." She winked at them. "Now, behave and talk about something else. Did you ever find that key thing?"

"I did. Finally. It was under a leaf by the pond. It was driving me crazy. One of the boys at school looks up the tricks online. Do you?" Rebecca asked.

"Nope. At least I try really hard not to look that stuff up. I play in tournaments and stuff. I use a different name, though." Bailey looked up when Beth walked back inside. "How'd it go?"

"Mom agreed, but she'll keep them at my place. It's hard for them to bike anywhere from there," Beth said when she came back inside. "Do you mind if I take them home and change clothes? If you give me about twenty minutes after we leave here, I'll be ready."

"Gladly." Bailey picked Jacob up and swung him over her shoulders. "Just leave the bikes here. I can drop them off tomorrow."

"Good. I think they should be without them for a few days anyway." Bailey could tell Beth was still upset. She wasn't smiling.

"Mom!" Rebecca and Jacob howled.

"It's only fair," Bailey said as she deposited Jacob in his car seat. "See you in a few minutes."

"I look forward to it."

BAILEY USED THE twenty minutes she had been allotted to change into something more than ripped jeans and a T-shirt. She called for reservations at the Italian restaurant in town only to be told they didn't take them. For some reason she found that funny. She was still laughing when she pulled into Beth's driveway.

As they drove to the restaurant, Beth told Bailey about her day. She was in charge of some of the larger accounts at the bank. As a result she often saw the greedy and petty sides of people. She entertained Bailey with stories from the house to the parking lot.

"How'd you find out that he was embezzling?" Bailey asked when they were seated. She looked over the menu once and made her choice.

"Long story. Mind if I get a drink?" Beth looked at the wine menu. "It's been a bit stressful."

"No, go ahead." Bailey was oddly flattered she had asked. "Most people don't ask if I mind."

"Well, I just thought that since you don't, it might make you uncomfortable."

"Not at all. It used to, but I never was big on wine anyway. Now cigarettes I miss like I'd miss my arm." She sighed. She missed more than that, but she didn't want to dwell on anything.

"I for one am glad you don't smoke any longer. I don't think you realized how badly it smelled." Beth wrinkled her nose in disgust.

"I do now. Have you decided on what you're going to order?" Bailey sat her menu down. She had decided on the same thing as last time, the chicken Parmesan.

"Yeah. Why'd you pick this place anyway? You're not hoping to see that waitress are you?" Beth arched an eyebrow.

Bailey said. "No, I liked their chicken. I love good Italian food. Thanks for coming with me anyway."

"No problem. Mom has the kids, so I had time. But you knew that. Forgive me, it's been a day and half." Beth shook her head as if to clear it.

"She helps out a lot?" Bailey asked after they placed their orders. She was pleased it wasn't the same waitress. That could have been a little awkward.

"Yeah she does. Even before Jerry left she helped out by watching them after school while I was at work."

"Speaking of, you owe me a story. Or several really, since we've plumbed the depths of my failed relationships, both of them." Bailey grinned. "Shall we do the same for yours?"

"What did my children tell you?" Beth's voice was full of suspicion.

"Nothing much." She didn't want to get the kids into trouble, but she did want to discuss what they'd said. "Just that you and the bastard fought some and that they wanted to know if he stopped loving them too."

"He is a bastard," Beth agreed. She nodded her head to the waitress who had just sat down a glass of wine. She took a long sip. "You know, I should have realized I had made a terrible mistake when I cheated on him just a few weeks after the wedding."

"You cheated?" Bailey was amazed and very surprised.

"Yeah. I did. Believe it or not, you're the only person I've ever told." Beth met her eyes. "Did you know I was pregnant at the wedding?"

"Liz told me not too long ago," Bailey answered. "She said you miscarried."

"Funny term, that. Miscarried." Beth took another longer sip of wine. "That implies that something went wrong, that I did something wrong or my body did something wrong. No. The baby died. I was roughly 18 weeks and her heart stopped beating. We found out at the ultrasound."

"Oh man, I am so sorry." Bailey was almost speechless.

"Yeah, well, I called you. Not to blame you or anything, and please don't feel guilty. I guess you were in rehab. Anyway, after I was physically okay, I turned in that trip to Barcelona you sent. He didn't want to go so I went alone."

"And?" Bailey prompted. This was taking directions she wasn't expecting.

"Thanks for that, by the way. I was surprised you remembered. In fact, I had thought you might have met us there, but obviously." Beth shrugged and took another long drink of wine.

"I'm sorry. I had no idea," Bailey said in the silence.

"I know. Bailey, I don't blame you for any of this. And I'm not mad anymore either. I had been mad, angry even, well we talked about that the first day you were back. I'm glad too. I really have missed you. It's nice to have you around again."

"I was thinking that earlier. I've missed you too. Thanks for being my friend again." It sounded sappy and for a moment, Bailey wanted to slap herself for saying it, but Beth's eyes lit up at the comment. That made it worth it.

"Where was I? Oh yeah, Barcelona. I met another American tourist there. We hung out. You know how things happen. The next morning, I thought I'd have been just riddled with guilt. I wasn't. At first I rationalized it. You know, had I slept with another man I would have felt guilty, but I don't think so."

"Why'd you stay with him then?"

"Well, that's a good question. I came home and for a while everything was fine. I did love him. I just wasn't really in love with him and it took me forever to figure that out. Anyway, he traveled a lot for work, which kept a lot of the pressure off. It was okay, really until I got pregnant with Jacob. I think that's when he started his affair. If he cheated before then, I don't know, but I'm pretty sure that's when the actual dating of another woman happened. It wasn't long after that we stopped sleeping together. Still, after I found out I had the full battery of tests just in case. He was either careful or I was lucky."

"That's good. Maybe the bastard does have a few brain cells." Bailey wasn't quite sure how else to respond to that.

"Yeah really good. I may have killed him otherwise." Beth's tone was serious.

"How'd it end?" Bailey was fascinated despite herself.

"We had a bad fight about a year ago and he slapped me. I kicked him out. He never came back. He's wanted for embezzling. He got away with something like 1.4 million. I don't think he'll come back. Rumor has it that he's somewhere on an island. They asked me all kinds of questions, but I had no idea about any of it. We had separate accounts and one just for house stuff. They seized that one, but I got it released after a forensic accountant went through everything."

"He hit you? Just the once?" She had to know for certain. She was seeing red.

"Yes. Just once." Beth met and held her gaze. "Just once. I'm fine. It was over a year ago or so. It's okay. Everything's okay."

"Yeah, okay." Bailey took a deep breath. "Sorry."

"It's okay. Don't be sorry. It's kinda nice having someone get that upset on your behalf. It's been a long time since anyone cared enough."

"Yeah, well." Bailey searched for a different subject. "Are you guys going to the festival tomorrow?"

"We've planned on it. You?"

"Yeah. It's been years since I've been to one of our festivals. You guys want to meet at my house? We can walk down together. It'll beat trying to park anywhere else," Bailey said. "Maybe we could order pizza after, or something. The kids can watch a movie and we can hang out on the porch and talk."

"Are you trying to organize an after festival party?" Beth's smile was enormous. Bailey felt herself flush. "You are. Wow."

"Yes. I've thought about it. Wasn't that the thing adults did when we were kids? They had festival parties. Come to think of it, they had parade parties too. We'll have to plan a few of those." It felt good but strange. Bailey had never invited people over to any house she lived in before. She'd never wanted to subject her friends to her mother, and in LA she'd never been able to afford to entertain until a label signed the band. After that, she was too busy touring, recording and promoting the band to arrange parties.

"I just can't believe you're intending to have people over to a house you inhabit," Beth teased.

"I finally have a house to be proud of," Bailey answered simply. "Does that mean you'll come to my festival party?"

"I wouldn't miss it for the world."

Chapter Eighteen

BAILEY WAITED PATIENTLY with Ian and Eric while the rest of the group used the facilities the festival had so thoughtfully provided. The live band was pretty good. She was enjoying their performance. It was mostly hits from the 40s and 50s, but every once in a while they would slip in a classic rock ballad, the kind she remembered hearing out of the jukebox growing up at her mother's bar.

Sarah ran and pounced on Bailey when the group returned. "Bailey, dance with me!"

"Okay." She allowed Sarah to pull her into an open grassy area in front of the stage. Not many other people were dancing. It didn't take long before Mike had pulled Cindy out on what they had just claimed as the dance floor. Liz and Ian joined them during a slow song.

"You should go ask Jacob to dance," Bailey told her diminutive partner. "He keeps trying to get Rebecca to dance and she looks a little skeptical about dancing with her brother."

"Okay." She ran off at the suggestion. The kids hadn't reached that shy stage around one another yet. And Jacob was still seen as a baby brother and cute.

Beth came up to her. "Thanks," she said. "He really loves dancing."

"He looked like he was about to force Rebecca to come out here," Bailey said and then caught a good look at Beth. Without thinking, she offered her hand.

The next thing she knew they were dancing slowly to a 1970s power ballad. The world narrowed. No one else existed. She wasn't aware of anything other than the woman in her arms and the beat. She pulled her close. Beth smelled of springtime, her perfume gardenias. It was intoxicating. Bailey let her arms rest at the small of Beth's back, the other woman's arms around her neck, her head on Bailey's shoulder.

For the first time in a very long time, Bailey felt out of control of her actions. As the beat changed, she slowed and looked down at Beth. They were at a festival in a small southern town. They were surrounded by friends, family and complete strangers. It didn't matter. Nothing else mattered at that moment.

Beth's lips were softer than Bailey expected, than she had

dreamed, than she remembered. At first, it was just a brief meeting, so soft and quick that they could both pretend it didn't happen. Bailey wasn't content with that. She brushed her lips against Beth's again, this time staying for a moment, capturing her bottom lip and brushing a light tongue against it. And that was when the world turned upside down.

At first it took her a split second to realize what pulled her attention from Beth. Then she heard Cindy yell and turned to see Cindy's ex-husband, Roger, standing toe to toe with Mike. Eric struggled to get between them. Whether to protect his father or soon-to-be stepfather, she didn't know.

"Shit."

"What?" It took Beth just a half second longer to catch up. She seemed a little dazed. "Damn."

"Here." Bailey handed over the keys. "Take the kids, all the kids, back to the house. Go. They don't need to be here for this."

"What? No," Beth protested.

"Go. I don't know what's going to happen, but the kids don't need to see or hear any of this. Go. Please. I'll see you later."

"Okay. Be careful." Beth turned to find her children and Sarah.

A circle had formed around the two groups, Roger leading one and the other supporting Mike and Cindy. Bailey elbowed her way through the crowd to her other cousin's side. Liz and Ian were just behind Mike and Cindy. They looked at her questioningly when she joined them.

"I sent the kids with Beth. What's going on?" She whispered.

"Roger objects to his son being seen in public with Mike." Liz looked close to angry tears.

"Bigoted bastard," Bailey said. "Ian, get your phone out and start recording."

"No, Bailey. You can't do anything. He'll sue if you touch him," Ian said.

"Just do it." Bailey pushed ahead even farther to stand level with Mike. "Everything okay?"

"Oh look, the dyke rocker has joined the freak show. Guess it's almost complete. Where's the last one of your little group? Heard she needs a man." Roger was obviously drunk.

"Roger, why don't we all have a seat and talk about whatever's bothering you?" Bailey suggested.

"Shut up, dyke bitch," Roger yelled.

"Hey, don't you talk to her like that," Mike shouted.

"It's okay, Mike. I've been called worse by better," Bailey scoffed.

"Oh, the freak is going to stand up for someone else other than itself." Roger stepped closer, pushing his son out of the way. Bailey grabbed Eric and kept him from falling. "Let go of my son. Your whole family is nothing but perverted little freaks."

"No," Bailey responded calmly. She held Eric as Roger attempted to grab the young man and pull him across the invisible boundary between them. "Eric, are you okay?"

"No." He leaned into her shoulder. "Don't make me go with him, please."

"Okay. He stays here. You're drunk, Roger. Go home." Bailey never let go of Eric. The young man was shaking.

"Not without my son. He's not living with that freak. I told that bitch not to marry the freak, but she must have lost her goddamn mind like the rest of you. That abomination shouldn't have been allowed to live much less live among the rest of us." Roger seemed to forget there were other people listening. He spoke only to Bailey. Perhaps it was because she was responding calmly to him. She remembered a lot from her time as a bouncer.

"Roger, it's okay, man. Everything's going to be okay. We just all need to talk about this later. It's not a good time right now, okay?" She looked around at Roger's friends, silently pleading for one of them to help.

"C'mon, Roger. Let's go over and look at the cars again," one of his friends said, attempting to direct his attention elsewhere. "It's not worth talking to them, man. They're not like us."

It didn't help.

"Fucking right. Weirdoes. Freaks. Cockless motherfucker thinks it's a man and wants to raise my son?" Roger took an unsteady step back.

"Shit." Bailey released Eric and grabbed Cindy, pulling her behind them right as Roger's drunken aim collided with the side of Bailey's face. Mike started to swing in retaliation, but Ian was there to grab him. Liz now had the phone, recording the entire thing.

"Let me go!" Mike struggled to get away as Roger's friends helped the drunken man off the ground. He had swung a little too wildly and overbalanced himself.

"Enough," Bailey yelled. Her jaw hurt, but it wasn't as bad as it could have been. "You assholes get your king out of here. Go sober up somewhere. Mike, chill. Get your family and get your asses home. Don't one of you look at the other. Just go."

"No." The surly answer was from a place she little expected it. Mike stood his ground. "I'm not leaving."

"Mike." Bailey waived Ian away. "C'mon man. You don't want to get arrested before your wedding, do you?"

"Come on, babe. Let's go get the car and go home." Cindy took him by the arm. Reluctantly it seemed he allowed her to lead him away. "Eric, you okay?"

"I'm fine, Mom." The young man looked a little shaken but seemed to be fine.

"You okay?" Liz asked as she joined Bailey and Ian to watch the others leave.

"Yeah. He didn't hit that hard. He over swung by a mile." Bailey rubbed her jaw. "What an asshole."

"Yes he is," Liz said. "But on a happier note, I noticed your dance. You looked good together."

"You both looked cozy," Ian agreed.

"Yeah." Bailey couldn't help it, she smiled, surprised to find herself slightly embarrassed.

"I think that was pretty damn awesome." Liz hooked arms with Bailey and Ian and started the walk back to the cars. "So, was it worth the wait?"

"As of right now it was worth every day. But ask me again after the excitement wears down. I could have been about to get slapped had Roger not shown his ass."

"I doubt that," Ian said.

"Bailey! Liz!" Cindy yelled as soon as they turned the corner to Bailey's road.

"Oh no. What now?" This was getting a little worrying. "How'd you people survive without me?"

"The same way you survived without us. Poorly," Liz said. "And with extremely high telephone bills."

"True that." Bailey took a good look at the house ahead of them. "This doesn't look good." Everyone was outside in the driveway. Cindy's car was missing.

"What's up?" Liz asked as they came within speaking distance.

"Mike took off." Cindy was in tears. Eric didn't look much better.

"What?" Bailey turned to Beth.

"They got here. We heard yelling. Mike took off. That's it," Beth answered. "What all happened?"

"Roger rattled Mike's cage," Bailey said. "Did you want to—"

Cindy pulled Bailey's attention away from Beth. "You have to go after him. I don't know what he could do. Bailey, please."

Bailey looked at Liz who nodded. "Okay. We'll find him and

keep him from doing anything stupid." She shook her head. "Beth, I uh..."

"Go," Beth said. "We'll talk later. I'll get the kids and Ian home."

Bailey nodded at Liz. "You drive." She got in the passenger's side of Liz's car.

"I have too many brothers," Liz grumbled.

"You'd miss being the only girl," Bailey reminded her. "Where's he hang out these days?"

"The shop. Cindy's house. Granddad's," Liz said. "He practically lives in that shed back there when he's not at Cindy's house."

"Has Roger made any trouble beside this?"

"Not much. You know today had to be for show. He rarely sees Eric and has only kept his parental rights because of his mother. She's been very involved in his life. Roger not so much."

"Yeah, I know. Last time I saw the three of them, Eric didn't know about Mike. I never asked Cindy if they'd told him. Did they?"

"When's the last time you saw them together?" Liz asked as she pulled through the parking lot of Mike's shop. Cindy's car was nowhere to be seen.

"Last summer. They came out to LA. I took Eric to all the amusement parks and stuff while Mike and Cindy went to see his doctors."

"Oh yeah. I remember hearing about that. Well, they told him. He took it pretty well. I suggested the three of them see one of my colleagues. Eric still sees him twice a month. I wish Mike would."

This was news to Bailey. "I thought he had to stay in therapy? Wasn't that some legal condition?"

"Nope. He met the requirement and stopped. And of course the first real test after that sends him off in a snit." Liz pulled the car around behind their grandfather's house. "Let's go see how this shit show turns out."

"Liz, are you okay?"

"Yeah, I'm just a little tired of being the responsible one and helping him clean up his shit."

"I know. I guess we sometimes focus on him so intently we forget about you." Bailey said.

"I know. I know you're always there. Ian's there and Beth and Cindy. But it would be nice if for once Mike was there. I mean I even asked him." She paused and took a deep breath. "The only thing we've ever really shared was a womb. I'll be fine. Let's go make sure he will be too."

MIKE WAS SITTING in the dark on a couch that had seen better days long before they were born. There were two empty beer bottles on the floor at his feet. He was drinking from another in his hand. He had maybe a twenty-minute head start on them after he left Bailey's house. From what Bailey saw, he'd used that time to work on getting inebriated.

"Have a beer," he offered when he saw them.

"No thanks," Bailey said. Liz accepted.

"Too good to drink with your freak cousin?"

"You know better than that." She waved off his comment as she pulled up a chair from the small kitchen table. "What's up?"

"I should have wiped the floor with that asshole," he growled.

"And what would that have proven?" Liz asked.

"Nothing. Just would have felt good."

"No it wouldn't have," Bailey said. "Eric wouldn't have appreciated it either."

"Bastard never raised him. I'm more his dad." Tears formed in Mike's eyes. "And I can't give him a sister. He needs a sister or a brother."

"Sure you can. They sell sperm over the Internet. They have for years," Bailey reminded him.

"It's not the same," he grumbled.

"Mike, you know I love you. I've been with you since the three of us wore matching baby blankets but drop the funk," she said.

"What would you know about it?"

"Obviously not as much as you. But I know you can't get through everything alone. Maybe you should go back to therapy."

"You go to meetings?" he asked.

"Sometimes I still do, when I need them. I went to one before I flew here actually. And I talk to Liz or my sponsor when I need to." That was true. Sometimes she felt as if she needed the positive reinforcement.

"And then Dad." Mike seemed determined to wallow.

"Dad will be okay. And really, there's not much we can do about it anyway," Liz said.

"Mike, it's okay to be sad. But I thought we worked through

all that back in LA."

"I did too," Liz added.

"I don't know. I love Cindy so much, and she's had to go through hell because of me. Eric is like a son. Most people don't know or can't tell, but..." He was close to tears.

"But Roger brought it up, in public when you were least expecting it," Bailey finished for him. "He's an asshole. Mike, you're twice the man he is even with a low sperm count."

He reluctantly smiled at the old joke. "Bitch."

"Bastard," Bailey shot back. "You know I never did ask you why you chose Ferdinand for a middle name. So why?"

"It's all I could think of at the time, honestly. Beats the hell out of Crystal."

"True," Liz said. "Your names sucked. My name sucks. Elizabeth Lea. What were our parents thinking?"

"Could have been worse," Bailey said. "Two little blondes? You guys could have been something really twin-ish like Mary and Kerry or Monique and Unique."

"You have no room to talk, Bailey Ray," Mike pointed out.

"Also true, but I didn't change my name to Ferdinand." She stuck her tongue out at him. "You better?"

"Yeah. Can one of you take me home?" He asked. His mood had improved. Bailey was grateful. She'd been worried it would be an all-night thing.

"Sure." Liz rose and offered him a hand up. "Come on, pain in my ass. I'll take you home."

"I'll follow with your car," Bailey said.

"Nah. Just leave the keys in it. I'll pick it up from your place tomorrow."

"Will do, big guy."

Bailey drove Cindy's car back to her house to find everyone had left. She was disappointed but understood. She had followed Mike to soothe him and abandoned her guests. She was torn between relief and disappointment. She'd almost hoped that Beth would still have been there.

As she unlocked the house and let the dog out she debated calling her. It was late. She wasn't ready to discuss the kiss. She wasn't ready to discuss what happened with Mike either. She let Elvis back inside and turned on her game console. She could deal with everything else later.

Chapter Nineteen

"BAILEY?" THE VOICE that called out to her crossed from dreams to reality.

"Beth?" Bailey opened her eyes to see Beth standing over her. "Elvis is so fired as a guard dog."

"Good morning." Beth had a very determined look on her face.

Bailey checked her phone. "Yeah, I guess it's still morning. Sorry. I was up late last night fighting a fierce campaign. Okay. I see that you want to talk. Before we start, can I brush my teeth and get dressed?"

Beth looked taken aback. "Yeah, I'll meet you downstairs."

"Could you do me a huge favor and make some coffee?" Bailey asked as she got out of bed. She heard Beth's gasp.

"I forget sometimes that you're a natural blonde," Beth said in a strangled tone.

"Yeah, I'm thinking of going back to it." She was amused. Beth kept looking everywhere else. "Go downstairs. I won't be long."

"Yeah. Coffee. Right." The blush on Beth's face made her almost glow.

Bailey took the time for a full shower. She'd been slightly concerned when she woke up and saw Beth standing there. After the kiss they hadn't had time to talk, but if the way Beth looked at her was any indication, Bailey suddenly felt a lot more confident.

"Smells good in here," Bailey said as she padded barefoot into the kitchen.

"Coffee's made," Beth said unnecessarily.

"Thank you." Bailey poured a large cup and added sugar. "So, you wanted to talk?"

"Yeah. How's Mike?" Bailey could tell that Beth was a little rattled and needed to work up to the conversation.

"He's fine. Roger just rattled his cage. So what's up?" She tried to act casual. She leaned against the counter and tasted her coffee.

"You kissed me," Beth said. She brought a hand to her lips as if in memory.

"I did. You seemed to be okay with it at the time. Did that change?"

"No. Yes. I mean. Why?" Beth asked after a deep breath. "Why did you kiss me?"

"Well." Bailey paused a moment. She wanted to phrase it correctly. "I've wanted to do that since you walked into Ms. Miller's first grade class."

"You what?" Beth looked confused. "But in Vienna."

"In Vienna you were drunk and married," Bailey said patiently. "And I thought you didn't remember that?"

"I lied. I was embarrassed and dejected. I wanted you so bad. I felt rejected." Beth crossed her arms in front of her.

"Oh, baby, I wanted you too. It almost killed me to stop you." It was Bailey's turn to take a deep breath. She half turned and put the coffee cup on the counter. For all her bravado, she couldn't meet Beth's eyes as she said it. "I love you. I always have. I didn't know what to do about it when we were kids. I was too caught up in being a rebel bitch."

"Bailey. You talk too much." Her voice was a bit strangled.

Bailey hadn't noticed Beth move, but suddenly she was in her arms. It wasn't grasping as if to keep from drowning, rather it was passionate and fierce, full of promise and wonder. She wanted it to never end. Unfortunately, like all good things, there was an end.

"It's about goddamn time," Liz shouted. The shout startled them so much they broke apart.

"The fuck are you doing here?" Bailey asked as Beth buried her head in Bailey's shoulder. "Elvis really sucks as a guard dog."

"I was going to take you out to brunch, but it seems like you have other plans." Liz was nonplussed.

"Yeah. I think we have some talking to do. You?" She asked her companion.

Beth's cheeks went scarlet. "Yes. Lots of talking and stuff."

"Okay. So I'll leave you ladies to do whatever you're going to do." Liz exited gracefully. They could hear the laughter linger in the hallway.

"Well that cat is out of the bag," Beth said as she stepped away.

"Liz won't say anything." Bailey was sure of that.

"I know. So, you said something that kinda made my heart stop for a moment." Beth prompted.

"Did I?" Bailey teased gently. "I can't believe you didn't know. But I do. I love you."

"What are we getting ourselves into? What about our lives? My kids? What do we do now?" She stayed a few feet away. The look on her face was serious.

"It depends on you. Really. I'm not quitting the band. Kat and I are kinda in it until we keel over. But I'm not touring often. We're doing one of those semi-retirement things. So I'll be around a lot. Not sure if you're okay with that. I wasn't sure how you feel about anything." Bailey found herself rambling.

"Wow. You are not your typical confident self. Where's your swagger?" Beth asked.

"After Vienna I knew I wasn't over you. I knew I couldn't be with anyone if I didn't love her as much as I love you. That kiss scorched me. When I came back and they told me about the divorce I thought maybe it was time I said something and found out how you feel about me." Bailey pushed her hair back from her eyes. "I'm in a strange position. I can't be friends with you because I want so much more. I don't think I can be strong enough. So if you don't want anything more you need to let me know. And wow that came out of nowhere."

"You don't know?" Beth pushed off the counter and walked over again. "Bailey Ray Cooper. I have loved you since you fell off the jungle gym and broke your arm. I would have jumped head-first off the train bridge for you had you asked when we were in high school. And then in college, Bailey, you broke my heart."

"I'm so sorry. I never want to hurt you again." It was hard to speak around the lump in her throat.

"I know. I'm not blind. I know how hard it was for you without any parental support. We were kids and it didn't make sense then. It does now. I never appreciated how much pain you were in." Beth reached up and brushed Bailey's hair back. "I don't know what we're going to do. I don't know if this will work out, but I have to stop wondering and find out."

"Does this mean we're okay?" Bailey wrapped her arms around Beth.

"Oh yeah. Definitely. I just don't know what we're going to tell the kids or what they're going to think about it."

"Are you kidding?" Bailey looked her in the eyes. "That day they biked over here? It was to ask me if I would date you."

"Are you shitting me?" Beth roared with laughter. "That's what those rascals wanted? You all just said they wanted to talk about their dad."

"They did. I'm sorry we stretched the truth a bit. I mean they did want to talk about that, but they also seemed determined we should hook up." She pulled Beth over to the couch. "They are smart children."

"So I guess we tell them the truth. At least how we understand it." Beth rested her head on Bailey's shoulder. "What is the truth, Bailey?"

"That's a good question. My first response is a wimpy one, which would turn it back on you and ask what you want. I can't do that though. I would like to try a real adult relationship with you. You know, dates, flowers, candlelight, sex."

"I honestly never would have thought of you as such a romantic. I knew you had it in you, but I never thought you'd bring it out without coaxing." Beth paused for so long that Bailey started to get a bit worried. "Hey, no reason to look scared. I love you, Bailey Ray Cooper. I always have, but I don't think we'd be having this conversation if neither of us had grown up. I mean, what I'm trying to say is that I would love to build a relationship with you, one that is built on love, trust, friendship and of course sex."

"Those were a lot of words for a question that could have been answered: Yes Bailey, I will date you." She felt like laughing, but she also fought back tears.

"Yes, Bailey, love of my life, I will date you." Beth's eyes were sparkling with unshed tears.

"See." Bailey's voice was a little strangled with emotion. "That wasn't so hard now, was it?" She leaned in for a long kiss.

"I know. But this next part is. I have to go. I have to take Rebecca to a party and Jacob to soccer registration. And then I have to get them in bed early because tomorrow starts another work week for me and day camp for them." She looked regretfully at Bailey.

"Well. Dating implies not living together, and seeing one another on occasion, right?"

"Right." Beth looked at her expectantly.

"So we'll do that then." Bailey nodded as she came to that conclusion. "We'll have to schedule time to talk and work on our relationship."

"Is that what you're calling it?" Beth raised an eyebrow. "We will. I love you, but I have to go."

"Ah, already with the 'I love you, but's'." Bailey grabbed her chest in mock dismay. "I love you too. Go on. I have furniture to put together, boxes to unpack and all that shit. Is it trite to say I'll call you later?"

"Not at all." Beth disentangled herself and straightened her clothes.

"IAN SAID SOMETHING about how hard the bastard may have found it to compete with me. He never did explain what he was talking about. You have any idea?" Bailey asked Liz. She had surprised her again with lunch the next day.

"Yep. So you know how we're taking trips as a group every two years, and of course you bought Beth the Barcelona trip as an apology for acting an ass at her wedding, right?" Liz prompted as she put dressing on her salad. Bailey had skipped the obligatory fast food and ordered take out from a local chain.

"Yeah," Bailey said with uncertainty.

"While we see it as you being you, I don't think the guys saw it that way. At least I know Ian has had issues sometimes that you can do things for us that he can't, but then hell, I make more money than he does and sometimes that galls him. And then with Sarah." Liz shrugged.

That caught Bailey off guard. Liz rarely complained about her relationship with Ian. "Wow. And here I thought you had the perfect relationship out of all of us."

"You know there's no such thing." Liz shook her head. "Anyway, after Jerry proposed, we all went to Oslo, remember? That's where she told us about it."

"Yeah. I can't forget that. By the way, you know they make some kick ass drugs in Norway?" Bailey said as an aside.

"I figured you did some self-medicating after that news. I think if Beth had been able to see your face, she would have known in an instant and called off the wedding."

"What makes you say that?"

"You looked like your heart was broken. After that you really went off the deep end, culminating in that wonderful performance at the wedding."

"Need you remind me? Worst six months of my life. At least they moved up the date. Had they waited I may have..." She stopped short.

"May have what?" Liz looked at her closely. "You did wreck that motorcycle, didn't you? You never did answer that question. We got back to LA and you didn't have any transportation. Said your bike was in the shop. It was, but only because you wrecked it, didn't you? That's why you were limping that weekend."

"Yes. I wrecked it. I spent a lot of time doing a lot of stupid things, more so than normal, during that period," she admitted. "I have some amazing scars now. Not as awesome as Mike's badass arm scar, but definitely one that has garnered some sympathy."

"Fucking hell, Bailey." Liz put her head in her hands. "You two are going to drive me crazy. Why didn't you tell me? Why did you let it get so bad? I'd have helped. I did help."

"You know how I was raised, or not, as the case may be. I never knew how to deal with pain and anger. The only thing I knew was not to take it out on someone else. So I took it out on me. And yes, I let it get bad. Hell, I came close to death a few times during that period. I couldn't say anything because there was a large part of me that thought I deserved it. I don't anymore. I got through it. I guess in a way Mike and I are a lot alike."

"The three of us may as well be triplets." Liz sighed. "You know; I still have nightmares about that night. How old were we? Fourteen? Kyle and Will. I would still love to wring their necks."

"Yeah that certainly counts as one of the worst nights ever." Bailey closed her eyes against the memory, but it didn't help. "It's amazing we made it out alive."

"Not all of us did." Liz's voice was choked with tears.

"We couldn't save Diana, we weren't out on that date with her and Robert. I wish we would have been. I wish that they would have stopped by wherever we were at for five minutes at least. But they didn't. So we couldn't have done anything," Bailey said. "But we saved Mike. He almost killed himself that night."

"I know." Liz sighed. "And that's the night I see so often. Yeah, I have guilt with Diana. I didn't like Robert. I always wondered if I'd said something maybe she wouldn't have gone out with him. Maybe she'd still be alive today."

"Liz, they were hit by a drunk driver head on. Robert hadn't even been drinking. There wasn't anything we could have done." Bailey had told Liz the same thing several times, but their friend's death was one thing Liz took harder than everyone else.

"I know," Liz said. "It's just we lost her, we lost Mike for the most part after that night with Kyle and Will. Then you up and left because that's what you do. Hell, I can't even think about what would have happened had you gotten yourself killed either by accident or overdose." It was rare, but Liz seemed headed for a full meltdown.

"I made it. Mike made it. Hell, you can barely see the scars after the chest reconstruction," Bailey said. "Dude's got awesome pecs."

"Do you ever wonder if he tried to kill himself that night? I mean he took a knife and tried to have a self-directed double mastectomy."

"I asked him that after he came out to California and we

found him a good doctor. He says no, but I'm still not sure." If Bailey closed her eyes again, she could still hear the yells, the cries of pain, the taunting. "I'm just glad Cindy and Beth weren't there. I don't know if that would have potentially impacted their relationship or not, but it was tough. You know, I wonder if Arnoux should have been there. Maybe had she seen the hell he was put through she'd have a little empathy for him."

"I doubt it," Liz said. "I haven't seen Will since graduation, but Kyle has never said anything nice to Mike after he found out who he was. I doubt that's from shame."

"How did we get off on this subject? We were talking about Bastard and how he thought he was in competition with me." Bailey wiped her eyes. There were some memories she never wanted to relive.

"Well, we've established that Beth is bi, right? I mean I can show you pictures of previous girlfriends you've never met if you need more proof."

"No. I'm good. What's the point?" She wasn't overly worried about past relationships.

"Anyway, she and Jerry started dating and I don't think he believed that she knew you until they visited her parents. You know how the Forsyths feel about you. Anyway, so he finally believes it. Then after he proposes she runs off to Oslo with us. He can't afford to take her to Oslo. They went on a cruise for the honeymoon, just an inexpensive one around the Gulf of Mexico, but she loved it. You know Beth, she's pretty appreciative of things, but then you send her to Barcelona. And then there's London. And then there's Aspen. Every two years like clock-work you're whisking us away on some grand adventure. He couldn't keep up with that."

"It wasn't a contest. I didn't do all that to get in her pants," Bailey said.

Liz looked at her. "Of course you did. Almost everything you've done from standing on the top of the jungle gym to crafting a gold record has been to impress her. You never did have to show off, you know. Anyway, for a while he tried to keep up. I think he eventually gave up. Ian told me that Jerry once said if anyone was going to take Beth away from him it would be you. So he knew."

"But I didn't. He did that himself. She told me he was cheating on her and then he embezzled a shit ton of money from clients and took off. That can't be laid on my doorstep. I never did like the bastard, but I sure as hell didn't have anything to do with that."

"You're right. Completely, and there's no reason for you to feel guilty. You just asked so I answered. How's it going between you, anyway? I thought you were going to kill me yesterday."

"That's what you get for walking into my house unannounced." Bailey stuck her tongue out at her. "We've decided that we're dating. Where does one go on a date around here?"

"La Maison. It's a French restaurant. It's highbrow. And then there's Maven's for top dollar steaks. A couple of the casinos have decent restaurants in them, but because they're in casinos they don't have that dress up appeal." She leaned back in her chair. "I guess this means you two haven't slept together yet?"

"Nope. After you left yesterday, we talked for a bit, made out for a bit and then she had to go take the kids places."

"You're not scared anymore, are you?"

"A little. Wouldn't you be?"

"I suppose I would." Liz said. "You know, your habit of bringing me lunch at my office is pretty awesome."

"It's the only time I get to talk to you alone, really," Bailey replied. "At your house we have Ian or Sarah. Well I suppose there's my house, but all the kids have been making it a habit to drop by unannounced. So has Mike. Actually, how did my house suddenly become the center of everything?"

"You are the only one who lives downtown. We all either work or go to school here. So your house is convenient, much like Beth's house was when we were kids, remember?"

"Fair point. All right. Well, I've things to do and you've patients to see. Thanks for keeping lunch open for me." She stood as she heard the signs of life returning to the clinic. Fortunately, the front door chirped when someone opened it.

"You know I always have time open for you, Bailey." Liz looked at her.

"Likewise. I may not be your twin, but you're as close as I have to a sister. I'm always here if you need me." Bailey eased the door closed behind her. She heard the surprised gratitude and it made her smile. Then she heard the phone and knew lunch was certainly over.

Chapter Twenty

BAILEY HAD COMPLETED putting together most of the furniture that had been delivered. She'd almost unpacked everything from LA. She bought paint and all the necessary supplies that went with that and had even drawn rough designs for the studio she wanted to make in the garage apartment. However, she was bored. She hadn't left the house in three days. Beth was busy at work, Cindy and Mike were busy with wedding preparations and for the last day or so she'd been unable to locate anyone she knew in one of her games.

"What's the matter, boy?" Elvis was lying on his dog bed, whining. It wasn't a normal noise either. She could tell he wasn't in pain. It was low and pitiful and reminded her a bit of children's sobs. "Are you sad, buddy? You miss the kids, don't you? I do too."

His ears perked up at that. That decided it for her. She stood up, found some shoes and called him to her. She was bored. He was bored. It was time to do something about it.

Bailey wasn't a big fan of walking, running or jogging on anything other than a treadmill for exercise. However, she knew she would have to do something until she joined a gym that offered the classes she was used to taking. Taking a clue from the kids, she bought a bike. To protect Elvis, she had also gotten a trailer to pull behind it.

"Come on, boy. It's like a sidecar only behind a bike. You'll be fine," she said. "Okay. I haven't done this in forever."

Bailey soon realized the truth and fallacy about riding a bike. While she did remember how, it was harder than she remembered. It also hurt. It was much different than the stationary bike she rode for miles at the gym in LA.

Beth's house was less than a mile away. It didn't take long for them to get there, but Bailey was sweating and straining with the effort. The kids were out in the yard when they pulled up to the house and ran to meet them. She put on a brave face for them. She didn't want them to see how out of condition she was.

"Bailey? Is that Elvis in there?" Rebecca ran up to the trailer. "Elvis!"

"Everyone loves to see the dog more than me," she pretended to complain. "I think he missed you guys."

"You know, you're the only person I could envision riding a bike in jeans and work boots," Beth said from the door.

"I don't really do this whole exercise in public thing very often. Usually it's a private gym type thing," Bailey said as she got off the bike and parked it in the yard. Rebecca was already freeing Elvis.

"Come in," Beth said. "Kids, you guys play with Elvis out here."

"Hi." Bailey grinned as the door was closed. "We missed you guys. Actually, I missed you." She leaned in for a kiss. "This okay?"

"Yeah." Beth pulled her close. "Man I missed you. Wanna stay for dinner?"

"I could do that if I'm not imposing."

"Not imposing. Just..."

"No dessert. The kids are here. I got it." Bailey sighed against her.

"You okay with that?" Beth asked.

"Yes, ma'am. Hey, I haven't had sex in almost three years. And I've wanted you since before I knew what love was. I can wait. I may die from it, but I'll wait," she teased. "Seriously. It's okay."

"Three years?" Beth looked askance.

"Don't judge." Bailey kissed her again.

"Never. Um, baby, we should stop. Kids. Dog. Dinner."

"Oh yeah. Right." Bailey rested her head on the door and immediately regretted it when someone tried to open it. "Ouch."

"Mom," Rebecca called through the slightly opened door. "Elvis needs water. He's panting."

"He does that," Bailey said.

"Come on in." Beth motioned for Bailey to move and opened the door. "It's time to wash up for dinner anyway."

"Is Bailey staying?" Jacob asked when he bounced through the door.

"I am. Is that okay?" She smiled at him.

"Of course," he said. "I'll go wash my hands."

"You too, Rebecca," Beth ordered. "And then set the table, please."

"Okay." Rebecca ran down the hall to do as asked, Elvis at her heels.

"He's a people dog. I didn't realize he was lonely for more than just me until today," Bailey said as she watched them.

"He's your dog. Of course he needs people. You do too." Beth took her hand. "Help me get dinner out of the stove?"

"Sure. What are we having?" Bailey tried to guess by smell. It smelled heavenly, like tomato sauce and garlic.

"Lasagna. It's fairly easy and gives great leftovers. Besides, it's easy to sneak vegetables in the sauce and not have the kids notice." Beth pulled lettuce, cucumbers and tomatoes from the refrigerator. "Here, cut the cucumber up for me."

"Ah, an ulterior motive." Bailey said as she took the vegetable and found a cutting board and knife. "Excellent. By the way, do you have any plans for Friday night?"

"Friday? This Friday?" She shook her head. "No. I don't think so, why?"

"I thought maybe we could have an official first date." Bailey waggled her eyebrows. "Seriously, we can do dinner and beach and a motorcycle ride."

"I like where this is going," Beth said as she bent over to pull the tray of lasagna from the oven.

"I'm glad my hands are otherwise occupied," Bailey teased. "That was a very tempting sight, Ms. Forsyth."

"Thanks." Beth blushed. "So, dinner? On Friday? Yeah, I'll get a sitter."

"You seem a little flustered." Bailey was enjoying seeing her discomfort. It was almost as if it made everything real.

"Bailey, does Elvis need to wash his paws?" Jacob asked as he raced back into the kitchen.

"No. He's fine." She spared his feelings and didn't laugh. She knew Beth's kids had wanted pets but Jerry hadn't allowed it.

"Mom said we can get our own dog maybe around Christmas," Rebecca said proudly as she entered the kitchen.

"That sounds awesome. What type do you want?" Bailey asked. Rebecca was attempting to get four plates from the cabinet and seemed stuck. "Here."

"Thanks." Rebecca smiled up in relief as Bailey handed them to her. "I don't know. I want a Golden Retriever or a Yorkie."

"I want a hound dog or a police dog," Jacob said.

"I want something that's not bigger than they are," Beth added. She had the salad bowls and was handing them to Jacob so he could place them on the table.

"Well, I've had a Lab and then bulldogs. So I guess I'm biased to bulldogs now, but they do have some health issues," Bailey told them. "I never could have a pet when I was kid."

"Really?" Rebecca's eyes went big and round. "Why?"

"My mother wasn't fond of helpless creatures," Bailey said

after a moment's thought. "She didn't like pets."

"That stinks. Pets are awesome," Jacob said.

"That they are," Beth agreed. "Well, let's eat."

Beth and her little family had a wonderful tradition that Bailey loved immediately. As they ate, they each told everyone what the best and worst things that had happened to them were that day. It was nice. The kids even insisted she participate. She did so, although she was unable to fully articulate how amazing it was to be sitting there with them.

It sparked an idea so much that after dinner, after she had helped clean up and the kids had gone to bed, after a brief few minutes with Beth, Bailey rode home and got out her guitar. She was up most of the night, but she finally wrote something she didn't hate.

"WHY DID CINDY send you two over here?" Bailey asked as Mike and Eric walked up the driveway. She'd heard the car and looked outside to see Mike's truck. She decided to meet them on the porch.

"She said you had a hot date and couldn't go in leather pants," Mike answered.

"She also said we needed clothes for the rehearsal dinner," Eric said. "She was acting kinda weird."

"She was weird on the phone," Bailey told them. "So do we insert ourselves into whatever is going on or do we do as requested and go shopping?"

"I vote shopping," Eric said.

"She probably just wants some time alone." Mike shrugged.

"Oh well. Wanna take the car? It was just delivered yesterday." Bailey picked up her car keys from the table inside the door. The rest of her stuff hadn't been delivered yet, but at least the car had made it in one piece.

"Yeah." Eric grinned. He liked the car and it had a great sound system in it.

"Cool. Where are we going?" She asked as she unlocked the car and waited for them to get inside.

"The mall I guess." Mike shrugged when she looked at him. "Only place I can think of to go."

"All right. The mall it is." Bailey pulled out of her driveway and set the car in the direction of the mall.

"What side of the store are you shopping on today?" Mike asked as Bailey parked the car twenty minutes later.

"Good question. I don't want to wear a dress. I want to take the motorcycle. I hate skirts. And women's pants have zilch for pockets," she said.

"Mom is always hollering for pants pocket equality," Eric said.

"I've often thought that if we all boycotted women's pants things would change, but there are way too many women who wouldn't participate," Bailey said. "Guess it's guy slacks for me today."

The trio walked into a large department store and looked around. It had been a long time since Bailey had been in any mall, much less the one at home. The store was so full of merchandise it was almost suffocating.

"Where to?" She turned to Mike for guidance.

"Upstairs I think." He led the way to the escalators.

The second floor was indeed home to men's wear. It was also where children's wear, home décor, and shoes resided. They walked around the displays of plates and sheets to a section containing suits and more casual attire.

"So I'm assuming you both need suits. I just need a pair of slacks and a shirt. I can't wait until the rest of my stuff gets here."

"Did the house sell yet?" Mike asked.

"Not yet. But they packed everything up and it's supposed to be on its way here. I'm actually surprised the car got here as when it did. Guess they found a truck coming this way pretty quickly." She turned into the casual clothes. "A pair of black slacks can't hurt, right?"

"Can I help you find something?" A salesman asked. He was in khakis and a dress shirt with a name tag efficiently placed over the shirt pocket.

"Yeah. I just need a pair of black slacks and these two need suits," she said.

"I'll be glad to help the gentlemen find something that fits them. I'm sure one of our ladies would love to help you downstairs." He spoke in a slightly dismissive manner. "Sir? Would you care to follow me?"

"Actually, I was looking for pants here," Bailey told him.

"This is men's wear," He said condescendingly.

"And?" She raised an eyebrow. "Are you unwilling to help me find something?"

"As I have said, ma'am, I'm sure the ladies downstairs would be more than happy to help you find something suitable."

"No thanks. I bet the people at your competitor down the hall will though," Mike said. "Come on, Bailey. We're not getting anywhere with this jerk."

"Did he say Bailey?" A young man poked his girlfriend in the shoulder and pointed in their direction. "He called her Bailey. That's Bailey Cooper."

"Wow. It is." The young woman seemed excited. She grabbed her boyfriend's hand and they rushed over. "Ms. Cooper. Man, you're amazing. I totally forgot you were from here."

"Ms. Cooper, it's a pleasure. I'm Peter. This is my girlfriend, Brooke," he gushed as he shook her hand.

"Thanks," she said. Eric seemed to be standing taller and looking around to see who hadn't noticed the disturbance. "I'm always happy to meet fans, especially ones close to home."

"Fans?" The salesman asked Mike.

"Yep. Why don't you do a Google search for her?" He offered the salesman his phone, which was not taken. Mike pocketed it and turned away. "Later."

"We were just on the way out of this store," Bailey told them. "Care to walk with us?"

"Of course. Thanks," Peter said.

"Were you done shopping?" Brooke asked.

"We decided it was too socially confining to shop here," Mike said with a smile.

"Big words, cousin, I'm impressed." Bailey said. "But he's right. We were sent to get those two suits and I need a pair of pants for a date tomorrow night. The salesman here didn't want to help me."

"That's a shame, but awesome." Brooke's eyes lit up at the thought. "I work at a men's clothing store here. No one there would have the slightest problem assisting the three of you."

"Excellent. Lead the way." Bailey waved them ahead.

"Do you get that a lot?" Brooke asked as she led the way back to the escalators.

"Not much anymore. Actually that's the first time in a long time, but it's also the first time in a long time I've tried going shopping here."

"I imagine it's a bit more liberal in LA, a bit easier to go shopping," she said. Mike snorted.

"One thing I've learned touring the world over is there are bigots everywhere. So we move on and spend our money where it's welcome."

"Well it and you will be welcome at my store," Brooke promised. Her boyfriend was engaging Mike in conversation about the tattoo on his forearm. "So when are you guys going back out on tour? Do you have a new album coming out?"

"No tour plans yet," Bailey hedged. "And we're all just taking a breather. We'll get back in the studio soon."

"Awesome. I really hope you guys play around here again. I missed the last concert," Brooke grumbled.

"Well, if we do, I'll hook you up with a few backstage passes," Bailey promised.

Three hours later they were heading back home. Eric had managed to get not only a suit for the rehearsal dinner, but a new pair of shoes as well. Mike just got the suit and Bailey splurged. She left with shoes, pants and a few shirts. All in all, it was a good and productive afternoon.

Chapter Twenty-one

BAILEY PARKED THE motorcycle in Beth's driveway and took a deep breath. For the first time she was actually nervous before a date. It took a few moments for her to will her heart to slow. She had to remind herself that it was Beth, but that thought alone was almost enough to set off a panic attack. It was worse when the door opened and Beth came outside.

Beth was wearing a short black dress and had her auburn hair swept back in an elegant knot at the base of her neck. She had even brought out heels. Bailey suddenly found it difficult to breathe.

"Your chariot, milady." Bailey held out the extra helmet with a slightly shaking hand. "You look amazing."

"Thank you." Beth blushed. It took her a moment to get the helmet settled where it would not make too big a mess of her hair.

It was tempting to turn the motorcycle around and go back to her house, but Bailey didn't want to rush things. She had reservations at a nice French restaurant and had planned a ride along the beach after dinner. When she felt Beth's arms around her waist, she smiled and headed to the restaurant.

Le Maison had always sounded a bit pretentious, but Cindy had raved about the place. Even Liz suggested it when Bailey asked for recommendations. She pulled into a space near the door, the benefit of riding a motorcycle.

"Dinner for two?" The maitre d' asked.

"Yes. Reservations for Cooper," Bailey answered as Beth excused herself to the ladies' room.

"This way, please."

Bailey followed the older gentleman through a darkened interior. From what she saw, the restaurant didn't have a table that sat more than four. It was certainly an intimate setting. She took a seat at the table he indicated.

"Hi. I'm Linda. I'll be your server this evening. Can I start you out with something while you wait?" Linda asked.

"I would love a glass of sweet tea, please."

"And your companion?"

"I don't know. Perhaps you can bring the wine list and maybe another tea."

"Certainly. I will return with your drinks."

"Thanks." Bailey fidgeted with the menu. She looked up when Beth joined her. "You take my breath away."

"Thank you. You are remarkably easy to please," Beth said modestly.

"It's true. You're beautiful."

"Again, thank you."

"Do you need a few minutes to look over the menu?" Linda asked as she delivered the drinks. "Would you like a glass of wine?"

"No thank you." Beth answered.

"We need a few minutes if you don't mind."

"I'll be over there." Linda indicated a place in the shadows. "Just let me know when you're ready."

"Thank you." Bailey waited until the waitress was out of earshot. "The service is pretty prompt."

"That it is. Have you ever eaten here before?"

"No. You?" Bailey asked. She didn't know how often Jerry and Beth had gone to dinner by themselves. She knew though that eventually they would have a place or five in common. At least they hadn't dated locally. They had only moved back after the wedding.

"No." Beth said. "I feel like a real grown-up out on a real date."

"Me too." Bailey grinned and opened her menu. "Cindy said the coq au vin is good. She actually recommended this."

"I was wondering. I thought you were pretty much a steak and potatoes person."

"I am usually. But I thought this was a bit more romantic than a place where you throw peanut shells on the floor," Bailey said.

"You were right. This is nice." Beth put her menu down. "I guess you can call the waitress over."

Linda appeared out of nowhere. "Have we decided?"

"Yes, ma'am."

"So what made you go back blonde?" Beth asked as soon the waitress left.

"Two things really. The first is Cindy asked. Which is not really the important one. I just thought you would like it better."

"I do actually. Not that I don't think you're beautiful with multi-colored hair, I tend to like the blonde." Beth smiled.

"I'll be honest with you. It's the first time I've cared," Bailey said.

"Really? I feel honored," Beth teased. "So I was wondering. You mentioned that racing cycle you had to the kids, and I've not seen you in shorts lately."

"Ah. Well Uncle Dwight has always said there are two types of bikers: those who have laid one down and those who haven't yet."

"And you? Which are you?"

"I've laid one down. Actually a few, but all the rest were dirt bikes when we were kids. This one. This one scared me."

"Tell me about it?" Beth asked softly.

"You don't want to hear about it, do you?" Bailey wasn't sure she wanted to talk about it, but Beth had asked. She'd promised herself that she would answer all questions honestly. She wanted this relationship to work more than she'd wanted anything before.

"Yes. I do."

"You know, I think the only person who knows is Brian. I never even told Liz, until she got it out of me a few days ago. Then I didn't even tell her everything." Bailey took a long sip of tea. "It was late. I'd been drinking. Probably done something else illegal. I don't remember. I was wearing a full helmet and I was wearing leather. But I still got some horrible road rash. I bruised pretty much everything and tore something in my knee. It was honestly one of the few times in my life I was certain I was about to die."

"When did that happen?" Beth asked. Bailey thought she looked radiant.

"Before rehab, obviously." Bailey attempted to grin. "It was a long time ago. I kept the big bike, sold the racing one and bought a car. Some guy found me, took me to the local hospital. I called Brian. He paid cash and we used someone else's name."

"You didn't want the bad press?" Beth leaned back in her seat, crossed her arms and looked at her.

"No. I didn't want you guys to find out. I didn't care about the public, but I didn't want my friends and family, the people I love, to find out about it. Not long after you got married, Liz kicked the shit out of me and I went to rehab. End of story."

"Maybe." Beth reached across and put her hand in Bailey's hand on the table. "Want to talk about something else?"

"What do you have in mind?" They had to lean back to allow the waitress to set their plates in front of them.

"This looks amazing."

"So do you." Bailey grinned.

AFTER DINNER, BAILEY helped Beth back on the motorcycle and headed for the beach. The moon hung low over the water. The air was slightly cool. She felt the warmth of Beth's body pressed against her back. It was too nice an opportunity to miss. Smiling a little at the sudden romantic thought, she pulled the motorcycle over and parked near the seawall.

"What's going on?" Beth asked, her voice slightly dazed.

"Well it's a nice night. Full moon. Thought a stroll along the beach would be nice."

"Or just making out on the seawall?"

"If you'd rather. Come here."

"With pleasure. I feel like I've been waiting my entire life to get here." Beth looked up and met Bailey halfway. The kisses started out slow and gentle. They didn't last that way for long.

"I, uh, think we need to either stop or we're about to scare some pelicans." Bailey struggled to catch her breath after several long minutes.

"Your place. It's closer," Beth panted.

"As you wish." Bailey helped her back on the motorcycle and headed for home.

She pulled the motorcycle into the garage and waited for Beth to dismount. She quickly did the same, tossing her helmet on the shelf. It wasn't real yet, but it was becoming so.

Bailey held the kitchen door open. She had done this many times before, but not with someone for whom she had real feelings. "You thirsty?"

"Actually, yes."

"Water, juice or soda?" she asked as she got two glasses out of the cabinet.

"What, no tea?" Beth asked.

"I've never gotten the hang of making it. I buy the gallons but I'm out," she explained just to keep an awkward silence at bay. "So here's your juice, m'lady."

"Thank you, ma'am." Beth curtsied. "The furniture looks really good in here."

"Thanks." Bailey put her glass down before walking up to Beth and taking her hand. "You look amazing."

"You are such a flatterer."

"Tis true." She placed her hand beneath Beth's chin and guided her into a very soft kiss. It didn't remain soft for long. "Upstairs?"

"Yes please."

"Right this way." Bailey was never sure how they managed

to get upstairs, and in the bedroom, but suddenly they were there. "You okay?"

"Yeah."

"I uh. Before this." Bailey took a deep breath and cupped Beth's face in her hands. "I love you and I want you so much, but this is the point of no return. I can't go back to just friends after this."

"You won't have to," Beth whispered. "I've waited decades for this. Make love to me, Bailey."

Bailey had dreamed of hearing those words. She needed no further encouragement. She dropped her hands down and wrapped them around Beth's waist before leaning in for another kiss.

Beth's heels made them the same height. Bailey took advantage and traced a line of kisses across her jawline to her ear. She felt hands explore her arms and the back of her neck and shoulders as she let her hands roam down Beth's sides, her back and finally under that little black dress. It wasn't long before that dress had to be removed.

"Holy shit." She stepped back for a moment to take in the view before her.

"What? You've seen me naked or nearly naked before." Beth seemed slightly self-conscious.

"Yeah. But never like this and never about to be in my bed and sweetheart, that is one sight I don't think I could ever get tired of." She gently guided her until Beth was sitting on the edge of the bed.

Bailey kicked off her boots and started to take her shirt off before catching the look on Beth's face. She took the hint and unbuttoned it slowly, letting it fall to the floor before joining her on the bed. There was more skin touching between them than there had been. It wasn't enough. Bailey laid them both on the bed and stretched out next to Beth.

Bailey turned her mind off for the moment, giving up any thoughts of doubt or awkwardness. She felt the rush, the desire to make it hard, fast and intense, but she slowed down and started over. No matter what, she wanted it to last. Every inch of Beth deserved a thorough exploration. Bailey let her mouth and hands map the scene.

"Bailey," Beth moaned as deft hands removed her bra and tossed it to the floor.

"Hmm?" Bailey was too intent on her mission to verbalize an answer. There were breasts that needed to be caressed, nipples that needed to be sucked and more, so much more to explore.

"Naked. Need naked," Beth managed to say.

Wordlessly, Bailey rose on her knees and removed her undershirt and bra. She arched an eyebrow at Beth and continued down to unbuckle her belt at the expectant nod. Soon she was in nothing more than her underwear and melted beneath the heat of Beth's gaze.

"This as well?"

"Oh yeah."

That task finished, she stretched out beside Beth, ready to pick up right where she left off. A warm mouth was suddenly surrounding her breast while a gentle tongue coerced a nipple into hardness. Beth's hands pushed her back on the bed and Bailey soon felt them everywhere. For a moment she thought about fighting to take control, but there was no need. It would be a long night for both of them. Hopefully only the first of a lifetime.

BAILEY SAT UP and looked down at her sleeping companion. She had never classified herself as emotional or a romantic, but this was hard to believe for a moment. The very thought took her breath away and made it feel as if there was a large balloon inflating in her chest.

"You've changed a lot, you know." Beth's voice was soft in the darkness.

"I thought you were asleep."

"I had the feeling I was being watched. It's a parent reaction. Everything okay?" She rolled over and faced Bailey.

Bailey smiled. "Wonderful. Absolutely wonderful. You?"

"I'm so very good."

"Yes you are," Bailey agreed. It had been amazing.

"Silly. No this. I'm amazed. I can't believe it took us so long to get here, but I don't think I'd change anything."

"No?" Bailey stretched back out and raised herself on her arm.

"Well, you've changed a lot. I noticed it a bit in Vienna, but I guess we haven't been around each other as much as we have recently. And I've changed too. Plus I wouldn't change a second of being a mom."

"No, that role suits you and your kids are awesome." Bailey leaned over for a kiss.

"Thanks." Beth pulled her closer. "Less talk."

"Definitely," It was the last thing either of them said until names were cried out in ecstasy.

"WE HAVE TO do something about the state of your larder, baby," Beth called upstairs.

"There's food in there," Bailey called back down.

"True. There is food," Beth admitted. "I was going to make breakfast, but is all you eat cereal? And dry pasta? Holy shit you have like every type of jarred pasta sauce known to man. You didn't go vegetarian, did you?"

"No. There's sandwich meat in the fridge," Bailey answered as she entered the kitchen and put her arms around Beth. "Morning."

"Morning." They broke apart after a lengthy kiss. "So, breakfast?"

"Any place around here to do brunch?" Bailey asked. "And when are the children supposed to be returned to you?"

"Not until this evening and yes there are several places that do brunch. Did you want to go somewhere?"

"Well that would require putting on actual clothes." Bailey indicated her cutoff sweats and t-shirt and then the robe Beth was wearing.

"Cereal it is, then. So what's up with all the dry pasta?" Beth asked.

"Well, as we know, Fiona never taught me to cook. And a few of the places out in LA didn't even have access to a working stove. I never learned to actually cook, you know. But it's not that hard to boil some water and heat up some sauce. When I'm not eating out or touring, I live off salads, pasta and sandwiches. It beats microwave dinners. Easy meals." Bailey shrugged. "Noodles, sauce, and some rotisserie chicken is a pretty quick and easy thing to make. And it's pretty hard for me to fuck that up. One of the guys on our very first tour taught me that."

"At least you try."

"Thanks. You know I always thought about taking a class or two, but I must admit I have a bit of fear."

"Fear of what?"

"Being the dumb kid in the class," she admitted. "Anyway, I manage. So. What did you want to do today?"

"I have no plans. I just have to be home by five to greet my monsters."

"What do you say to a lazy afternoon watching bad movies

and making out on the couch?"

"I think that's one of the best ideas I've heard in a very long time."

Chapter Twenty-two

BAILEY SPENT THE morning painting the master bedroom. She decided to take a break around lunch. She was hungry, tired and wearing as much paint as the walls it seemed. She took a glass of water out to the porch and sat on the swing. She gently pushed it with one bare foot, watching the street. She was surprised to see Beth's car turn into her driveway.

"You look comfortable. And paint spattered," Beth said when she got out of the car and walked to the porch.

"I'm taking a break and annoying my neighbors," Bailey said happily.

"How can you be annoying your neighbors already?" Beth asked.

"Well just one particular neighbor. You remember Mr. Braddock? He remembers me. Dude already tried to file to get an ordinance against me buying the house."

"Wasn't he the guidance counselor in junior high?"

"Yep. He was convinced that Mike, Scott and I egged his house two years in a row," Bailey said.

"But you did, didn't you?"

"Yeah, but he couldn't prove it."

"So he's holding a grudge?"

"Something like that." She patted the space next to her on the swing. "Here take a seat."

"Thanks." Beth sat with one foot tucked beneath her.

"My pleasure. Anyway, he's been glaring at me every time he sees me. It's like he's waiting for me to break some ordinance so he can call the cops." She pointed to his house. "I can see the curtain draw back. It's like he's checking every so often to see what I'm doing or where I am."

"What are you going to do about it?" Beth asked.

"I have a whole campaign of intimidation planned. Wanna help?"

"Sure. What do you have in mind?"

"Making out on my front porch." Bailey wagged her eyebrows.

"That I'll help with anytime." Beth leaned in for a long, slow kiss.

"So I have a question. Do you want to be my date to the

wedding?" Bailey asked when they came up for air.

"The matron of honor and the best person? Of course."

"You're still a matron of honor even though you're divorced? Doesn't that re-maiden you?" Bailey asked.

"I don't think you can be re-maidened. I'm not even sure that's a thing, goofy. But that does lead me to a question I have for you. When Kat gets here how are you going to introduce me?"

"As my girlfriend. That's the appropriate title for now, right?" Bailey asked. She'd heard from Kat the day before and they had planned the upcoming visit.

"I suppose. I feel a bit old for girlfriend. Hey what do you mean by for now?" Beth looked at her with an eyebrow raised.

"Nothing. So you wanna see the color you picked out for the bedroom and how it looks on the walls?" Bailey changed the subject.

"It looks pretty good on you." Beth leaned in again and began lightly kissing Bailey's neck.

"You're just on lunch aren't you?" Bailey asked with some difficulty.

"Yeah. Why?"

"I was wondering how you'd look paint splattered. How about after work you and the kids come over for pizza?" She pulled back before she caused Beth to be late back to work.

"That sounds good. Should we plan for the night?"

"Of course. It's Friday, right? Want to see the room?" Bailey got off the swing and held her hand out. Beth took it without hesitation.

"Have you decided what you're going to do with the other rooms?" Beth asked as they went inside and up the stairs.

"I have a plan. First I have to get the apartment over the garage done. I have some sound engineers flying in next week."

"Still going to make it a studio?"

"Yep. Here. What do think?" Bailey pushed open the door to the master bedroom.

"I think your talent as a musician is second only, well third only to your ability to paint a wall." Beth smirked.

"Third? Need I ask what my first talent is?" Bailey said. She had a good idea what the answer would be.

"You can remind us both tonight. It looks great."

"Thanks. Did you skip lunch?" Bailey asked. She mentally went through what food she had on hand to offer.

"Nope. I ate between calls so I could run an errand and stop by here during my lunch hour."

"How much longer do you have before you have to leave to get back?" Bailey asked.

"I have enough time for one really good, long kiss on the porch." Beth held out her hand. "Come on. Let's go give Mr. Braddock something to get upset about."

"As you wish." Bailey felt like skipping down the stairs.

"HEY, BAILEY, CAN you come down to Fortune's?" Liz asked when Bailey answered the phone.

"Why?" Bailey sat the guitar to the side. She was taking advantage of her recent events to mine inspiration from them. Plus, she had no plans with Beth as she had a Chamber event to attend. "I'm trying to write here."

"Because your girlfriend is here wasted off her ass. And Kyle is circling," Liz said. "I swear I only saw her drink a glass of wine. It's strange, Bailey. I think you should come and get her."

"I thought you said Beth doesn't need a hero to ride in on an iron horse and save her?" Bailey said.

"Don't throw my words at me, Bailey Ray Cooper. I'm serious. I've already gone over there to ask her to leave, but she won't budge. Come on before Kyle tries something."

"I'll be right there. Shit." Bailey disconnected, pulled on her boots and grabbed her keys. This was going to be interesting. Right before she walked out the door she called Elvis. She didn't want to leave him home alone just in case.

When Bailey got to Fortune's, she found Beth practically cornered by Kyle. At first she saw red. She knew she could easily get all of them into a lot of trouble, so she took a deep breath and centered herself before walking over.

"Bailey!" Beth greeted her. "Thought you were writing something."

"Hey, baby. I was." Bailey walked over and put her arms around Beth. "Thought I'd take a break and come hang out. You having fun?"

"Kyle was just asking me something. He just bought me another glass of wine. I've only had two. Weird." Beth shook her head. "I'm glad you came."

"Me too." Bailey couldn't help the smile that crossed her face when Beth snuggled closer. "Hello, Kyle."

"Bailey. How ya doing?" Kyle looked a bit startled. He tried to ease the empty glasses from the table.

"Leave those," Bailey told him. "Unless you want to tell me

what you put in that."

"Really? Are you accusing me of tampering with a lady's drink?" he said indignantly. However, she noticed he didn't raise his voice above a quiet conversation volume.

"Yes. I've seen this woman down half a bottle of wine and not act like this. I've also seen way too many people act like this on one drink or less when something was put in their drink. I can call the cops and they can test it or you can fess up now." She stood just in front of Beth and crossed her arms. She wanted to see just how far he would take this.

"Seriously, I have no idea," he stammered.

"Fine. Let me put it this way. Stay away from my girlfriend. If I have to take her to the hospital, that glass is going to the police. You come sniffing around here again and it goes to the cops. I hear this happens to anyone else, and again, it goes to the cops. Got me?" She knew he was too thick to question what she said. Like most bullies, he was scared also of having his crimes brought to light. Bailey promised herself she would see him get his just desserts one day.

He tried unsuccessfully to turn on his charm. "Now, Bailey."

"Nope. There's no wiggle room. Again. Do you understand me? You better, asshole or I'll rain down a fuck-ton of trouble on your head." She didn't flinch.

"Yes." He slunk away.

"Hey, you wanna go home?" She asked the woman who was suddenly in her arms. She felt Beth yawn and relax against her.

"Am I not?" Beth roused a bit. "Yes. Take me home, Bailey."

"Okay then." She grabbed a napkin and used it to pick up the wine glasses Kyle had left on the table. She placed them gently in Beth's purse and then helped her out of the restaurant. He was watching her from across the room.

Bailey put an arm around Beth and helped her out of the restaurant. She nodded to Liz as they left. She had parked close to the building and had left the truck running. She escorted Beth to it and opened the door for her.

"Hey it's Elvis." Beth exclaimed when she looked inside the truck.

"Yes it is. Come on." Bailey helped her get in the truck. "Let me know if you feel sick."

"I so don't feel sick. You staying with me? I missed you. I don't like waking up without you."

"Boy you're very talkative tonight." She was amused. It wasn't the first time she'd seen Beth drunk, but it was the first time after they'd become involved.

"You could do something about that, you know." Beth let her hand run up Bailey's thigh. "How come you're never wearing the leather pants?"

"I don't usually wear those just around the house." Bailey concentrated on the road. It was difficult. She pulled into the driveway with relief. "Let's get you inside."

"Yes, please. And let's get you into bed. Shit. My folks are here." Beth groaned.

"It'll be okay. You're an adult, remember?" It was hard not to laugh. Bailey helped both passengers out of the truck. Elvis went immediately to the door.

"Yeah I know." Beth sighed. She blinked a little when her father opened the door. "Hi, Daddy."

"Beth? Bailey? What's going on?" Mr. Forsyth held the door open for them.

"I'll explain in a minute." Bailey directed Beth to the couch. "Hang out here a minute, Okay? You need some water."

"What happened?" Ms. Forsyth asked. The concern was obvious in her voice.

"I think her wine was laced with something." She took the glasses out of Beth's purse and put them in a plastic bag. "She'll be okay. She just needs rest and water."

"You sure? Do you need us to stay?" Ms. Forsyth asked.

"Nah, I got it." Bailey waved them away. "I'll stay with her."

"The kids have to be up early and they get dropped off at eight in the morning at day camp," Ms. Forsyth said. "And they usually take their lunch."

"She's got this," Mr. Forsyth reassured his wife. "Call us if you need us, Bailey. Thanks for taking care of our little girl."

"Anytime, sir." She poured a glass of water and took it back to Beth as the Forsyths showed themselves out. "Hey, baby. You need to drink some water."

"Thanks. So did you get rid of the old folks?" Beth asked when Bailey joined her on the couch.

"Your parents have left, yes." She struggled not to laugh. "I'm not sure your mother would like hearing herself be called old, but they have left the building."

"Good. Come here." Beth pulled her down on the couch and kissed her. "I have a serious question. What exactly is a fuck-ton?"

"It's a standard unit of measurement. See there's a ton, a butt-ton and a fuck-ton." Bailey answered distractedly. Beth was letting her hands roam.

Beth murmured. "Do me a favor and don't help the kids with math, okay?"

"You don't want them using that on a test?" She stood. "I need to check and make sure they're asleep."

"You really care about them, don't you?" Beth asked as Bailey crept down the hallway. The doors to both rooms were open. Jacob was asleep with his arms wrapped around his favorite stuffed animal and Rebecca was sprawled across the bed, taking up way too much space, just like her mother.

"I do. Your kids are pretty amazing." She answered when she returned to the living room.

"Have you ever thought about having your own?"

"No," Bailey said sharply. "Sorry. No, I'm not a mother. Do you want more?"

"I don't know. Depends on whether I have a full partner or not. I don't think I could be a good single parent to three kids, especially if one were an infant. At least I couldn't be the parent I would want to be."

"I can see that. I think you're an amazing mom, but I will say based on my own mother, I don't have much to compare to. But your parents are pretty great." She offered her hand. Beth used it to pull herself off the couch.

"That reminds me. I saw some paperwork with your name on it over at dad's house. What's up with that?" Beth asked as Bailey lead them to the bedroom.

"You don't know?" Bailey looked at her oddly. "Your dad's my accountant."

"How long? He never told me." Beth fell back on the bed and struggled with her shoes.

"Funny story actually." Beth was still drunk but making sense. Bailey felt it was safe to talk to her, although she knew there was a good chance Beth wouldn't remember the conversation in the morning. "There I was out in LA working three jobs just to stay in microwave noodles and your dad calls me up. He says he and your mom are going to Hawaii and they have a pretty long layover in LA. Your mom apparently wanted to see the sign. Anyway, they invited me to lunch. So I met them at the restaurant at their hotel."

"I remember they went to Hawaii, but he never said anything about seeing you in LA."

"I don't know why. Well actually I do. I just can't believe he stuck to it. I asked him not to say anything. I mean I met them for lunch and then got the dad speech from your father, you know the 'be careful, take precautions, don't trust' speech. He told me if I ever needed anything to call him. Then he took me to a bank and we set up an account. He put me on a very strict budget. He's handled everything since."

Beth stopped getting undressed and watched her. "Wow. Why didn't you want him to tell me?"

"Well at first it confused me as to why he was doing this. I mean here he was acting like a father and I've never had one. So I asked. Made him laugh. Anyway, after that I just didn't want y'all to know things were so bad. I danced on a very fine line between homelessness and severe poverty. If it hadn't been for your dad's guidance I'm not sure what would have happened. And I was kind of ashamed."

"Why?" It was a simple question without a simple answer.

"Because I left because of you." Bailey smoothed Beth's hair away from her face. She felt bad, using this time to tell the story. She knew Beth would probably not remember much if any of it, but it was safer this way. "You remember that fight we had at that frat party? I was insanely jealous. And it served me right of course. I had assumed you would always be there when I wanted you. You see, I knew already that if I ever got you it would be forever. I don't know how, I just knew that if I allowed us to exist it would be a lifetime thing. In high school I was too full of myself, too determined to be someone other than just another Cooper, and too interested in the variety of girls around. College scared me. It was too big, too much. I couldn't deal with classes of two hundred. So I partied and fooled around and expected you to be there."

"I couldn't wait anymore. It hurt too much. You broke my heart, Bailey. When I saw you that day at lunch, I didn't know if I wanted to hit or kiss you. I never, never got over you. You can't run away on me this time. Not now. Not after this."

"I'm not going anywhere," Bailey promised. "But I need you to know that I'm not all sunshine and roses. I don't have a normal schedule and I don't live a normal life. I don't want to control you or let you exist because of me. I mean I want you to work and be your own person. I think it's damaging otherwise."

"Good. I know and I agree. I love you, Bailey. I always have. I loved Jerry, but not as much. Honestly, he wasn't a bastard until the end. It's gotta be hard knowing your wife is in love with someone else." Beth looked slightly confused.

"I never hope to know. But know this. I'm not running

anywhere. I'm staying here; staying with you for as long as you let me stay. And I'm so, so sorry. I will spend the rest of my life making it up to you if you let me."

"I'll let you. You can start now."

"Now?"

"Please."

"Your wish is my command."

Chapter Twenty-three

BAILEY PICKED THE kids up from day camp a few days later. Beth was working and her mother and father were on vacation. She was glad to do it though. It helped break up the monotony of painting rooms. She knew she could have hired a crew to redo the house, but she liked it. She liked doing things herself, but it did get dull after a while.

"What's up, sport?" She asked as she noticed Jacob. He'd been quiet the whole way home.

"Nothing." Jacob looked miserable. He was sitting on the couch kicking his feet with his arms crossed.

"That's not a nothing look. That's a something's up look." She sat down next to him. "So what's up?"

"One of the kids in my group at the camp called me a sissy," he said very softly.

"Oh really?" Out of reflex, Bailey looked for his mother even though she knew Beth was still at work. "Why?"

"'Cause I wouldn't kick the turtle," he said.

"Good. I'm proud that you didn't kick the turtle. It's not cool to hurt something that can't defend itself," she reassured him.

"Really?" He climbed in her lap.

"Really. I know it's hard, Jacob. I really do. But when someone calls you a name like sissy you should try to not let it bother you." She put her arms around him and held him close. He seemed so small and fragile.

"Why?" He asked. He buried his head in her shoulder.

"Well, basically he called you a girl. Is that an insult?" she asked. She wanted him to think about it logically.

"Girls wear dresses though. He told me I should run home and put on a dress like the little sissy I am." Jacob didn't look at her. He sounded close to tears.

"Not all girls wear dresses. I don't always. And my cousin Scott sometimes wears dresses." She sighed and held him closer. "It took me a long time to understand that how you dress doesn't make you who you are."

"But what if you want to wear a dress? And you're a boy?" She had to strain to hear him. He barely spoke the words out loud.

"Well, do you want to wear a dress?" He shrugged into her.

"I'm sure we can find one of Rebecca's dresses that would fit you. You can try it out. You want to do that?" She knew from her own experiences that a safe space to experiment was golden.

"You wouldn't think it was silly or sissy?" He risked looking at her.

"Have you met my cousin Scott? He is so not a sissy, and look." She pulled out her phone and brought up her gallery looking for a certain picture. "Here. See that?"

"Are you in a suit?" he asked in awe.

"Yep. And that's Scott. In a full formal dress." She showed him the picture of the two of them at an awards banquet. She and Scott shared the desire to dress however they wanted. They had played it up for the event.

"Wow." He took the phone and examined the picture closely.

"Yeah. So see, boys can wear dresses and girls can wear suits. It all depends on what you want to do." She moved him to where he was sitting up and not hiding in her arms any longer. "I have an idea. When I was in Germany once, one of the bands had a thing. They all wore this matching pink dress. Guys and girls. Let's get your sister and we can play pretend. What do you think?"

"Okay." He seemed encouraged by that idea. "Will you wear one too?"

"If we can find one of your mom's that fits me," she said. "Go get Rebecca."

"Okay, Bailey." He bounded off to find his sister.

It took a little digging, but they all found something that would work. The dress she borrowed from Beth's closet didn't fit anywhere. It was too short in length and too big in the bust. They didn't find anything too absurd for Rebecca, so they improvised and threw an old belt around a T-shirt Jerry had left behind and paired that with some leggings. Jacob fared better. He ended up in a large sundress and socks. They looked absurd and loved it.

Bailey played several different types of rock songs. They improvised with tennis rackets for guitars and a bucket for drums. Rebecca and Jacob took turns singing. They played like that for hours, at least until it was time to order dinner.

They spent the rest of the evening eating pizza, talking in funny accents and perfecting their air guitar. Finally exhausted, they settled down to watch a movie. When Beth found them, all three were asleep.

Bailey felt a gentle hand shaking her shoulder and woke to see Beth's puzzled face staring at her.

"Bailey, sweetheart. What were y'all doing?"

"Playing rock group." Bailey stretched. "Someone called Jacob a sissy at camp."

"And putting him in a dress to play tennis racket guitar was your solution?" Beth asked.

"Well not really. Hang on." Bailey managed to extract herself from the sleeping children and followed Beth into the kitchen.

Beth grinned. "I don't know if that dress is right for you or not."

"I can't quite fill it." Bailey pulled at the loose fabric on her chest. "I seem to be missing something."

"I don't know about that. It seems to me that you are not missing anything." Beth waggled her eyebrows. "So, about the dresses?"

"Oh yeah, so some kid called Jacob a sissy because he wouldn't kick a turtle. That got a conversation going on how people dress because the kid told him to run home and put on a dress. I think he was intrigued by the idea. So I came up with a safe way for him to try it. Rebecca volunteered an old sundress and he kept his own socks. You're not mad, are you?" Bailey realized at that moment she may have overstepped her bounds. She was scared for a moment that Beth would be mad. She cringed against the expected anger.

"No. Not at all. Hell, my brother went through a phase at four where he carried a purse." Beth took Bailey's hand and dispelled all of Bailey's doubts. "That was pretty clever. Thank you for being there for him. Did it make him feel better?"

"Yeah. We ate pizza, rocked out and had a great time."

Jacob ran into the kitchen. "Hey, Mommy. We played German band. I was the lead singer sometimes and Rebecca and I took turns playing drums. Bailey showed us pictures of a band and we dressed up like them. It was so much fun."

"Great." Beth scooped him up and hugged him. "How was the rest of your day?"

"It was okay. But it was so much better after Bailey picked us up."

"It really was," Rebecca added as she stumbled into the kitchen rubbing her eyes. "Can we move into Bailey's?"

"We'll make decisions later," Beth said. "Now pajamas on and teeth brushed."

"That's a good question, you know," Bailey said after the kids left. "If things keep progressing, would you want to move in with me?"

Beth turned to face her. "Are you asking?"

"Yeah. I mean not right away, but if you want to stop dating and do the whole step two in the lesbian handbook and move in together, would you want to?"

"Bailey?" Soft fingers covered her mouth.

"Yes?"

"Those were an awful lot of words for a question that could have been asked: 'Beth, do you want to move in with me?'"

"Beth, sweetheart, love of my life, would you do me the honor of one day moving in with me?"

"I don't know. It's not like you have a pool or anything."

"That's what it would take? A pool?" Bailey raised an eyebrow. "Me and Elvis aren't good enough? You need a pool?"

Beth grinned. "Believe me, you're more than enough incentive. I don't need anything else. So provisionally I'd say I'll give my affirmative answer when you formally ask."

"Formally? Okay, you've been working too much, you're starting to talk in contracts." Bailey gave her a quick kiss. Her heart felt lighter than ever. "I saved you some pizza. Do you want me to heat it up for you?"

"I'd love that." Beth kicked off her flats and sat at the table. "You're amazing."

"Not really. I just figured you'd be hungry."

"While you do that, I'll go shoo my kids into bed and change into something less business casual. I'll be back in a minute, okay?" Beth picked up her shoes and walked down the hall.

Bailey had pizza ready and waiting when Beth returned several minutes later. They sat at the table for a long time talking about the day's events before they decided it was time for bed.

"DOES IT EVER bother you that you didn't know your father?" Beth asked quietly. She'd been so quiet, Bailey thought she'd fallen asleep.

"Sometimes. You worried about the kids?" Bailey asked.

"Yeah. It's a fear."

"They'll be fine. There were times when I wondered who it was or what he was like. My mother has issues, I know that. I've always known that. Naturally I wondered how it would be with a parent who loved me. Your kids have that. They will never doubt that you love them."

"How did you survive?" Bailey could see the years reflected in Beth's eyes.

"I had you, Mike, Cindy and Liz. I had your parents. Uncle Dwight and Aunt Ellen. My grandparents. I had enough people in my life who loved me that I was able to use that to keep from completely killing myself," Bailey answered honestly. Somehow she had internalized enough of the good influences around her to balance her mother's toxicity.

"It's amazing. You're amazing," Beth said in awe.

"No, sweetheart, I'm just real fucking lucky."

"Well I think you're amazing."

"Thank you." Bailey leaned in for a kiss. "And thank you for allowing me to sleep over."

"It was sleep, remember," Beth reminded her. "I've got to work in the morning."

"So, the rehearsal dinner is coming up," Bailey said. "Wanna go in one car?"

"Yeah. If you're okay with that," Beth said. "We're going to the wedding together after all."

"Why wouldn't I be okay with that?" Bailey asked.

"Just we've been together an awful lot since you came home. I didn't know if it was too much for you."

"No. Not at all." Bailey was amazed at that. "Matter of fact, I miss you guys when you're not with me. I really look forward to the weekends when y'all can stay over."

"And the random night you stay at my house." Beth grinned. "I'm glad you're not getting tired of us, because I can't seem to get enough of you."

"Believe it or not, that's how I feel with you and the kids. I never knew I liked kids until Eric was born." Bailey had never been around kids that much before then.

"He looks like you, you know, but not as much as Sarah does," Beth said.

"I know," Bailey said. "My mother swore he was mine when he was born. It would be a little hard for that to happen."

"Especially since I was in the delivery room with Cindy." Beth said. "I wonder if that's why Ms. Arnoux hates you. If old man Arnoux was your father."

"I've wondered. Not going to lie, but I've never asked." She hadn't. She was still a little scared of the answer.

Beth sighed. "I can understand why. That woman is scary. I'm worried she's going to do something drastic at the wedding. She's nuts."

"Is that your fatal flaw? Worry?" Bailey asked. "Not that it's fatal, but that's your big thing, isn't it? You worry too much."

"Yeah. I worry over everything. It's what I do. I gnaw at things until I either have to give up or find a way to make it work," Beth admitted.

"I don't think that's a fatal flaw, or a flaw at all. At least not for me, but then I usually jump in without worrying about consequences," Bailey said.

"Guess that's why we work." Beth smiled. "Now goodnight, Bailey. You have a long day of helping Mike with stuff tomorrow."

"I do," Beth said, "and you have to work, poor baby." She brushed Beth's hair back from her eyes. "Man I love you."

"I love you too. What brought that on?"

"I don't know. Just kinda welled up. Anyway, good night." Bailey let her hand drift a little lower.

"Goodnight, sweetheart." Beth closed her eyes. "Bailey, if you keep that up we'll never get to sleep."

"And that would be bad." She leaned over for a kiss. "Very bad."

"So bad," Beth responded. She gasped as Bailey's wondering hand caught a sensitive spot. "Evil. You are so evil."

"Should I stop?" Bailey asked without waiting for an answer.

"Fuck no." Beth pulled her close. "Do not stop."

Bailey pulled back and looked into Beth's eyes for a long moment. If she had any doubts left, the love and desire extinguished it. It was a long night, but eventually they did get some sleep.

Chapter Twenty-four

"THEY HAVE A pool?" Jacob asked from the backseat.

"No. They just made us wear swimming suits to be stupid," Rebecca answered.

"It's true," Bailey said. "There's no pool. It's just a large hole in the ground. We dress like we're going swimming to make it look more interesting."

"No way," Jacob said. "Mom said there's a pool. That you guys used to go swimming over there in high school because Mike and Liz were the only ones in your group with a pool."

"He's so knowledgeable for a little one," Bailey said to Beth.

"He gets that from me," Beth buffed her nails on her shirt. "I'm glad Dwight's got the all clear. I know Cindy's been worried sick about this wedding business."

"Well now that's one worry off their plates," Bailey said. She pulled into her uncle's driveway. "Okay, kids, don't let any of the cousins hold you under water."

"We won't," Rebecca promised. "Besides, Sarah won't let them do anything."

"That's probably true," Bailey agreed as she parked. Liz's daughter Sarah could get just about anyone to do what she wanted. "All heathens out of my car."

"What are you going to do if your mom's here?" Beth asked as she watched the kids run around the house to the back.

"Deal. It's all I can do." Bailey sighed. "I can't not face her, besides, I don't even know if she'll show up. She doesn't like to leave the bar."

"Well, if she's here you won't be alone. I'm here. I'll knock her down a bit if I need to for you." She flexed her arm as a show of strength.

Bailey snorted. "You're a goober, Elizabeth Forsyth. But I love you anyway."

"And here I thought you loved me because I'm a goober." Beth opened her door. "Come on, let's go congratulate your uncle Dwight for being able to live longer."

"I'm right behind you."

Bailey took Beth's hand and they followed the path around to the back of the house. Dwight was holding court there. He was ensconced in a lounge chair under an umbrella and was watching his children and grandchildren play in the pool. Mike and Scott were manning the grill. Ian was in the pool with Cindy, Eric and Sarah. Paul Cooper, Mike's older brother was sitting in the shade next to his father. His children were playing away from the others. Bailey didn't see his wife.

"Bailey!" Strong arms wrapped around her and lifted her off the ground.

"Jordan? Dude you've gotten strong." She laughed as he put her back down. "It's good to see you. How long have you been here?"

"I got in late last night. This must be Beth?" He let go of Bailey and offered his hand. "Jordan Cooper."

"I remember," Beth answered. "You were a bit smaller last time I saw you."

"Army life will do that to you." He stood up to his full height. He was the tallest as well as the youngest. "Heath won't be here. Mike said they left word."

"Well, at least he'll show for the wedding," Bailey said. "Where's Liz?"

"She's inside. Her and mom are getting the food seasoned. Celia is in there as well making sure no seasoning gets on her food." He rolled his eyes. "Honestly, Paul would marry someone as odd as him."

"You forget, Cuz, to them, we're the weird ones." she said and turned back to Beth. "I see the kids are already in the pool."

"Well, let's go get something to drink and sit for a few," Beth said. "We should talk to your uncle as well."

"Yes, Dad would love it if someone interrupted Paul. He's going off on the grandparents' estate again," Jordan said. "Beer is in the white cooler and everything else is in the blue one."

"Thanks, Jordan." They walked over to the patio while Jordan jumped in the pool. "Did you want to get in the pool later?"

"I don't know. It depends on how out of hand this gets," Beth said. "I remember when you guys would have parties in school. Y'all can get wild."

"Very true," Bailey said. "Guess I get to be the tame one this time around."

"Hey, Bailey. Beth." Dwight waved at them. "Y'all come take a seat."

"Thanks. Glad to see you out of the hospital." Bailey kissed him on the forehead. "You look good."

"You do look very well," Beth agreed as she turned her chair to watch the pool. Her kids were playing with Eric and Sarah.

"You both flatter me." Dwight winked at them. "Paul was just mentioning that we should sell the house your grandparents built on the land my grandparents owned."

"I think it would be a better use," Paul said. "It's just sitting there rotting." Unlike the rest of the Coopers, who were mostly blond and fair, Paul was dark like his mother. Bailey had always wondered if he refused to act like the rest because he didn't look like them.

"Mike lives in the cabin," Bailey said. "Of course after he and Cindy get married...actually I'm not sure what they're doing. I guess they'll live in Cindy's house."

Paul ignored everything Bailey said. "That property could be developed into something."

"I have a vague idea of what to do with it," Dwight said. "I'll need to speak with Fiona as well. It's part her decision too."

"Right." Paul rolled his eyes. "I'm going to check on my kids."

"He's still an ass," Bailey said. Beth and Dwight nodded. "I'll be right back. Anyone need anything while I'm up?"

"Nope. Thanks, baby." Beth squeezed her hand. "I'm just going to watch my kids play and keep Dwight company."

"I'll sit here and soak up the attention of a pretty woman," Dwight teased. "Liz and Ellen are in the kitchen if you're looking."

"That's not the room I need to visit, but I'll stop in and check on them. Thanks." Bailey walked inside and headed down the hall to the bathroom. She stopped when someone appeared just ahead of her.

"Guess this means you're fucking or are you just playing dad?" Fiona's voice was full of hatred. Bailey heard it clearly for the first time. The woman had appeared out of nowhere.

"My relationship with Beth and her children isn't really any of your business," Bailey said coldly. Fiona blocked the way forward. Bailey's line of escape was the kitchen to her right or the back door behind her.

"You talk tough, but you don't know shit." The bottle in her mother's hand was almost empty. Bailey knew it wasn't the first her mom had gone through.

"Tell me then," Bailey challenged. "Tell me what made you a bitter, lonely old woman. Tell me why you hate me. Tell the reason why things are what they are."

"I don't have to tell you anything." Fiona clenched her empty hand into a fist. "Everything happens so easily for you. You have no idea what hardship is."

"Really?" Bailey scoffed. She couldn't help it. "Easy for me? Woman, you have no idea what it was like growing up with you as a mother."

"Why? Because you had no curfew. I let you do whatever the hell you wanted to do."

"Mama, seriously," Bailey ran her hand through her hair, "Ellen and Grandma had to teach me about personal hygiene. I had hand me downs until I started playing at the bar to earn money and could go to the thrift store myself. Grandma made sure I ate vegetables and brushed my teeth. My grandparents took me to the doctor, the dentist, the eye doctor and even the gynecologist. For fuck's sake, Mama, all you let me do was sleep at your house, do your laundry and wash your dishes." Bailey felt tears start and fought them. She didn't want to give her mother the satisfaction.

"Oh right, the neglected diva. I forgot. You survived," Fiona spat. "Fucking millionaire. Let's all pity Bailey Ray with her German car and hot dates. Poor you. You have no fucking idea what true suffering is, you ungrateful little bitch."

"That's enough, Fiona," Dwight said from behind his sister. "Leave Bailey alone. Why don't you go home?"

"Kicking me out?" Fiona asked him.

"Yes," Ellen said as she came up behind Bailey and placed a reassuring hand on Bailey's shoulder.

"Don't you have enough kids? You needed to steal mine?" Fiona said coldly. "Between you and my fucking parents, everyone always tried to take her away."

"If you had done fuck at all for her, we wouldn't have," Ellen said. It was the first time Bailey had heard her aunt speak that harshly. "We should have gotten you help years ago. Hell, we offered. Your father offered. I'm sure Bailey has."

"I have," Bailey said quietly.

"Oh right. Like you're going to do something for someone else," Fiona scoffed.

"She does all the time," Beth said. Somehow she, Liz and Mike had entered the kitchen without anyone else seeing them.

"Most generous person I know," Liz agreed.

Mike crossed his arms and leaned against the counter. "Saved my life more than once," he said. "I think you're confused, Aunt Fiona."

"That's it then? You all pick her over me?" The blood drained from Fiona's face.

Dwight walked closer to Fiona. "It's not like that. We love you both. Bailey's had it hard. We know you have as well, but a lot of that was of your own making. We've asked you before and I'm asking you now. Let us help you, Fi. We can get someone to run the bar and get you into a great place where you'll receive all sorts of personal help."

"You gonna pack me off like you did that one?" Fiona pointed at Mike. "I don't need your fucking charity and I don't need your fucking rehab."

"It helps, Mama. It's not a magic wand that makes everything better, but man is it the right place to start. Believe me," Bailey said.

"Fuck you. Fuck all of you," Fiona hissed. "I don't need any of you. You can all go set yourselves on fire for all the shits I give."

"Mama." Bailey sighed. Whatever else she was going to say died in her throat as her mother turned around and stormed out of the house. They heard her car peel out of the driveway. "Fuck."

"Well, now it's officially a Cooper Party," Mike said dryly. "The only thing we're missing is some asshole throwing people in the pool with their clothes on."

"Damn it!" Scott entered the kitchen, dripping wet. "Mom, you got any rice? My fucking kid brother decided to toss me in the pool. My fucking phone was in my pocket."

"Now it's official," Bailey said. "This family. It's amazing any of us are sane."

"You ought to see my family gatherings." Beth put an arm around her. "Want to go check on the kids?"

"Yeah." Bailey looked up and caught Liz's eyes. "It's okay. For Mama, that was kinda mild."

"You sure?" Liz asked.

"Yeah. The situation sucks, but you guys were awesome. Thanks." She looked around at the people gathered in the kitchen.

"Yeah, yeah," Mike said. "Let's get outside and see what's going on before we all end up in a chick flick. Maybe I'll find Paul and push him in."

"Now that I would like to see," Scott said as he zipped up the bag that now contained his phone and a bunch of rice. "This better work or I'm taking the price of a new one out of his ass."

Mike threw a brotherly arm around Scott. "Come on. Let's go

get the little fucker."

"Now this we should definitely watch." Bailey turned to Beth. "Thanks for coming with me."

"I wouldn't have missed it for the world."

"Good. I still need to do what I came in for."

"Go ahead. I'll wait here for you," Beth said.

"Thanks." Bailey grinned. It was a nice thought that no matter what had just happened, she had someone who would wait for her.

Chapter Twenty-five

"RIGHT HERE," MIKE said unnecessarily.

"Been here before, buddy," Bailey answered as she put the car in park. "I should have brought the truck. I forgot this parking lot was gravel."

"I know. Sorry," Mike said sheepishly. "I'll help you wash it."

"It's okay. I don't know why I'm so protective of this car. I've had it for years. It's an ingrained habit." She'd grown up without the ability to replace things if something happened to them. That habit had followed her into adulthood.

"It looks brand new," Mike said.

"I hated driving in LA so I took cabs, public transportation and whatever else." She locked it as soon as Mike closed his door. "You're moving a bit slow, cousin. You nervous?"

"A little," Mike said. "Ms. Arnoux hates me and has tried everything to get us separated," he said as they entered the building.

"I don't think she's tried everything." Bailey stressed the last word. "But it doesn't mean she won't."

"Can I help you?" A pale looking young man asked from behind a counter filled with rubber masks and accessories.

"Tuxes?" Bailey asked. The young man pointed. "Thanks."

They followed the walkway through a row of costumes into a room with ball gowns and more expensive outfits. It was hard not to give in to temptation and play with the props and costumes they passed. Finally, they came to an open area where Scott seemed to be holding court.

"Bailey. Mike. How's it hanging?"

"Nonexistent," Bailey said.

"Have you gotten anything accomplished?" Mike asked.

"Yeah. I got her number." Scott accepted a high five from Bailey. "Was waiting on you, dude."

"What can I help you with?" the young woman, who gave Scott her number, asked.

"I called and..."

"The man here is getting married and wants full morning attire for his wedding. We're two of the groomsmen," Bailey said. She knew it would have taken five minutes or more for Mike to answer, and then the answer might not even be coherent. He got like that when he was nervous.

"Where's Ian anyway?" Scott asked.

"He'll be here in a minute," Mike said. "Beth's bringing Jacob and Ian has Eric."

"Why didn't we bring Eric?" Bailey asked.

"Ian is getting him a job mowing yards for a few of the rental houses the brokerage has," he said. "Why didn't you bring Jacob?"

"I couldn't get him from day camp, Beth has the booster seat. I'm supposed to take him home." She forgot to move the seat over this morning.

"Do you have a certain type of tuxedo in mind, sir?" The saleslady asked.

Mike wandered over to the counter. "They mentioned a book or a catalogue on the phone, you know something to look through for ideas."

"So how's it going?" Bailey asked Scott.

"Pretty well. We're almost ready to bring in an apprentice. When are you going to get your arm finished?" he asked.

"After the wedding," Bailey said.

"Sounds good. Hey. What's up with... Hi, Beth, how's things?" His abrupt greeting made her think he was going to ask about her relationship. She held back the laugh that thought caused.

"Good," Beth answered. "I saw you got a great write up in the local magazine."

"Bailey!" Forty pounds of six-year-old rocketed at Bailey. "Mama said you're taking me home after we get ticks."

"Tuxes," Bailey corrected gently. "And yes. I'm taking you home."

"Awesome."

"Will you guys be done by dinner?" Beth asked.

"Beats me." Bailey walked over to her. "I'll text you when we're done. You sure you're okay with this?"

"Of course." Beth said. "I sat the booster seat on your trunk. I hope it's still there when y'all are done. I've seen you install it before. I know you'll do fine."

"That's not what I meant."

"I know. And I'm not worried." Beth gave Jacob a hug. "Go over by Mr. Scott, sweetheart. I want to talk to Bailey for a minute."

"Okay." He scampered off.

"What's up?" Bailey asked.

"Well, I thought I'd say goodbye properly." Beth put her hands on Bailey's chest. "And remind you that I trust you. My kids adore you. I do too. So relax, baby."

"Okay," Bailey answered sheepishly. "I don't know where these bouts of self doubt come from."

"It's just part of you. One day you won't doubt anymore." Beth pulled her down for a kiss. "Now I have to go. I love you. Call or text me when you're heading my way and we'll decide what to do from there, okay?"

"Anything you want," Bailey answered. "I love you, too."

"Jacob, you be good, okay? I love you. Stay with Bailey."

"Yes, ma'am," he promised. "I love you too."

It wasn't long after Beth departed that Ian arrived with Eric. Bailey snuck out and installed the booster in the car while Mike chose what style of tux he wanted. By the time she returned, he had picked out the tuxedos he wanted for the wedding. The fitting took the most amount of time. There was only one person available to take measurements. She was older and a bit over cautious. She often took the same measurement three times to make sure she had it right.

A few hours later, all the tuxedos were ordered, the accessories, such as socks and suspenders, had been purchased and even the shoes had been chosen. Bailey was glad. The area where they had to try on all the parts of different suits to see which fit better was small and full of clothes. She was starting to feel a little claustrophobic. It was a relief to walk outside in the evening air and get away from the smell of mothballs and fabric.

"What are you guys up to now?" Mike asked everyone as they stood in the parking lot.

"I've got a few late tat appointments," Scott said. "Gotta keep the lights on, brother." He climbed on his motorcycle. "Take it easy. I'll see y'all later."

"Ian?" Mike asked as Scott roared away.

"We've got a family outing planned. Sarah wants us to take her to see some movie." Ian shrugged. "So it's family date night."

"We'll give Eric a lift," Bailey told him. She closed the rear door after making sure Jacob was secure in his booster.

"Thanks." Eric looked relieved. Ian listened to country music. It drove them all crazy. "I'm supposed to go to Grandma's tonight. She wanted to take me to some art show in the morning."

"I'm assuming not your mother's mother," Bailey said rather than asked.

"Right. Grandmother doesn't do stuff like that." He grimaced.

"Okay. Bailey? What are you and little man doing?" Mike asked.

"I don't know. I'm supposed to call or text his mom. We'll see from there. Eric, grab your stuff from Ian. I'll take you to your grandmother's house first. We'll go from there."

"It's a plan anyway." Mike shrugged.

"Hey, you'll have the house to yourselves tonight." She reminded him. "Maybe you shouldn't make plans."

"Oh yeah." He smoothed his beard. "Never mind then."

"That's the spirit." She clapped him on the back. "Now get in and let's be off."

THERE WERE NOT many locally owned jewelry stores in the area, but Bailey didn't want to buy anything at a national chain. She wanted something unique. The first store she tried was a bust. However when she walked into the second, she knew she'd walked into the right place.

"May I help you?" A well-dressed young man with barely tamed blond curls asked as Bailey approached the counter.

"Yes, please. I've got a question first. What do people usually get, just an engagement ring or the whole bridal set? Is it better to let the bride pick out the wedding rings?"

He leaned a little closer and asked. "First time?"

"Yes," she said sheepishly. "Does it show? I'm not one for buying jewelry anyway."

"It shows a little." He smiled and extended his hand. "My name's Wayne Castle."

"Bailey Cooper." She shook it. "Show me what you got, Wayne."

"Certainly. If you'd like to take a seat over here?" He came around the glass case and directed her to a chair. "Tell me about her? Do you have a picture?"

"I do." Bailey pulled out her phone and scrolled through the gallery. "Here."

"Very lovely. She down to earth or loud and flashy?"

"Definitely down to earth." Bailey grinned at the picture. It was a recent one. They had been at the park, lying back on the grass watching the kids play. Beth was smiling up at the camera.

"Pear, round or square?" He asked.

"Pardon me?"

"The cut of the diamond. Let me show you." Wayne stood up walked around the glass display. He pulled a lined tray from one of the cases and selected three rings from the tray. "Here. Pear. Square. Round."

"Oh. Um. Not pear." Bailey hadn't realized there would be so many decisions. "Hang on." She pulled out her phone again and dialed Liz's number. "Help."

"Where are you?" Liz asked.

"Castle diamonds." Bailey was expecting derision, but didn't get it.

"I'll be there in a minute," Liz said and ended the call.

"I have help arriving," Bailey told him.

"Well while we're waiting, do you want to look at something else?"

"Actually yes. I need to get a wedding present. I'm not the type to buy toasters or anything," she said.

"We have lots of imported cut crystal," Wayne suggested.

"Nah. I can't do that. What else do you have?" Bailey looked around and saw a display of watches. "Can I see some of those?"

"Sure. Would this be for you?" Wayne asked.

"No. My cousin Mike is getting married. His watch is crap. Do you have a matching set or something?"

"Seriously?" Wayne seemed impressed. "That's a hell of a wedding present. Sorry."

"No worries. I have to remind myself to keep the language PG rated." She looked at the watches in the case. "He needs something that can take a hell of a beating. She would like something pretty I'm sure. Do you have anything that's a good compromise?"

"How much do you want to spend?"

"Let's just see what you have. We'll decide on the rest later." She wasn't worried about cost. She knew she could afford it.

By the time Liz arrived with Sarah, Bailey had managed to find a set of matching watches for Mike and Cindy, and a different one for Eric. She had to exercise a lot of restraint. She found that funny. She'd never been one for jewelry before, but she kept noticing things she wanted to buy for Beth and a few things for Rebecca and Jacob. She decided to wait

"So what's the emergency?" Liz asked as she stood next to Bailey. "What's in the bag?"

"Wedding presents," Bailey answered. "I'm stuck. If you were a ring for Beth, what type of ring would you be?"

"Oh my god!" Liz threw her arms around Bailey. "Are you serious?"

"Yes. I'm serious. I haven't figured out when yet, but I'm going to ask." She had no plan in place for the asking, but she did plan to ask.

"Ask what?" Sarah asked.

"Bailey is going to propose to Beth," Liz told her daughter as she let go of Bailey.

"Awesome!" Sarah cheered. "Then Rebecca and I really will be related, and you won't leave us again. Can I see the ring?"

"Well, I haven't actually picked one out. That's why you two are here," Bailey said. "You get to help."

"Have you managed to make any decisions?" Liz asked.

"She did decide to exclude any pear-shaped diamonds," Wayne answered. He offered his hand to Liz. "Wayne Castle. I've been assisting Ms. Cooper."

She shook his hand. "Liz Cooper. I'll be helping I guess."

"So. Where would you like to start? Metal?" Wayne asked.

"White Gold or platinum," Bailey answered." I think that would be better than yellow gold. Don't you?" She asked Liz.

"Personally, no. I'm a big fan of gold. Beth, though, isn't. So yes, you've made one decision." Liz said.

"Great." Bailey sighed. "How many more to go?"

"Depends." Wayne pulled a padded mat from beneath one of the display cases and laid it out over the glass. "What's our price range?"

"That's up to you, Bailey," Liz said.

"For this? We don't have one," Bailey responded.

"Okay. No pear shaped and no yellow gold." Wayne looked around at his merchandise. He gathered a handful of rings and placed them gently on the pad. "First we'll look at round cut."

They looked at different styles of rings for an hour or more. Finally they found the perfect ring. It was a large, clear square diamond in a platinum setting. The thin platinum band had a subtle design flare to it and each side had a line of three tiny diamonds. Even Sarah found it breathtaking.

"Well, Ms. Cooper, if that ring needs to be sized please bring it back in and we'll get that done for you," Wayne said after he ran her card and boxed the ring.

"Thank you." She shook his hand. "And thanks for all the help."

"You are most welcome. Please come back and see us if you need anything else." Wayne handed her the bag with all her purchases in it.

"Okay, Ms. Romantic, you owe us lunch," Liz told her.

"There's a good seafood cafe not far from here."

"Okay. Where'd you park? I'll follow you," Bailey said as she held the door for them.

"Good. We can discuss how you plan to propose," Liz said.

"Thanks, but that part I think I can do myself," Bailey said when she reached the cars. "I'll wait and pull out behind you and then follow you to this seafood place."

"Can I ride with Bailey and hold the ring?" Sarah asked.

"I don't mind if she doesn't." Liz smiled fondly down at her offspring.

"I don't mind. Come on, squirt." Bailey handed her the bag after she unlocked the car. "See you in a few."

Chapter Twenty-six

IT WAS A nice night. The group met for dinner at a restaurant downtown that had an outdoor courtyard. Bailey was content. The food was excellent, the company was outstanding and the house band was surprisingly decent. She still hadn't decided when to propose, but she thought about it constantly.

"So any last suggestions before we start planning showers and parties?" Liz asked Mike.

"Start?" Mike looked startled. "I would've assumed for a bachelor party of epic proportions you'd need more than a month of planning."

"Nah. I got this," Bailey assured him easily. "I think Liz was actually trying to pull Cindy's chain."

"Good catch," Liz said. "I was, but someone doesn't seem to be listening. Earth to Cindy." She waved a hand in front of Cindy's face.

"I'm sorry," Cindy said. "I swear I was paying attention, but do you guys see that?" She pointed at a giant smoke cloud in the distance. "It wasn't there a minute ago. I wonder what happened."

"That white trash bar out off the highway caught fire. We just drove past it," a young man told them as he sat down at the next table.

Bailey leaped to her feet. "Did you call 911?" She knew instantly it was her mother's bar.

"Shit." Beth stood quickly. "C'mon, I'll drive." She grabbed the keys off the table.

"Fuck. Don't wait for us," Liz called. "We're right behind you."

Bailey made short work of elbowing her way through the crowd. She thought about asking for the keys but decided not to do so. She knew Beth would get them there as quickly and safely as possible. So for once she let someone else take control of the situation.

Beth pulled the car into the yard just as a large fire truck pulled in front of the building. Several people, Bailey recognized most of them as patrons, were crowded around the lone cop on the scene.

Smoke billowed through the windows, over the roof and the bricks seemed to be hissing. Bailey frantically scanned the crowd for her mother. She walked closer, only dimly aware of what was going on around her.

"I'll check the house," Mike called as he jumped out of Cindy's car. "Don't let her near that fire."

"What?" Bailey asked vaguely. There was too much noise, too much going on at one time. It was a nightmare. She walked closer to the crowd, desperate to see Fiona. All her anger at her mother gave way to overwhelming fear. "Mama? Mama!"

One of the regulars caught her attention. "She's still in there. She ain't out yet."

"We have to get in there." Bailey started to the door but was held back by several hands.

"No, sweetheart." Beth pulled her close. "Let the firemen do their jobs. They'll get her."

"But." She wanted to argue. For a moment she really believed she would be able to survive the inferno, find her mother and make it out unscathed. Beth's next words stopped her cold.

"Stay with me, Bailey. You can't leave me now." Beth's voice was soft in her ear, but it managed to penetrate the torrent of sound around them.

"But she's hurt, Beth. What if they can't..." She couldn't complete the thought.

"I know." She let herself be pulled tighter into Beth's arms. "I know."

"We're here, Bailey." Liz's arms slide around her. Her voice was tight with unshed tears.

At the cop's urging, they pulled one another a safe distance away. Bailey wasn't aware of much, not even the passing of time. She knew at some point Beth had stepped away, probably to call her parents. She knew that Ellen and Scott had joined them at some point as well. She vaguely realized it had started raining. It wasn't until a young man in a firefighter's uniform approached that she took in her surroundings again.

"So what happened?" Liz asked when the fireman came within earshot.

"Supposedly something on the grill caught fire. Some asshole threw water on it." He looked around at them. "Is Ms. Cooper's family here?"

"Yes," Bailey answered in a hollow voice.

"I, uh..." He turned to Liz and pulled her aside.

Liz said in an overly calm voice when she rejoined them,

"Let's go into the house for a little while. We should sit down. Maybe we can have some coffee."

They followed her wordlessly. Bailey was silent, content for the moment to be led. She didn't want to make decisions and she certainly didn't want to acknowledge what had happened. If she thought, if she did more than exist, it would be real. She let Liz be in charge. It was easier that way.

"Why the fuck was the grill going? Fiona rarely made food there. Always said it was a bar not a cafe." Mike rubbed his eyes after he collapsed on the sofa.

"I don't know," Bailey answered. She was exhausted. She felt the warm weight of Beth's hands on her shoulders and leaned into them. They steered her to a chair and guided her to sit down.

"What about a funeral?" Liz asked delicately.

"But do we know for sure she was in there?" Ellen asked. Everyone looked first at Bailey, who shrugged, and then Liz.

"They recovered two bodies. That's why they wanted us to come in here," Liz said in a tight voice.

"I, uh, guess I can make the funeral arrangements. I'll go up there tomorrow, to Cobb's," Bailey said. It was difficult to speak.

"Do you need me to go with you?" Liz asked.

"I'll take the day off," Beth answered. "If you need me, I'm here."

"Thanks, babe." Bailey sighed. She didn't want to face it alone. "Let's group trip it. Hell, Fiona would love the attention."

"What time?" Mike asked, he looked at his watch. "Damn thing. It's tomorrow morning now. Let's go home and get some sleep."

"Good idea. We can meet later this afternoon. Bailey, how about you call us when you're ready, or have Beth do it," Liz suggested. "We'll meet you when you're ready."

"Okay." Bailey let out a deep breath. She was fighting the urge to cry and wondered who all knew that. Then she realized she didn't care and neither did they. She was among family. They would not think badly of her if she gave in and cried.

"Is it safe to go out, do you think?" Cindy asked after a long few minutes where everyone seemed lost in his or her own grief and thoughts.

Mike pulled the curtain back and checked outside. "It looks like it. All the fire trucks and the county vehicles are gone."

"Let's go home." Bailey stood up and looked around and her eyes fell on the kitchen counter. A bottle of vodka and a container of frozen orange juice were still there. She wiped a few tears away with the back of her hand.

THE RAIN BEAT down on the sidewalk. Bailey didn't care. It was soothing. Her jeans were soaked. Every bit of her was soaked. She still didn't care.

Everyone in the house was asleep. She wished she could be as well. Every time she closed her eyes she saw her mother in flames. It was hard to keep from seeing it. It was hard to keep from imagining it.

The only thing she was thankful for was there was no alcohol in the house. It was late. All the liquor stores were closed. She didn't want to leave, to drive, to see another person, but it was tempting. It was so tempting to do something crazy. But she was a rock star. She had done crazy. She had tattoos and piercings. She had shaved her head and dyed her hair every color imaginable. She had picked up strangers and tried to skateboard down arena ramps. There wasn't anything else to do. So she paced barefoot in the rain, wishing for something to take her mind off what happened.

"Bailey, come in out of the rain." She hadn't heard Beth approach.

"It feels good." She turned to see Beth standing behind her, wrapped in an old robe Bailey had stolen from some hotel early in her career.

"I know. But you're soaked and it's cooling off. Please come in."

"You shouldn't be out here." Concern for the woman in front of her overrode the pain for the moment. "You'll get sick."

"I'll go in when you do," Beth said gently. "Let's go inside and dry off. Come on, we can lay on the couch and watch one of those cheap B-rated horror movies you love."

"Okay." Bailey let herself be led back into the house.

"Here. Strip." Beth helped Bailey take her wet clothes off and handed her a towel.

"The kids?"

"Are still at my mother's house." Beth quickly shed the robe. Her pajamas underneath were fairly dry. "Here."

"Thanks." Bailey's throat felt raw. "You're too good to me."

"No, I'm not. Here, put these on." Beth brought out a pair of sweats and a baseball jersey. "Now come here."

"Okay." She didn't resist. It was easier to let someone else take control.

"Tell me about it?" Beth asked as she helped Bailey sit down on the couch.

"It burns."

"I know." Beth wrapped her in an embrace and held her close. "So what were you thinking out there?"

"What to do. And how to scrub my brain of the images I keep seeing."

"What do you want to do?"

"Cremate her, but what about the ashes?"

"Um. Good question." Beth was obviously taken aback. "You want a funeral?"

"I don't know." She sighed. "I'll have to ask the guy at the place about ashes. I don't want to keep them."

"What about a memorial service instead? It would be more casual than a funeral. Less stress," Beth suggested.

"Yeah. That sounds good." Bailey was relieved. One decision was made.

"I can't help you scrub your brain, sorry baby. But you want to tell me about it?"

"It's tough. Every time I close my eyes I imagine what it was like for her. And I feel guilty for not being there. And for being mad at her. And I just want to curl up with a bottle and go to sleep for days. And then I feel bad for that. And I know getting lost in a bottle is bullshit. It doesn't dull the pain. It just puts it at a distance and that's not enough."

"I know, sweetheart. I know." Beth pulled Bailey's head into her lap and stroked Bailey's hair.

"It hurts so much. Why? I mean she was mean and hateful and abusive, and at times wonderful and fun."

"She was your mom. You guys had a complicated relationship. And the last words you spoke to one another were in anger. That's going to lead to some complicated emotions. I wish I had answers for you, but all I have are arms, ears, shoulders and a fierce love for you. And no matter what, as a parent I know your mother loved you. You have to remember that."

"Are you sure?" Bailey asked softly. "How could anyone?"

"No. No. We're not going to let you fall into self-pity," Beth said with a quiet fierceness in her voice.

"Okay."

"Okay. Now just lay here. There's no reason to move. It's a nice storm outside. We're safe and warm in here. And I can hold you all night." Beth gently massaged her shoulders.

After that they were silent. Bailey tried to concentrate on nothing more than Beth's touch. It was relaxing where nothing else had been. It wasn't long before the tears started. This time they were less angry and more healing. She finally fell asleep with her head still in Beth's lap.

Chapter Twenty-seven

"HOLY SHIT. LOOK at you all domesticated and shit."

"Kat! You were supposed to call from the airport so I could pick you up."

"Why when I can get a cab and surprise you?" Kat asked. Kat spread her arms wide.

"You look great. How was Japan?" Bailey asked as she returned the hug.

"Japan was wonderful. It would have been better had I been able to see my husband more often."

"Fuck. You guys didn't get any time together?" That was disappointing.

"Not much." Kat took a seat at the breakfast bar.

Bailey washed her hands to get the paint off. "Something to drink?"

"Yeah. What you got?"

"Soda, juice or water."

"Juice is fine." Kat was a reformed drinker as well. She preferred that term over recovering alcoholic.

"Here ya go. So what's up? Seriously?" Bailey asked. It seemed a way to break through her own confused grief.

"Not much. What's up with you? You look almost happy. What did you do?" Kat raised an eyebrow.

"I took your advice." Bailey couldn't help the smile that broke out across her face.

"You got laid?" Kat asked.

"Well yeah, but." She was unexpectedly embarrassed. "You know, the funeral thing."

"I understand. It's okay to be happy and sad at the same time, you know." Kat looked around the kitchen. "Is that a kid's drawing on your fridge?"

"Yes. That is." Bailey smiled at it. It was one Rebecca had drawn the weekend prior.

"Holy shit. You got her, didn't you?" They hadn't talked much while they were on different continents. Both preferred to catch up in person. Kat had rescheduled her trip to make it earlier so she could be at the funeral.

"What do you mean?" Bailey asked, slightly confused.

"That Beth chick. The hottie you went to school with. Spill.

What happened?" Kat didn't hide her excitement.

"The short answer is yes, we're dating," Bailey replied carefully.

"Dating? Okay. That's a step. Does this step include sex?" Kat asked. She chuckled as Bailey's cheeks turned red. "So that's step two. Being that you're a lesbian is step three the moving van or the ring?"

"The ring, actually. I don't know for certain if she'll say yes. I think she will." Bailey admitted.

"Oh yeah? That serious?" Kat raised an eyebrow again.

"Kat, do you love Ross?" Bailey asked unexpectedly.

"Yes, but I wouldn't compare us right now." Kat lost her look of happiness.

"Why? Something happen in Japan?"

"Nothing happened in Japan. That's part of the problem. I'm honestly thinking about leaving him. Not sure he'd notice," Kat said.

"Of course he'd notice," Bailey scoffed and then stopped as she remembered being around them and the distance evident between them. "Maybe he would. I don't know."

"Me either," Kat said. "But back to the good news. There's a ring? Have you bought one yet? How are you planning on doing it?"

"Wow. When did you get interested in other people's love lives?" Bailey asked. Kat was usually a very private person.

"Not others. Just yours. And only since you've fallen in love, then fallen out, and back in again," Kat said. "Maybe it's a vicarious thing."

"Fallen? Kat, I never fell out of love with this woman," Bailey said.

"But she has kids. You don't do kids except from a distance. Is that drawing from one of them?" Kat asked.

"Yeah. Rebecca drew it one night when they were over," Bailey answered.

"You know, I thought it would be tough seeing you as a stepparent, but you seem ready to cannonball into domesticity."

"I've never had it, really. Well, you know my mom." She choked down another wave of guilt and grief.

"Yeah I know." Kat walked a little closer. "How are you doing with that?"

"It's tough. The last time I saw her, we fought. She was sick, Kat. She was so twisted from her own bitterness that she couldn't be happy for anyone else." Bailey paced the floor.

"That woman was a piece of work, if you don't mind my saying so," Kat said. Kat and Fiona had never gotten along. Kat didn't play games and refused to placate the older woman.

"I know." Bailey sighed. "I just wish things could have been different. That maybe just once she could have been proud of me or happy for me. Hell, anytime anything good happened she tried to ruin it. I finally have what I've always wanted and all she wanted to do was tear me down." That was all part of the battle going through her head. Bailey was as much confused about how she felt about her mother as she was how her mother felt about her.

"Did she know?" Kat asked.

"Know what?" Bailey asked confused.

"About the kid?"

"There are only three other people on the planet that know, Kat." Bailey went cold. "You know that."

"You haven't told Beth?" Kat was incredulous. "Bailey, believe me when I say this, you can't hide something like that from someone you want to spend the rest of your life with."

"I know." She collapsed on the couch. "It was so much easier to live in LA and whisk my friends and family away on vacations when I felt the whim. This coming home shit is for the birds, I tell you."

"Well?" Kat crossed her arms and looked down at her.

"I have to tell Beth. I will tell her. I just don't know how." She rubbed her eyes and then changed the subject. "Are you staying for the wedding?"

"I don't think so. I may come back for it, but I can't impose on your hospitality for that long. Besides, I have a few things to do back in LA."

"Fair enough." Bailey pushed herself off the couch and hugged Kat again. "It really is good to see you, Kat."

IT TOOK A lot of soul searching and discussions with one of the planners at Cobb's funeral home for Bailey to decide on the most appropriate send off for her mother. It also took a lot of hours with her attorneys to make sure she was still judgment proof when it came to her mother's estate. She had almost forgotten to do so until Brian and his wife called. They wanted to attend, but Bailey asked them not to. She wanted a small, more intimate gathering.

"Here we go," Bailey said as they pulled into her mother's

driveway. Beth put the SUV in park and placed a hand on Bailey's thigh.

"I'll be okay."

"I know," Beth said. "I just wanted to take a small moment to reassure before you have to face everyone."

"Me too, Bailey." Jacob put his thin arms around her neck.

"Yeah. We're here with you," Rebecca said with all the self-importance and reassurance she could muster.

"Me too, Superstar," Kat called from the back row of Beth's SUV.

"Thank you all," Bailey told them. "All right, let's do this."

"You got a spot in mind?" Mike asked when they got out of the car. Cindy hit his arm. "What?"

"Tact. Concern. Empathy." Cindy told him.

"It's okay, Cindy," Bailey said. "I know he cares. And yes, I've picked out a spot. Got shovels?"

"I do," Mike said. "I leaned them up against the house, I'll grab them as soon as everyone else gets here."

"It looks like we're just waiting for Uncle Dwight and Aunt Ellen." She scanned the small group of family and friends, most of whom were starting to walk slowly forward.

"There they are." Rebecca pointed out the car pulling in behind them.

"Awesome. Guys, give me a second so I can go talk to the gentleman from Cobb's, please." Bailey turned and walked away from the group over to the hearse. "Mr. Salatore?"

"Ms. Cooper. Again, my condolence." A large man with a very deep voice leaned away from the car and offered his hand. "We have everything ready as you asked. The only thing we haven't done is the digging. Did you want us to do that?"

"No, sir. Two of my cousins and I will do it. It's kind of a family tradition. But thank you for the offer." Bailey looked around at the gathering. "I guess it's time."

"Ms. Cooper, would you prefer to take the smaller one now?" He handed her a small wrapped package. "We'll bring the rest out when you're ready."

"Thank you, Mr. Salatore." She put the small box in her pocket and walked back over to her family. "Okay. Let's dig a hole."

Scott claimed one of the shovels. "Just tell me where." It appeared as if he was holding the shovel away from his father. "Dad's not allowed, but he keeps trying to muscle in."

"Dwight, I appreciate that, but please, allow us," Bailey said softly. She knew it was painful for him to relinquish that duty to others. He nodded and went back to stand by Ellen.

Bailey chose a spot halfway between the house and the bar. She felt that was fitting. It put her mother between both parts of her life. Silently they dug a shallow hole, each taking a turn at shoveling a small pile of dirt.

"Damn. I don't wanna know what it's like to dig a whole hole," Mike muttered when his shovel got tangled in a root.

"Thought you were macho," Scott teased.

"Right? Next relative we're renting a backhoe," Bailey said. "Okay. Guess that's deep enough."

They stood back from the hole, leaving their shovels stuck in the ground around it. Mr. Salatore took that as his cue and carried the carefully wrapped package toward them. Everyone else followed.

"I, uh, want to thank everyone for coming today." Bailey felt something she hadn't felt in years: stage fright. She felt Beth take her hand and then willed herself to calm down. "Mama didn't leave any wishes for this. I had to, with a lot of help, make this up as I went along. I hope maybe that this is what she would have wanted. It certainly seems to fit. I had Mama cremated. Her ashes are in this container. In time a tree will grow in this spot. Karmically, hopefully, this will right some of the wrongs that were done to and by my mother."

Mr. Salatore handed the container to her. Bailey carefully unwrapped it revealing a tiny oak sapling. With infinite gentleness, she placed it into the hole while Scott and Mike covered it. Liz used an old alcohol bottle they had cleaned to water it.

"I'm not one for speeches. I'm not sure what else we should do here, but if someone would like to say something, I'm okay with that."

"I think we should just each say something positive and affirming to the tree." Ellen suggested. "Just a word, even one of parting. I'll go first. You'll be missed, Fiona."

"Goodbye, sis." Dwight wiped tears from his eyes.

One by one they all said something, even the children. Bailey was the last to go, reluctant to speak her feelings in front of others.

"Goodbye, Mama. Despite everything, I loved you and I'll miss you." It was all she could manage.

Bailey stood there, staring at the little tree as the rest of the group slowly dispersed. She had a wild desire to dig it up and tear it apart. She wanted to stomp on it and yell at it. She clenched her fist around the box in her pocket and fought the urge to throw it as far as she could. The pain she felt was new, raw, and seemed unmanageable. It threatened to control her and then destroy her. With an amazing amount of willpower, Bailey allowed Beth to take her hand again and lead her away from the sapling, away from her mother's house and away from thoughts of anger.

THE HOUSE SEEMED too full. It was suffocating. There were kids in two rooms, a guest in another, and a woman in her bed. The press of people, the weight of responsibility and the grief she still felt battered at her. Bailey began pacing. Places seemed to come to mind. It was a great time to visit Peru. She'd always wanted to go back there. Or she could go to one of the video game launch parties in New York or San Francisco that she'd been invited to last month. It was tempting. She hadn't felt the pull to leave everything so strongly since Beth had announced her engagement to Jerry all those years ago.

"Hey, superstar. Pacing? Where you heading?" Kat asked from the living room.

"What do you mean?" Bailey asked.

"I mean you're pacing. I've known you long enough to know you're planning to leave. So where we going?" Kat turned around and faced her over the back of the couch.

That stopped Bailey in her tracks. "We?"

"Why not. Russ is still in Japan. Our relationship has hit the rocks. So where are we going?" Kat asked again.

"I can't go anywhere," Bailey answered automatically. "Beth."

"Has lived for years without you. I'm sure she can wait longer. Besides she's got kids, man. You can't go from being a freewheeling rock star to a stick in the mud stepmom in this small town. You'll go nuts."

"I grew up here." Bailey felt slow. Her thoughts were heavy and hard to organize. "It's not so bad."

"Really?" Kat raised her eyebrow. "You always talked about how glad you were that you weren't stuck here, about how backwards they were here, and of course all the shit your cousin went through."

"I was angry," Bailey said.

"And you're all zen now? Come on, Bailey. Let's go

somewhere neither of us have ever been. Or we can get an acoustic guitar and snare drum and do that guerilla concert series we always talked about."

"Why, Kat? What's the point?" Slowly the wheels in Bailey's brain started to turn. "Running away the first time didn't help matters. The only person who followed me out there was Mike. And I wouldn't have lasted out there without you and Mr. Forsyth. The last time it didn't change anything. Beth still got married. And I ended up wrecking my motorcycle and going to rehab. So what do I get by running away this time?"

"Nothing," Kat answered. "Absolutely nothing. But you know that now, don't you?"

"Well, yeah."

"But you were seriously considering it, weren't you? Admit it, Bailey, if I hadn't interrupted your train of thought you'd be booking plane tickets for you and Elvis now," Kat said.

"I thought about going to Peru," Bailey admitted softly. "How did you know?"

"Cause I know you. You're so very transparent. You still thinking about it? Cause you know, and this is just based on what I've seen since I've been here, she won't wait for you again. You're lucky to get this one shot."

"I know. I know if I were to give in to temptation and leave, I'd cut all kinds of ties. I can't be selfish anymore. If I miss the wedding, damage. My whole family will never forgive me. If I leave, I'll break those kids' hearts. And I don't even want to think about what Beth would think. I know that we'd both survive. I'm just not sure if I would want to live any more of my life without her. I love her so much. Hell, I love those kids. I can't do that to them or me. I need them."

"And we need you," Beth said from the stairs. "You weren't in bed. I wanted to make sure you weren't standing out in the rain again."

"How much did you hear?" Bailey asked defensively.

"Enough." Beth said. "Come back to bed? Please?"

"Go on, rockstar. You made the right choice," Kat whispered.

"Thanks, Kat." Bailey pulled her into a hug.

"Anytime, my friend."

"Hey. Sorry." Bailey stopped a step right below where Beth was standing.

"For what? "Beth brushed her hair away. "Being human?"

"For thinking of leaving. For wanting to run away." She rested her head on Beth's chest.

"Sweetheart, if you only knew how often I've wanted to run away in my life."

"But you never have. You still stay here," Bailey said in awe.

"And you've never had reason to do so before now," Beth said. "I'm honored and flattered that I'm part of that reason, but I don't want you to stay if you don't want to."

"I do. I love you. I don't want to be without you again. And next time I go somewhere you'll come with me."

"I'd like that. I love you, too." Beth kissed her. "You've had a very rough day. You want to get some sleep."

"Eventually." Bailey smiled for the first time all day. "I want... I need."

"To take that to your room, please," Kat called from the couch.

"Yes, ma'am," Beth called. "Come on." She offered her hand.

Bailey took it and allowed Beth to guide her up the stairs and into the master bedroom. Beth lay down on the bed and patted the space next to her. Bailey submitted willingly.

"What do you need, baby?"

"You," Bailey answered. "I just need to feel close to you."

Beth pulled her close and allowed her hands to roam. Gentle kisses were peppered from Bailey's ear to her mouth. A soft hand explored her side under her t-shirt. It amazed her. Beth was a more than willing partner, eager to both give and take the initiative when it came to lovemaking. Bailey really hadn't known what to expect that first night. She had a better idea now. She relaxed; content to let Beth take the lead.

Beth rose up on one elbow and looked down at her. She smoothed Bailey's hair away from her eyes and leaned in for a long and slow kiss. Finally, she pulled back and looked down at her again.

"I can't believe it sometimes."

"What?" Bailey asked.

"That I get to make love to you. That you allow me to do so."

"Why wouldn't I?" Bailey asked as she ran her hand along Beth's cheek.

"I don't know. It doesn't matter. Especially not now." She rubbed her hand farther under Bailey's shirt. "I just love you. I love to touch you. I love to taste you. I love to hear you whisper my name right before you get to that point where you can't say anything until after."

Chapter Twenty-eight

"HEY, YOU NEED some help?" Beth asked from the doorway.

"I think I've got it. Thanks." Bailey finished tying the tie and turned to face Beth. "How do I look?"

Beth grinned and leaned against the doorframe. "You look hot as a Mafioso type. Can I be your gun moll?"

"Seriously? How's it look? I've never done a gangster thing before." She turned on her heel, trying to see it from all sides.

"You look good," Beth said seriously.

"Thank you." Bailey stopped at the look on Beth's face. "What? You want to say something. What is it?"

"It's nothing."

"Sure it is. Whatcha thinking? You're not thinking about that waitress, are you?" Bailey teased.

"No. Besides, she's a bit butch for flapper dresses." Beth said. "I admit I can be a bit jealous and possessive, but I wasn't even thinking about that."

"Then what are you thinking?" Bailey walked closer and put her arms around Beth.

"Bailey, I love you. I mean holy fuck do I love you."

Bailey's heart froze. "There's a but there. What?"

"I'm just a little worried about you. It seems so soon after the funeral and you were pretty wrecked." Beth walked behind her and put her arms around her.

"I know." Bailey sighed and adjusted her suspenders. "I almost wish I could cancel it. But. And there's the but. But. I can't. This is Mike's bachelor party. I've rented the entire Italian restaurant for the night. It's decorated like a mob movie. After the pasta, sauce and sausage and whatever the hell else, it's going to be a turned into a speakeasy. Fuck, baby, I'm in a zoot suit."

"It's okay, sweetheart. So is Jacob and y'all look adorable. Well he does. You look oddly sexy in that outfit. Almost androgynous and I've got to get my mind out of the gutter." Beth shook her head.

"I think it's cute when you get flustered," Bailey said. "And for the record, I think you'd look sexy in a garbage bag. But. And here's that but again. We just said farewell to my mother and you're wondering if this party is a bit too much, too soon, right?"

Bailey personally thought it was oddly fitting. Her mother had always tried to make any family event about her.

"Yeah, kind of," Beth said. "One of the many things I love about you is your strength. I'm worried that maybe you've been pushed to the end of it." Beth hurried on at the look on Bailey's face. "I'm not worried that you're going to fall off the proverbial wagon or anything. I'm just concerned that you'll keep it all in until you implode."

"That's a perfectly understandable fear." Bailey said calmly. "However, between you and Liz and then my real therapist, I know better. I've learned how to cope. Plus, I think I've come close to cracking and you and Kat kept that from happening."

"I know. I know you have. And I trust you." Beth pulled her down for a quick kiss. "Now shouldn't you be taking the boy to the party? I'm supposed to come get him at eight, right?"

"Right. Thank you for being concerned. It's nice, in a way. And your empathy and heart are two of the many things I love you for." Bailey pulled her close again. "Now I need to go or I'll be late and Mike will never let that go."

"I know." Beth gently pushed her away. "I love you. Have fun. I'll see later."

"Love you too."

Bailey had rented a 1934 Buick with suicide doors. It had been interesting, to say the least, to get the booster seat in the back. Thankfully the owner had retrofitted the car with seatbelts. She got Jacob safely tucked in the back and then got in and started the car. Mike had no idea what was in store. She had his suit delivered to the house but without any instructions.

"Bailey, what's a mobster?" Jacob asked from the backseat. "Isn't that what we're dressed as?"

"It is. A mobster was someone in organized crime, like a gang thing I guess, only they've made a lot of movies about that time period. Mike is a big fan of those type of movies," she explained. "So I chose that as the theme for his party."

"Are those movies I can watch?" Jacob asked as they turned on the road where Mike and Cindy lived.

"Not usually. They're pretty violent." She pulled into the driveway, put the car in park, honked twice and waited. "I should have hired a photographer."

Mike and Eric came out and got in the car. Mike's expression was one of pleasant surprise. Eric looked mildly interested. He had helped with the party planning process, so he knew what was going to happen.

"What is all this?" Mike asked as he got in the front seat. "Zoot suits and suicide doors?"

"Welcome to the mob, big guy," Bailey said as she backed out of the driveway. "Let's go celebrate your upcoming nuptials."

"Don't say nuptials. It sounds so weird," Mike said. "This is awesome, Bailey. Thank you."

"Don't thank me yet. The night is just beginning."

The dinner was just for the groomsmen. Scott and Ian met them at the restaurant where they were served a feast of food that started with large antipasto salads. They had pasta with marinara, sausage, chicken parmigiana, lasagna, baked ziti, and osso buco, all served on a giant platter placed in the middle of the table. There was enough for each of them to have a full serving of each. There were plenty of leftovers sent home with Beth and Cindy when they came to pick up Eric and Jacob.

After dinner, the party started. More family members arrived as did plenty of Mike's friends. The party room was decorated as an old speakeasy. Bailey had opted for an open bar. She knew more people would attend then. However, she did think ahead and hire a limo service to get anyone who needed it a ride home.

About an hour into the party itself, she started to get bored. It was hard being the sober person when everyone else was drinking and having fun. She was still a little raw emotionally as well. Fortunately, she'd placed a firm time limit on the party. It wasn't easy, but she was able to make it to the end.

She paid the check after everyone else left. Mike was happily humming to himself at a table. Scott and Ian were waiting on the limo. The party was a success. She was amazed. There were several Coopers in attendance, and not one fight broke out among them.

"I can give you guys a ride home if you want," she told them when she was finished making sure everything was paid and finished.

"That works for me." Ian swayed a little as he stood.

"I'm so glad I hopped a ride to this thing. I do not want to try to remember where I parked my bike tomorrow," Scott said. "I'm going to have one bitching hangover. I can tell already."

"Not as bad as Mike's going to have," Ian said. "This was a great party, Bailey."

"Great party." Mike still had a little beer left in his mug. He lifted it up in a toast. "Great, great party."

"You're about to pass out, big man," Bailey said. "Let's get you home. Please don't puke in the car though. I don't want to have to buy it."

"Here, I'll help." Scott grabbed an arm and attempted to help his brother stand. Bailey ran to assist. Together they managed to get Mike on his feet.

"Good. Now one step then another and we'll get you out to the car." She bit back her laughter. It reminded her a lot of the parties they used to have, and how drunk they would get when they got together. At least she would remember this evening. There were plenty she didn't.

Somehow Bailey managed to get them all home. Mike rode in the front seat and made machine gun noises as they went down the road. Scott sang Irish folk songs badly and Ian liked to quote sci-fi movies randomly. Before they left the parking lot, she turned on her phone and left it recording for the ride. Blackmail material always came in handy.

"YOU SURE YOU want to stay for this?" Bailey asked. She looked at the clock. It was almost time for them to arrive. She was dreading this meeting, but she didn't want to cancel it.

"Of course. What type of girlfriend, much less friend, would I be if I let you face this alone?" Beth asked.

"How did I get so lucky?" Bailey rested her head against Beth's chest.

"I ask myself the same thing every day. How did you get so lucky?" Beth teased. She ran her hands through Bailey's hair and held her close. "Now are you sure you want to do this? You have no idea what Dwight's going to tell you."

"I may not want to hear what he says, but I need to hear it. I don't think I can let the anger I have toward her go until then. Does that make sense?" She'd thought about it enough. She had spoken with her therapist and her sponsor, both back in LA, about it and decided it was time to know the truth.

"It does, but baby, you have to be prepared to learn stuff that might make you angrier." Beth put a gentle hand under her chin and made her look up. "Whatever he tells you though, remember that I love you. You are an awesome person. There are four children who adore you. And you have friends and family who love you. And whatever he says, I'll be here."

"Bailey, there's someone at the door!" Rebecca called from downstairs.

"So here we go. Thanks, babe. I don't think I could face this without you." She stood up. "Ready?"

"If you are." Beth stood back and then took her hand and squeezed.

Together they walked downstairs to meet their guests. Beth took a moment to shoo the kids upstairs. Bailey awkwardly invited Uncle Dwight and Aunt Ellen into the formal living area.

"You look good, Uncle Dwight."

"Thanks. I feel pretty good, all things considered." He grimaced a bit as he sat down. "So far everything's clear. The tumor was completely removed. We'll see from there."

"I'm so glad to hear that."

"Me too." Ellen rubbed his arm. "So, I told Dwight you had questions."

"Thanks," Bailey said. "So."

"Can I get y'all anything to drink?" Beth asked when she reappeared. When everyone declined, she sat down beside Bailey and took her hand.

"It's nice seeing you two together. There were times I wished Mike was just gay." Ellen sighed. "I know how that sounds, but his life would have been much easier."

"It's worked out," Bailey said. It wasn't a subject she liked to discuss with them.

"True," Uncle Dwight said, "and we're here to talk about you and your mother. So, where do you want me to start?"

"The beginning, I guess. I have tons of questions, but I can't remember any right now."

"Fair enough," he said. "I'll start at the beginning then. Interrupt me if you know this already or if you remember a question, okay?"

"Okay," Bailey agreed and leaned back in her chair.

"Not long after your uncle Sullivan died, your mom got pregnant. She didn't tell anyone at first. She was young, only nineteen. She wasn't married. She'd been taking courses at the college, but had to drop out. I didn't find out until much later who and how. Several times we tried, and your grandparents tried, to get guardianship or custody, but your mother fought us every step of the way. Believe it or not, she loved you. I just don't think she knew how to separate you from the circumstances surrounding you."

"What does that mean?" Bailey asked. "And you guys tried to have me move in with y'all?"

"Yes. You may not remember, but around the time you were three you actually lived with your grandparents for a year or more. Your mother attempted to run off with some asshole who beat the shit out of her. Or another asshole I should say. She never got over our brother's death and I think she kept finding these guys to punish herself, you know?"

"Yeah. She stuck pretty hard to that pattern when I was growing up." Bailey felt Beth tighten her grasp.

"Remember that summer you guys went to Houston?" He asked.

"Yeah. That was almost fun." Bailey was nine and they'd stayed with a friend of her mother's. It was the only time Fiona had closed the bar for anything. It was also the only trip they'd taken together.

"That summer your grandparents filed official papers to adopt you. Your mother ran with you and wouldn't come back until they called it off," Dwight said.

"Fuck. I never knew that." Bailey felt that like a punch in the gut.

"Yeah, well. That was the last time any of us tried that. We kept you with us as much as possible of course," Ellen said.

"Yeah," Bailey said. "I remember spending a lot of time over there, and then I wouldn't see you for a long time."

"That's how it would go. Bailey, your mother wasn't always so mean and hateful. I know that doen't excuse anything." Dwight shrugged.

"No. What about the man who helped my mother get pregnant? Who was he?" Bailey braced herself for that.

"I think you know the answer to that question already," Dwight answered.

"What? No. Who?"

"Who do you know who hates the very sight of you?" Ellen asked.

"Cindy's mom," she answered instantly. "Fucking shit. So old man Arnoux knocked up my mother? No. Was it, did he?" Beth squeezed her hand again. She'd almost forgotten Beth was in the room.

"As far as I know it was consensual. It went on a little while before Ms. Arnoux found out and, by all reports, lost her shit on everyone. She was pregnant with Cindy at the time and her marriage was failing. It was a shit show if there ever was one," Dwight said ruefully.

"Damn." Bailey whispered.

"Here." Dwight pulled an old cigar box from the seat next to him and slid it across the table. "They exchanged letters. I'm not sure, but there was talk at one time of them running off together.

I know when Shelia flipped her shit he had to go make nice with her for a while. She could have taken him to the cleaners, you know."

"But they obviously stayed together, I mean he didn't die until we were in fifth grade. And they were still together because Toby was born two years after we were." Bailey shook her head. "Damn. It must have been hard for Mama. Thank you for telling me this, Uncle Dwight. But this doesn't make anything better or easier. In fact, it makes a few things worse. Does anyone else know? I mean Cindy's my sister for fuck's sake."

"No. Your mother only told me grudgingly and I had to swear not to tell you unless she was dead," Dwight said. "It's up to you if you want to tell anyone else. I know you'll have a hell of a time with Sheila if you do, but the DNA test she demanded is in there. I think your mother was relieved when you came out looking like us instead of them, but you can see some Arnoux in you. Hell, you can see it when you look at you and then that boy of Cindy's."

"Yeah, Mama once accused me of spawning him. I figured it was just a coincidence." She stood. "I'm going to go to the rehearsal dinner and the wedding and everything like normal. I'll deal with some of this later, but I think maybe I'll have a nice little chat with Sheila Arnoux before the wedding. If nothing else, maybe I can convince her to give Cindy and Mike a break with a little judicious blackmail."

"For what it's worth, Bailey, I'm sorry. Ellen and I wanted to raise you. We should have tried harder, but we were scared, you know?" He looked older at that moment and slightly weak. It was disconcerting.

"I know, and thanks. I wish things could have been different, but Mama let her circumstances shape who she was. I did too for a long time. I won't do that again." She put her arm around Beth, who then put a hand on Bailey's leg.

"Well." Dwight stood. "I hate to dump that on you and leave, but even a recovered old man is still an old man and needs his sleep."

"He's getting his stamina back, but it could take a while," Ellen said as they all stood as well.

"Bailey, we love you. We always have. Thank you for everything you do for us and our kids." Dwight pulled her into a hug.

"Thanks for being there, Uncle Dwight. I couldn't have made it this far without you." She clapped him on the back as he tightened the embrace.

"Love you, Bailey Girl." Ellen kissed her on the cheek when it was their turn to hug. "We'll see ourselves out."

"Are you sure?" Beth asked.

"Certainly." Ellen smiled at them both. "Goodnight, you two."

"Good night, Aunt Ellen. Thanks." Bailey watched them walk down the hallway and out the front door. She waited, knowing Beth would want to talk about it, to mention something, and she wasn't sure she was ready to do so yet. Beth would also want to know that Bailey wasn't going to jump headfirst off the wagon of sobriety.

"Want to go for a walk?" Beth asked instead. "I think the ice cream place is still open."

"Yeah." Bailey was surprised into a smile. She looked questioningly at her, but Beth went to the end of the stairs and called the kids.

"Who wants to walk down for ice cream?"

"Me." Jacob barreled down the stairs.

"Can we bring Elvis?" Rebecca asked as the dog followed her downstairs.

"Of course," Bailey said and went to get his leash.

"Awesome. It's a like a complete family outing," Jacob said.

"That it is," Beth said. She ruffled his hair, but her eyes were on Bailey. "A full family outing."

"Well then, let's go get ice cream." Bailey was suddenly not worried about anything else than the moment she had with two kids, Beth and Elvis.

Chapter Twenty-nine

THE KIDS WERE finally asleep. The excitement of the rehearsal and the dinner, coupled with the anticipation of the wedding had them both wired so tight it took a long time for them to wind down. Finally, Bailey banished Beth to the front porch, piled both kids in one bed and pulled out her acoustic guitar. They were asleep five minutes later. Even Elvis was snuggled on the bed with them.

Bailey sighed in contentment, put up her guitar and grabbed a small box from a dresser drawer. She'd been thinking about it for days, weeks, and years if she were honest with herself. It was time. She could think of little else.

"Hey, they asleep?" Beth asked when Bailey walked outside.

"They are. Even Elvis is piled in the bed with them."

"That's sweet." Beth moved over to make room for her on the swing. She looked so comfortable, snug in a pair of cotton shorts, barefoot with her auburn hair pulled back. It was like nothing stressful had happened at the dinner. "What's wrong?"

"Nothing." Bailey remained standing. "Actually, I wanted to talk to you. Man it's a nice night."

"It is." Beth patted the seat next to her on the swing. "Bailey, sweetheart, what's the big secret?"

"It's not just my secret, but Kat reminded me that I needed to tell you and how honesty is a necessity and all that." She sighed and ran her hands through her hair, but then sat down and looked at Beth. "Did you know that Liz can't have children?"

"What?" Beth frowned. "But she gave birth to Sarah. I was there."

"She found out in high school. Anyway, it was crushing because she always wanted children. Before Mike's operation, the one that removed all female organs, Liz asked him to donate eggs. She figured they were identical twins and it would be the same thing, you know the same amount of DNA and everything." Bailey spoke fast. It was hard to let some secrets go after carrying them around for so long.

"What did he say?" Beth asked.

"He said no." Bailey hung her head. "Liz was devastated. I swear I almost beat the hell out of him, but it was ultimately his choice."

"So that's why Sarah looks and acts just like you," Beth said slowly.

"Yeah. I donated. I'd been clean for about a year and tested then so it was okay. It's Ian's sperm. We did it out in California. Took four fucking tries before we got Sarah. There are still some eggs in storage I believe. But we didn't tell anyone. Kat knows. She helped find the doctor. Her sister used the same one. But that's it. Dwight and Ellen don't know. My mom didn't know, Mike, Sarah, no one else."

"So it's a level one secret. I won't say a word, but one day you'll want to tell Sarah," Beth said.

"That's up to Liz. I lay on a table and spawned. Liz has done the hard part. She's Sarah's mom and she and Ian will tell her when, and if, they think the time is right." Bailey shrugged. The easy part was over.

"Why are you telling me now?" Beth asked. "You didn't have to, you know." She slipped an arm around Bailey.

"I know. But I want this to be right. I want everything to be open and honest. That was the biggest secret I had left."

"You all are amazing," Beth said. "I can't believe none of us knew." She nuzzled Bailey's neck, her mind clearly elsewhere.

"It's easy to hide things when you're a continent apart from everyone," Bailey said wryly. "How long do you think we've been officially together?"

"About two months, I think." Beth paused her assault on Bailey's neck. "You know I hadn't really thought about it. Seems like longer. Why?"

"It does to me too. I think maybe because we've known each other for so long that it makes some things easier."

"Maybe. I was expecting a bit more of an adjustment period, but we don't really seem to have needed one. Are you having second thoughts or something?" Beth stopped her assault on Bailey's neck and looked at her.

"Not at all. I've never done this before, bear with me." Bailey abruptly stood and turned to face her.

"Okay."

"Elizabeth Marie Forsyth, I love you with everything that I am and everything that I hope to be." Bailey sank to one knee and pulled out the box. "I want to stand before our friends and family and shout my intentions to the world. I want to spend the rest of my life with you. I want to fall asleep and wake up next to you until I fall asleep forever. Will you marry me?"

"Bailey. I. Oh. Yes." Beth slid from the porch swing and into

Bailey who fell back until they were both on the porch as much as each other.

"You sure?" Bailey asked when they came up for air.

"Never been surer," Beth said as shaking hands placed the ring on another pair of shaking hands. "It's beautiful."

"I thought you deserved something as beautiful as you are. This is as close as I could find." Bailey sighed deeply.

"Keep that up and you're going to end up writing love songs," Beth warned.

"I'll keep that in mind." Bailey said as relief flooded through her. "Perhaps we should go inside before we give my neighbors a show."

"I thought you wanted to have a campaign against Mr. Braddock."

"Yeah, but I don't want to give him an instructional video," Bailey murmured as she began kissing Beth's neck. "So inside?"

"Yes. Please. Now."

"As you wish." Bailey stood up and offered her hand.

"When should we tell everyone? I don't want to say anything tomorrow and take away from Cindy," Beth said.

"I know. I had actually planned on doing this at the wedding, but after tonight, well, they deserve a special day with nothing to take away from that." Bailey pulled her close. "But that's tomorrow. Tonight though."

"Yeah tonight. We should certainly focus on that. Now come to bed. Let's celebrate our engagement by not getting a lot of sleep, having a fuck-ton of sex and showing up tomorrow as zombies for the wedding." Beth waggled her eyebrows.

"Elizabeth Forsyth, you are twisted. I love you so much." Bailey felt as if she would never stop smiling.

"Then let's go to bed." Beth held her hand out. Bailey took it and felt herself being drawn into something new, something she'd never had before and she was grateful.

They made it upstairs and to the bedroom before they were back in one another's arms. It was late. They were tired. They had to be up early for a wedding between two people they loved very much. They managed to get a little sleep. It was worth it.

"BAILEY, I'M SO glad you're here," Scott said as they pulled into the parking lot.

"What's up?" She asked as she got out and then opened the backdoor for Jacob. She was a little sore and a lot tired, but she was looking forward to coffee to help with at least one of those.

"Someone has trashed the reception area. It's bad. Hey, Beth. The other ladies aren't here yet."

"I figured," Beth said. "We kinda wanted to be here early just in case."

"Apparently you did too," Bailey said to Scott. "Is Mike here?"

"No. It's just us. I guess great minds think alike. Last night as we were leaving the restaurant, I thought I saw Cindy's ex-husband and some of his buddies. Then I remembered how weird Ms. Arnoux was acting so I thought it would be a good idea to get here early. I'm glad I did," He said.

"Can the kids go in there?" Beth asked. "Should I call Liz?"

"I already did," Scott said. "She and Ian are on the way." He leaned against the car.

"Good. We'll leave the dress clothes in the car. What are we looking at here?" Bailey asked. She thought she was prepared for anything. She wasn't.

"Come on and I'll show you." Scott led them through the double doors to the reception hall.

At each table, instead of the elegant display of lilies and blue hydrangeas, plastic flowers spray painted black were there. Someone had removed the engagement photos and replaced them with pictures of Mike as a kid and worse. There were post op pictures of top and bottom surgery someone had printed off the Internet everywhere.

"Oh shit." Beth turned back to the kids and told them to wait on the steps.

"Fuck!" Bailey said. "What asswipe did this?"

"I have no idea." Scott ran his hands through his hair.

"Well, enough gawking at it. Let's get this cleaned up." Beth began by attacking the first table.

"Oh, geez. This is disgusting. Y'all didn't take these, did you?" Scott held up a particularly graphic picture showing a half-healed incision that looked infected.

"No." Bailey examined it. "I don't think any of these are actually Mike. We never took graphic pictures. Just the normal before and after shots were all we did. I bet someone printed them off the Internet."

"That only makes it slightly better," Scott said.

"Do we know where the flowers that were supposed to be here are?" Beth asked. She had removed all the fake ones.

"What the hell?" Liz asked as she entered.

"That's what we were wondering." Bailey resisted the urge to laugh. Liz still had her hair in curlers. "Where's Ian?"

"He's outside with the kids. This is unbelievable." She looked at one of the pictures posted to the wall. "Damn, I'm glad they aren't here yet."

"We've got an hour before the limo is supposed to pick us up," Beth said. "Has anyone checked where the ceremony is going to be?"

"No. I got here a few minutes before you guys did. I saw this and then called Liz. You pulled up as I was dialing your number," Scott told them.

"I'll check the ceremony area," Bailey volunteered. "We need to check the changing rooms too."

"If we can get the graphic pictures down in here, the kids can get the school pictures," Beth said. "We'll get that done."

Scott squared his shoulders. "I'll check the changing rooms."

"Okay." Bailey sighed. "This is so fucked up. I'll meet you back here."

"Dude, who would do such a thing?" Scott asked as they left the room.

"I've a few suspects. You okay?"

"Yeah. You know intellectually I knew what all he went through but damn. I never wanted to really know, you know," Scott said.

"You thought they waved a wand and poof instant penis?" Bailey was beyond tired and irritated and she couldn't keep the sarcasm from her voice. Fortunately, Scott didn't seem to mind.

"Not really, but damn. The man has some sort of inner strength." Scott seemed a bit shaken.

"Yep. That he does. Let me know if you need help or if you find anything," she told him.

"Okay."

Bailey took a deep breath and squared her shoulders before opening the door. It was dark inside. She turned on the lights and was unsurprised to see the madness. This made the reception area look like an act of love.

Each wall was covered in spray paint. Someone had badly misspelled several bigoted epitaphs as well as threats and other gay and transphobic phrases. More pictures were plastered on the walls. Dildos and other sex toys were placed where the candles had been. The floor was covered with black petals and skull confetti.

"Hey, what did...oh shit!" Liz shouted.

"Yeah. Think you can help? We need something to cover these walls. Can we send Ian and the kids to the store?" Bailey was thinking fast.

"Yeah probably. What are you thinking?" Liz looked around. "I think we've got flowers coming. We couldn't find the real ones. I strong armed the florist."

"Awesome. We'll need sheets. Tarps. Plastic sheets." Bailey shrugged. "We don't have enough time to paint. But we can staple the shit out of the walls."

"Yeah I'll go send him to the store." Liz turned to leave.

"Here." Bailey tossed her wallet over. "Let him use that."

"You sure?"

"Yeah. Tell him to hurry. And to get a staple gun," She called.

Bailey started with the floor. She found a broom and started sweeping up the confetti. She was almost done when Liz returned.

"I had him pick up something for lunch too. I know the kids will be hungry."

"Awesome. Can you hold the thing so I can sweep this shit into it?" Bailey was glad she hadn't gotten dressed in her formal attire already.

"Yeah." Liz chuckled. "I'll hold the dustpan. You know the sad part?"

"There's a sad part? I would say it's all sad."

"No. Sick. Not sad. The sad part is someone spent a lot of money on toys we just have to throw away."

Bailey shuddered. "They may have been part of someone's private collection."

"Then that tells us a lot about something they wouldn't want us to know. I'd guess bought or stolen," Liz said.

"Too bad it doesn't tell us who did it," Bailey said. She shook her head. "Let's get the pictures down. I want to put all the toys directly into a garbage bag before one of the kids comes in."

"You got it. I brought in some garbage bags." Liz waved to the mass of black plastic she had piled up on one of the chairs.

"Thanks."

It didn't take long to throw everything away. By the time they were finished Ian had appeared with two rolls of white plastic and two staple guns. Scott followed with a stepladder.

"This is going to look like shit," Scott said.

"Well, you're the artist. Make it pretty," Liz said.

"I can't give a pig a face lift and expect it to win a beauty contest," he protested.

"Look. This shit isn't everywhere. What if we drape it?" Liz asked.

"We could do that." He scratched his chin. "Does this place have any props or anything?"

"I'm on it," Bailey said. She was relieved. She wasn't visually creative.

"Hey how's it going?" Beth asked when Bailey left the room. They met in the hallway.

"Eh we're cleaning it up." She stopped for a moment. "Whoever did this is one angry asshole."

"Yeah. You okay?" Beth wrapped her arms around her.

"Yeah. Ours will be much less stressful, right?" She leaned into Beth.

"Of course. They'll be doing everything. All we'll have to do is look pretty and say I do." Beth smiled at her. "Very easy."

"I like that."

"Hey, stop making out in the hallway," Mike called out, making them jump.

"Mike," Bailey called loudly. "What are you doing here so early?"

"That was my ear," Beth complained.

"Sorry, baby." Bailey patted her on the back. "We gotta get him outta here."

"What's going on?" Mike sounded suspicious.

"Nothing. We're just making sure your day goes off without a hitch," Bailey lied.

"Uh huh. Where's Scott? I saw his motorcycle outside."

"He's around. Maybe we should get you to the dressing room so you can start getting ready," Bailey suggested.

"Yeah, you don't want to be out here when Cindy shows up you know." Beth took him by the arm. "Come on. I need to make sure the dressing area for the bridal party is set up and ready to go."

He seemed to accept that. "Okay."

"Scott and I will be down there in a few," Bailey called to him. She raced back into the other room and stopped. "This is not going to work. It looks like shit. And Mike's here."

"What about setting everything up outside?" Liz asked. "They wanted that but it was supposed to rain so they moved it inside."

"Then let's get this set back up outside," Bailey said. "We get wet, then we just get wet."

"All right." Ian dropped the plastic he was holding. "Start tossing stuff out. I'll get the kids to help place chairs."

"Emergency door. Right here." Scott pushed open the door and started tossing out chairs.

"Didn't they hire people to help with this shit?" Liz complained.

"You. Go." Bailey told her. "Your curlers are falling out."

"Okay. Good luck." Liz hurried out of the room.

Bailey and Scott tossed chairs outside. Ian and the kids grabbed them and ran to put them in place. The hired crew finally arrived and Bailey commandeered them and sent them out to help. After that it didn't take long to set everything up again.

"Damn. It almost looks like they intended it to be out here." Scott wiped his forehead with his sleeve as he looked around. "Too bad we can't shower here."

"Guess we'll have to suffer," Bailey said. "It's time for all of us, kids included, to go get dressed."

"All right." Ian whistled and the kids ran over. "Come on, younglings, it's time to put on our pretty clothes."

"Excellent." Rebecca ran to the building.

"Great." Sarah didn't sound happy but grudgingly trudged behind her friend.

"Jacob, you ready?" Bailey asked. He nodded and took her hand, allowing her to lead him inside to get dressed. It was such a small gesture, but it felt huge.

Chapter Thirty

BAILEY SAW HER quarry at the end of the hall. "Sheila!"

"Excuse me?" Sheila Arnoux turned to face her.

"I need to talk to you," Bailey said, not bothering to keep her voice down as she approached Cindy's mother.

"Did you call me by my first name?" Sheila sounded astounded.

"I did. I'm a fucking forty-three-year-old adult and I will call you by your first name if I feel like it. We're all over these fucked up, childish games, Shelia. Call off your dogs. Cindy and Mike are getting married in less than an hour. If you have anything else planned, call it off. Scott, Ian and I have pulled the world apart and back together to give them a great day. And as of right now, they don't know a thing."

"It's not right," Sheila said.

"What's not right? Two people who love one another have the right to live their lives together regardless of how you feel about it. It's about time you learned that lesson." Bailey couldn't keep the very real anger she felt about that out of her voice. "You kept my parents apart. You're not keeping anyone else that way. Understood?"

"I don't know what you mean by that." She attempted to deny everything.

"Like hell. Look, Sheila. If you interfere again into Cindy and Mike's relationship, I will personally bust your ass. You may have been able to intimidate my mother and bully your husband, but you can't do shit to me. And if you try, I'll spread the word. Because so far I've not told anyone."

"Who told you?" Sheila sputtered. "That's not right. It's not true. He never would have cheated on me with your whore of a mother."

"Don't lie to me. I've seen the letters, the pictures, and most importantly, I've seen the DNA test." She raised her eyebrow as Sheila turned pale. "Mike and my sister, and yes I understand how fucked up a relationship that is, are getting married. You will sit in the front row. You will smile at your daughter. You will smile at your son-in-law. You may cry. You will not throw a fit. You will not make a single negative comment. If you can't, then you need to leave. Understood? You have twenty minutes to make a decision. They're starting to seat people now."

"I don't know what to say." The older woman seemed shocked.

"Personally speaking, there's not much you can say to me to make it right. You've treated me like shit since the day I was born and now, at least, I know why. Doesn't make it right, matter of fact it makes it a little worse." Bailey shrugged. "I'll deal with that later. What you can say right now to your daughter is that you're sorry. Apologize to them both and try to accept them. If you can't then you need to say goodbye to them until you can accept it."

"Bailey, C'mon," Scott hollered at her from down the hall. "We need to finish getting dressed."

"I'll be right there." She turned to look back at Sheila. "The clock is ticking, Sheila. You better make a decision."

Bailey walked away without waiting for a response. She knew why Liz was worried. She assumed Beth was as well, but Beth hadn't said a word about it. It had been difficult. Handling her mother's death, the revelations about her parentage, keeping the wedding from going completely off the rails and then the showdown with Sheila. It was almost enough to make her want to drink. Almost.

"What's going on?" Mike asked when Bailey re-entered the room.

"Just having a little chat with your mother-in-law," she said with a smile. "No big deal. Let's get dressed and then get you hitched, huh?"

"Yeah. I like that." Mike grinned in return. "I can't believe this. Seriously, Bailey. Thank you."

"You are welcome, my man." She shrugged it off.

"I'm just curious." Scott walked over to them. "But how did you know how to handle it?"

"Handle what?" She asked.

"Mike? I followed your lead, but you were way ahead of the pack. How?"

"Oh that." Bailey sighed as she finished buttoning her shirt. "My mom dated this guy named Ed for a while. He's the one who bought me my first guitar and taught me how to play. I think I was nine. Anyway, I'd see him around town from time to time and he'd check on me. When I was twelve he gave me a card and told me to go to this place or call this number when I was older and I had too many thoughts. I didn't get it. But when I was fourteen I went. Turns out it was his sister's number and she owned the only women's bar in town."

"That's the bar you played at, right?" Mike asked.

"Yeah. I played solo sets there for extra money. I also helped more at that bar than Mama's I'm sure." She laughed. "There was a woman there who was transitioning. I think she was going from Gary to Genny. Something like that. Anyway. She was a hell of a conversationalist and didn't seem to mind answering childish questions. It cleared up a lot about what Mike was going through."

"Ah. And here I thought you were just born wise," Scott teased.

"Nope. Mike, man you scared me that night. I know why, and I know why you reacted the way you did. But I've never felt fear like that before. I can't tell you how glad I am, how honored I am to be standing with you here today." Bailey felt tears and fought them back. She didn't want to go stand in front of their friends and family with red eyes.

"For a long time I resented being sent away, you know. I never blamed you and Liz. I've always kinda known that just the blood on my shirt alone would have gotten Mom and Dad's attention," Mike told her. They'd never really spoken about what happened as sober adults. "And I suppose it was less their idea than it was the hospital's."

"You did try to escape and finish the job," Bailey said quietly. "How are you handling everything today?"

"I'm wonderful." Mike looked around and then back at her. "Honestly, I could do with a drink. I'm worried that Cindy's mom will try something. Or that Roger will show his ass. Hell, I'm even concerned Kyle will be here."

"Whatever happens, Mike, I'm here," Bailey promised.

"I know. And I'm grateful. You seem good. Are you?" He asked.

"Yeah, actually. I'm really good. I have some grief, but it's lessened. I have answers to questions, I'm working on sorting out. Mostly though, I feel like an adult. I feel human, and thanks to y'all I feel like I have a family."

"DAMN, WE DID a good job," Scott whispered as they stood near the altar waiting for the music to cue the bride.

"What made y'all bring it outside?" Mike asked.

"Quit playing with your tie," Bailey told him. "It wasn't raining."

"Yeah, but..." Whatever else he was going to say was interrupted by an organ. It was time.

The entire audience turned in their seats to watch the bridal procession. Sarah and Rebecca walked solemnly down the aisle, carefully releasing flower petals. Jacob was concentrating so hard on holding the pillow with the rings that he wasn't watching anything else.

Bailey looked away from the kids and caught their mother's eye. She forgot to breathe for a moment. Beth looked amazing.

Scott elbowed her. "Breathe."

"Dude, I can't," she said quietly.

"Keep an eye on Mike. He's sweating."

"Shit," she muttered. It was true. While it was warm outside, Mike was sweating copiously.

Once the bridesmaids took their places, a different tune began. Eric looked both nervous and proud as he walked down the aisle with his mother. Cindy looked radiant, as if she was finally getting something she had always wanted. Bailey snuck a glance at Mrs. Arnoux. The woman looked shocked and thoughtful.

Mike stumbled for a moment. Bailey discreetly placed a steadying hand on his back. By the time Eric released his mother Mike was steady again.

It was over in moments. The officiant directed the newlyweds to face the audience. They received a standing ovation.

Unfortunately, Bailey soon learned that wasn't the end. The photographer and his assistant appeared and held them captive for almost another hour posing and smiling in various groups. At least the photographer paired her with Beth for a few shots. They even managed to get one with Rebecca and Jacob.

The last pose was the cutting of the cake. After that they were released and sent off to enjoy the reception. The deejay was playing a slow ballad. Everyone was either dancing or sitting and eating.

"Hey." She walked up to Beth. "Wanna dance?"

"Off course." Bailey led Beth onto the dance floor. "Well, we managed to pull it off."

"We did. I didn't think we'd be able to there for a few." Bailey sighed. "Do you want to do this all over again?"

"I don't know. I've had the full wedding thing. If you can live without it, I certainly can." Beth leaned closer. "Let's just enjoy this right now. Later we can fly to Vegas if you want."

"That would be awesome." Bailey smiled. "I didn't say

anything to anyone yet."

"Believe it or not Sarah noticed. She didn't announce it, but she did get Liz's attention."

"Well they did help me pick it out," Bailey admitted. "There were too many choices. Liz had to help me narrow it down."

"You all did an amazing job."

"Thank you. So how long before we can announce it, and how long before we can leave?" Bailey was ready to be done and go home.

"Anxious, sweetheart?"

"You look so beautiful. I just want to share how amazingly lucky I am. And I really want to take you home and ravish you. And then I want to sleep for twelve days."

"Well, we have to wait until the bride and groom have left at least. But," Beth put her head down on Bailey's shoulder, "let's just enjoy this."

"I have no problem with that at all." Bailey wrapped her arms tighter around Beth. "I love you. Thank you."

"I love you too. What are you thanking me for?"

"I finally feel like I have a home and family."

"We've always been here, sweetheart. You just had to get to a place where you could see it. Welcome home, Bailey."

"You are my home." Bailey leaned down for a kiss. "And I'm never leaving you again."

About the Author

Hope A. Milam lives on the Mississippi Gulf Coast with her wife, their daughter, three dogs and a cat. Hope would like the menagerie to be larger, but her wife is adamant that they limit the number of dogs to one dog per person. The cat is lagniappe.

Hope is a very passionate Saints fan, having followed the team since she understood what football was. Hope also is an affirmed geek and spends time educating her daughter on Star Wars and comic books. Attempts to assimilate the wife have failed, but their relationship remains strong despite that.

MORE REGAL CREST PUBLICATIONS

Melissa Good	Red Sky At Morning	978-1-932300-80-2
Melissa Good	Storm Surge: Book One	978-1-935053-28-6
Melissa Good	Storm Surge: Book Two	978-1-935053-39-2
Melissa Good	Stormy Waters	978-1-61929-082-2
Melissa Good	Thicker Than Water	1-932300-24-4
Melissa Good	Terrors of the High Seas	1-932300-45-7
Melissa Good	Tropical Storm	978-1-932300-60-4
Melissa Good	Tropical Convergence	978-1-935053-18-7
Melissa Good	Winds of Change Book One	978-1-61929-194-2
Melissa Good	Winds of Change Book Two	978-1-61929-232-1
Melissa Good	Southern Stars	978-1-61929-348-9
Danielle Grainger	Wrecking Bernadette: Book One in the Bernadette Series	978-1-61929-428-8
Jeanine Hoffman	Lights & Sirens	978-1-61929-115-7
Jeanine Hoffman	Strength in Numbers	978-1-61929-109-6
Jeanine Hoffman	Back Swing	978-1-61929-137-9
K. E. Lane	And, Playing the Role of Herself	978-1-932300-72-7
Kate McLachlan	Christmas Crush	978-1-61929-195-9
Kate McLachlan	Hearts, Dead and Alive	978-1-61929-017-4
Kate McLachlan	Murder and the Hurdy Gurdy Girl	978-1-61929-125-6
Kate McLachlan	Rescue At Inspiration Point	978-1-61929-005-1
Kate McLachlan	Return Of An Impetuous Pilot	978-1-61929-152-2
Kate McLachlan	Rip Van Dyke	978-1-935053-29-3
Kate McLachlan	Ten Little Lesbians	978-1-61929-236-9
Kate McLachlan	Alias Mrs. Jones	978-1-61929-282-6
Hope Milam	Welcome Home, Bailey	978-1-61929-438-7
Lynne Norris	One Promise	978-1-932300-92-5
Lynne Norris	Sanctuary	978-1-61929-248-2
Lynne Norris	The Light of Day	978-1-61929-338-0
Schramm and Dunne	Love Is In the Air	978-1-61929-362-8
Rae Theodore	Leaving Normal: Adventures in Gender	978-1-61929-320-5
Rae Theodore	My Mother Says Drums Are for Boys: True Stories for Gender Rebels	978-1-61929-378-6
Barbara Valletto	Pulse Points	978-1-61929-254-3
Barbara Valletto	Everlong	978-1-61929-266-6
Barbara Valletto	Limbo	978-1-61929-358-8
Barbara Valletto	Diver Blues	978-1-61929-384-7
Lisa Young	Out and Proud	978-1-61929-392-2

Be sure to check out our other imprints,
Blue Beacon Books, Mystic Books, Quest Books,
Silver Dragon Books, Troubadour Books,
and Young Adult Books.

VISIT US ONLINE AT
www.regalcrest.biz

At the Regal Crest Website You'll Find

- ~ The latest news about forthcoming titles and new releases

- ~ Our complete backlist of titles

- ~ Information about your favorite authors

Regal Crest print titles are available from all progressive booksellers including numerous sources online. Our distributors are Bella Distribution and Ingram.

www.ingramcontent.com/pod-product-compliance
Lightning Source LLC
Chambersburg PA
CBHW051130020726
47501CB00005B/1431